ROCKET HANDBOOK
Book One – Seraphim

R. Alan Blood

Dedicated to my wife, Michelle,

without whom there would be no story to tell.

Contents

CHAPTER ONE

West Wing

"Oh no," whispered a slender scientist in a lab coat. With a shaky hand, he wiped the sweat from his forehead as the sound of footsteps got louder. "No-no-no!" he said as he ducked behind some large crates. Seconds later, shadows emerged from the end of the corridor. Only three more levels, and then the airlock, he thought. Sweat continued to stream down his face, stinging his eyes. The scientist shook and cowered even more into a corner as three armed security officers walked by. After they passed, an involuntary sigh left his chest, causing one of the guards to stop and turn around.

"Wait," said the guard. "I heard something." He started back toward the crates, but after a few steps, water rushed through some pipes bolted to the wall that extended from ceiling to floor.

"It's nothing," said another guard. "C'mon. We have a

1

lot of ground to cover. We have our orders, and not a whole lot of time to carry them out." The sounds of their footsteps faded into the far end of the other side of the corridor.

Now or never, thought the scientist. It had been three months since he'd seen the surface – since he'd seen any sunlight. The hum of fluorescent lighting, the clanging of steel flooring, and the lifeless cement walls had worn for too long on his sanity. "I'm not crazy, I'm not crazy," he mumbled to himself. He reached into his large pocket and with a shaking hand, pulled out a small clear disk. "They won't think I'm crazy after they see what we found. If the Miras won't share it, someone must. The whole world must see it." He took a deep breath and leapt from the corner. After pausing at the elevator, he smiled and ran a bit further to a door leading to the stairs.

On the other end of the west wing of SeaLab IV, a tall uniformed man turned to his new supervisor. "Our firm was hired to provide security for the research projects on this station," he said, "Not to turn the station into a prison camp."

"Agent Thomas, you're getting too emotional and dramatic," said Agent Forsythe, the head of west wing security. "We all knew what would happen in the event that a discovery was made."

"What do you mean?" asked Thomas. "What kind of discovery justifies the level of security you've decided to impose on these civilians?"

"The sensitive kind. The kind of discovery that really

draws the Investor Consortium's attention," said Forsythe. He seemed suddenly to get irritated at Thomas' questions.

Thomas didn't care. He knew how far to push his old friend. "C'mon, Forsythe. Tell me what's going on. You've gotta be able to tell me something."

"I don't have any details to share, and even if I did, it would be need-to-know," snapped Forsythe. "Do you need to be reminded of all the contingencies to which we all agreed?"

"No. Forsythe, of course not," said Thomas, "But look what's happening. These people are scientists, not soldiers. They can't be expected to work under these conditions." Thomas was new to the west wing, having spent most of his time heading up security for the Miras over in the east wing. Now, the investors were pulling all available agents over to the west wing, without a clear explanation why.

"I haven't heard any complaints from the Miras. They seem to be just fine," said Forsythe. He folded his arms confidently and leaned back in his chair. "And if they're fine, the other scientists are also fine. Isn't that right, Thomas?"

"The Miras have no idea what the conditions are for groups with whom they have no direct interaction. Yes, SeaLab IV is their operation in general, but they've been insulated from the day to day routines of projects, that are not under their direct supervision," said Thomas.

"Yes, and they requested that it be that way," said Forsythe. His expression took a serious turn as he unfolded his arms and leaned forward. "And there's a good reason why their requests were so willingly granted. There's a lot at stake here, and the investors refuse to risk any sort of leak." He stood up and walked toward the door. "The less the different research groups know about the other projects around them, the better."

"What is it that the investors want to lock down? What happened to you, Forsythe?" asked Thomas. "Since when did this become all about the investors? Whatever happened to all that passion around scientific discovery and the improvement of mankind? What about the protection of all these people? Isn't that why we're here?"

Forsythe sighed. "Listen, Thomas, the game has changed. If any of those scientists ever leave, they could pose a serious threat to national security."

"What?" blurted Thomas. He stood up abruptly. "What country's security are we talking about here? There are over a hundred countries and private entities contributing to SeaLab."

"Well, it would seem that those entities are not completely aware of the nature of their investments," said Forsythe. "Listen, Agent Thomas. I've indulged your questions long enough. From now on, you call me sir. Is that clear?" Thomas sneered and walked toward the door, but Forsythe grabbed his arm. "Thomas, the orders have already been issued. Lock down the facility and prevent any more escape attempts."

"More?" asked Thomas. "What's going on here? Since when does anyone need to ...escape?"

"Three scientists carrying classified data have already been apprehended, and one is still unaccounted for. You will lead the search. If we fail to adequately secure this facility, we will have no choice but to move all less-critical staff to a holding area and put all other personnel under twenty-four hour watch – and that includes the Miras." Forsythe tightened his grip on Thomas' arm. "Am I clear,

Agent Thomas?"

"Yes ...sir," said Thomas. A thousand other questions and protests flooded his mind, but he thought it wise to bite his tongue for now. "What are we to do with the prisoners?"

"Leave that to me," said Forsythe. An empty darkness washed over his face, and there seemed to be no compassion in his eyes. "Now, go do your job."

With some difficulty, Thomas was able to conceal his disappointment, straighten, look Forsythe in the eyes, and say "Yes sir." Thomas walked out the door and didn't look back.

Thomas had almost returned to his quarters when his radio called out, "Agent Thomas, Agent Thomas, do you copy?"

"Yes, I copy. What is it?"

"We have found the scientist that went missing. We have him cornered in the west airlock."

"I'll be right there," said Thomas. He turned off his transmitter and hit the wall. "I signed up to protect these folks from the outside, not to be a prison guard." It had only been a few days on his new assignment in the west wing, but he already longed to be back with the Miras on the other side of the station.

In the east wing, there was no airlock and no transport, but it did provide the best views of the sea floor, and everything around the station – not that the extremely dense murky water allowed anyone to see very far. Nevertheless, video feeds from a host of external cameras projected onto the wall. Most of the time, Ray had the mode set to thermal, for the off-chance that some warm-blooded thing would swim by. Not down here, thought Raymond, too deep. Way too deep. He turned to his wife. "Jules, I need that latest data on the submersible," said Raymond.

"Sure thing, I just entered it into the research logs," replied Julia. She turned around and faced Ray who's gaze was still glued to his display. "Ray, something's not right. Our staff have been shuffled again on deck three. Did I miss something?"

Ray looked up from his display and turned to Julia. "Do a bulk transfer of the research data from the research logs to our personal logs. Use that special tunneling protocol I made so it'll be encrypted."

"Encrypted? Why the precaution? Did you hear something from Agent Forsythe? Is he worried about another security breach? You think something's been compromised?" she asked.

"I don't know, but we're too close to a critical phase to be distracted by any of that. We have no choice but to trust Forsythe to do his job," said Raymond, "But that doesn't mean we shouldn't take additional measures to protect our findings."

Julia sighed. "Are you at all concerned about the shuffling around of our staff?"

"Well, I'm always concerned when there's a change, but we have to stay focused," said Ray. "At the very least, we should make sure that the new staff proves themselves before we expose them to all the data we've been collecting."

Julia looked concerned. "Maybe we should just back the

data up to our personal logs, and just discontinue entries to the funded research logs."

"Why would we do that?" asked Raymond. "Our agreement clearly states that we are to–"

"–Ray," interrupted Julia, "Something is wrong. We made far more progress than anyone had anticipated. The game has changed. Do you know for sure just who is on the receiving end of all this data we've been collecting? We've received petabytes of data every hour from that neutrino stream, and it's coming from the center of the earth. We're dealing with an unidentified intelligence, and I seriously doubt it's from someone else on the planet."

"Whoa, hold on Jules," said Raymond. "Let's not jump to any rash conclusions. We still have a ton of data to process."

"Ray, come on," protested Julia. "You've got to be kidding me. What else could be sending all that data?"

Raymond sighed. "Fine, you're right, of course. Cut the feed to the research database. It's time we moved to plan B. Notify the kids and Agent Thomas."

"What about the report?" asked Julia. "The Consortium is expecting to learn what the recent fuss has been about. I'm not sure I can hold them off much longer."

"Just report on the five new species we discovered last week," said Ray, "And how there's a possibility of some new treatments for cancer. That should give them something to chew on."

Agent Thomas approached a group of security officers. Why is this happening? he thought. Thomas gritted his teeth in frustration. This should not have escalated to a stand-off in the first place.

"Agent Thomas, sir," said one of the guards, "We tried to tell him that everything would be ok, but he's so terrified."

"Well, of course, he's scared," said Thomas as he approached the security team. "Your guns are drawn, and it looks like he's been chased all over the west wing. Is this how you guys always treat folks over here?"

The other agent looked at Thomas incredulously. "Isn't the east wing locked down as well? How long since you've been transferred over here?"

"Just two days ago. I was told you needed extra help repelling break-in attempts from the surface," said Thomas.

"Heh, yeah right. No one on the surface even cares that we're down here at the bottom of the ocean," said the agent. "While you've been over there protecting the Miras on the east wing, we've been over here protecting the airlock from break-ins. It was getting boring around here until our job changed to preventing break-outs."

"Break-outs? You've got to be kidding me. Why?" Thomas' communicator buzzed. He looked down. It was an encrypted text from Julia Mira, and it read:

possibility of plan B, please advise

A cold sweat washed over Thomas. He looked up in shock. Has it come to that already? he thought.

"Are you ok, Agent Thomas? What are our orders?" asked the agent.

"I'm fine," said Thomas, as he ran his fingers through

his sweaty hair. "What happened to the other scientists who escaped? The holding areas are the only place we could keep them down here, and on my way to Agent Forsythe's office, I noticed that they were empty."

"Oh yeah, we had to round them up," said the agent, "About fifteen of them. They were apparently escorted back to the surface for questioning. This fellow here we have cornered is number sixteen, and there will probably be more."

"Agent Thomas," said Forsythe from Thomas' radio, "Ensure that the scientist you have found is escorted back to the holding area for the next transport to the surface."

"Yes sir," said Thomas. What has been going on over here? he asked himself. I've known Agent Forsythe for awhile, he should be able to explain. For Thomas, that was one of the perks of moving over to west wing security. He had been one of Forsythe's trainers, and now Forsythe was in charge of security for the entire west wing. Thomas was still wondering how he had pulled off that kind of promotion. It had been too long since he'd spent any time with Agent Forsythe, and now he seemed different. Something was wrong with his old friend, and he was determined to find out what.

On the other side of the station, Ray paced back and forth in front of a display which showed a schematic of the entire station. From here, Ray could monitor the status of all of the research projects being conducted on the station. Several of them were behind schedule, and others were losing personnel.

Julia ran into the room. "Ray, I heard back from Thomas. The situation in the west wing is not looking good. Scientists are fleeing to the surface." she said.

"What? Has there been an emergency? No alarms have sounded." said Ray. "Have you seen this?" he said as he pointed to the display.

"No alarms have been activated. According to Thomas, some personnel are trying to leave. He's trying to find out why." said Julia.

"That doesn't make any sense. Those scientists were scrambling to get down here and be a part of history," said Raymond. He paused and then looked concerned. "I hope the investors haven't decided to change the terms of our agreement."

"Well, if they did, that would put our friends at risk," said Julia. "We don't have a contingency in plan B for our scientist colleagues over in west wing."

"Yeah, I know," said Raymond. "What have we done?"

"Well, let's not freak out," said Julia. "I'll try and get ahold of our investor liaison."

Back in the west wing, Agent Thomas was able to get the scientist who was trying to leave the station to settle down. The correct protocol was to report to the wing administrator's office and file a grievance. A person shouldn't just leave. Why try an unscheduled departure? thought Thomas. Why was he so afraid? Thomas sighed and switched off his transmitter. He turned to another agent as they escorted the captured scientist to Agent Forsythe's office. "So, the investor liaison is dead? How'd that happen? When?"

"I heard the news from our wing administrator, and now she's gone as well. Some sort of extended leave. Either way, they're not replacing her." whispered the agent. "No administrator, and no liaison."

"That means Agent Forsythe is not just the head of security for the wing, but the director of the entire west wing,' said Thomas. His feelings of doubt and suspicion grew. What is he up to? he asked himself. What are the investors up to? Things were not adding up, and a seed of doubt grew in his gut. He wondered if this scientist knew anything more that could shed some light on this.

"Well, it's good to work for Agent Forsythe now, isn't it?" said the agent to the others. He smiled and lightly elbowed Thomas in the side. "Maybe we'll all benefit from being so close to him now."

"Yeah, right," said Thomas. He faked a laugh but wasn't smiling like the others.

As they approached Agent Forsythe's office, he stood outside to greet Thomas and the others. "Well done, men. You're dismissed," said Forsythe.

"Yes sir!" they said. Everyone, that is, but Thomas.

Thomas glared at Forsythe as the others saluted and walked away. "What's going on, Forsythe?" he said. "Both the investor liaison and wing admin are gone? What kind of messed up gig have you got going on here?"

"You're way outta line, agent," barked Forsythe. It almost seemed as if he wanted to confide in Thomas, but something held his tongue. "You're dismissed."

Thomas noticed rings under Forsythe's eyes. There was a darkness to him, and his uniform seemed to have an unusual amount of dried sweat stains. Forsythe nodded to

Thomas and quickly shifted his stare to the scientist. Thomas walked away, but not before noticing that there were a small handful of suited men in Forsythe's office. Thomas looked back as they escorted the scientist into Forsythe's office. His eyes were filled with terror.

Thomas decided to walk back to his quarters, but as he turned the last corner, he noticed that his door was cracked open. He quickly turned around and plotted the fastest route back to the east wing. "Geez, I can't catch a break – just wanted to get a little sleep." muttered Thomas. Time to text an update to the Miras, he thought. I can see why they wanted me to transfer over here to keep an eye on things. Now, I think it's time for me to go back.

"Ray, did you get that message from Thomas?" said Julia. "The situation over in west wing is worse than we thought. He'll be here any minute."

"Yeah, I guess that's why we couldn't get ahold of the liaison or the admin over there," said Ray. "My sources on the surface say that they were both killed in car accidents while on leave, during the same weekend."

"Yeah, that's no good. A takeover of west wing is underway, and we're next. Something has compromised Forsythe – he's out of our hands." said Julia. "I'm transferring Thomas back here to the east wing and starting the plan B protocol."

"Let's do it," said Ray, grimly. "I thought it would be years before we'd have to do this."

Agent Thomas walked into the room. "Tell me you

guys already got Tommy."

"And hello to you, Agent Thomas," said Raymond, smiling. "Yes, of course. Your son is safe and sound playing videos in our quarters. I trust your little fact-finding mission to the west wing was illuminating?"

Thomas heaved a sigh of relief and grimaced. "Forsythe's goons were already in my quarters after we handed over the last escapee."

Raymond and Julia looked at each other with concern. "What on earth is going on over there in the west wing? What happened to Forsythe?" asked Julia.

"Someone has really gotten to him. Probably the investors," said Thomas. "He's not himself, seemed really stressed. He's over the whole wing now that the admin and the liaison are vacant."

"Yeah, we know about the so-called car accidents of both the west wing admin and our investor liaison," said Raymond. He stared at Thomas. "They were killed in the same weekend."

"This reeks of a take-over," said Thomas. "What have you guys been up to over here to cause such alarm?"

"We'll get into that later, Agent Thomas," said Ray. "Right now, we need to stage an evacuation-level event."

"You mean, plan B, right?" said Thomas. "You're sure that we'll come out of this in one piece?"

"We'll be just fine," said Julia. "Go be with your boy. We'll take care of the rest." She nodded to Ray. "I'll use our secured channel to alert the kids. Marc and Liz haven't heard from us for awhile. It's time they did."

* * *

The scientist, now strapped to a metal chair with nylon zip-cords, wondered if he'd ever make it out of that office in one piece. At first, he was okay with the idea of filing a grievance with the wing admin, but then he found out that there was no wing admin.

"One last time. Where's the disc?" hissed one of the men in a dark suit.

Who are these guys? thought the scientist. This is not what I signed up for, and the protocol for catching someone trying to leave the station with classified data did not involve... this. The scientist looked up. "I-I really don't know what you mean," he said with a shaky voice. He looked nervously around at the others in the room. "Please, I can't take this anymore. Just let me go. My family will call the authorities if they don't hear from me soon. I have rights. If you don't let me go, I'm filing an incident report with the Investor Consortium. The SeaLab charter clearly states–"

Agent Forsythe stepped forward. "That kinda sounds like a threat, Dr..." he looked down at his badge, "Dr. Lee."

"No, I-I didn't mean it like that," said the scientist. His panic-stricken eyes darted back and forth between Forsythe and the suited man across from him. A thin red line of blood ran down from his split lower lip, and bruises started to redden on his face, and small spatters of blood littered his white lab coat.

One of the suited men opened a briefcase and pulled out a syringe. "This should help clear up the details of this quaint conversation," he said as he jabbed it mercilessly into the scientist's neck. The scientist shrieked in pain and jolted in his chair. "Now, please, kind doctor, be good and tell us what you did with the intelligence you planned to take to the surface." Two other suited men drew long dark blades and approached the scientist.

"Wait, we're just going to question him, and then turn him over to the authorities, right?" asked Agent Forsythe. "We don't need to hurt him."

A fourth suited man stood and approached Forsythe. "It would seem that you are slightly confused as to the chain of command here, Agent Forsythe. We will do precisely what we need to do, and you will remain silent unless we ask for you to speak. Understood?"

"Yes sir," said Forsythe, reluctantly. This whole deal is getting worse every minute, he thought. "May I ask what happened to the other scientists who were taken to the surface?"

The fourth suited man nodded to the two with blades drawn. Before Agent Forsythe could mutter another word, he dropped lifeless to the floor — a pool of blood quickly spread out from his body. The suited man then turned to the scientist whose eyes were only half-opened. His drugged head leaned to one side, and drool dropped from the corner of his mouth. The suited man smiled. "Now, kind doctor, what have you done with the intelligence you tried to take to the surface? Where is the disc?"

The scientist smiled and with some effort turned to the suited man. "I... I gave it away," he muttered.

The suited man gritted his teeth and nodded to the two other men. As they approached the scientist, the room rocked sideways, knocking everyone to the floor. The fluorescent lights dimmed and emergency horns started to sound.

"Uh-oh, that doesn't sound good," said the scientist

with a slur.

The suited man nodded again, and they all left the room, but not before slitting the scientist's throat.

Back in the east wing, the Miras initiated their plan B protocol. It was designed as a way of shutting down the entire station temporarily in order to evacuate all personnel so that critical research could be secured.

"Forsythe's branch was last to get shut down, right? The others got into pods, right?" asked Thomas as he ran back into the Mira's control room.

"Yes, of course. They'll have plenty of time to get to their pods," said Raymond. "We did build this place, you know."

"What on earth made you guys think to build in such a contingency?" asked Thomas.

"Jules is the most paranoid person I know," said Ray, smiling broadly. "And I always listen to Jules."

"Well, all escape pods have been activated in both the north and south bays. Nothing clears the house faster than a fire drill," said Julia. "When they get to the surface, they'll be ok, but they'll need to spend some time in compression chambers until the nitrogen bubbles leave their system."

"Doesn't sound like much fun." said Thomas.

"More fun than dealing with deep-sea martial law and violent new management," said Raymond. "Besides, we can't let our most recent data fall into the hands of the Investor Consortium."

"Yeah, good point," said Thomas. He put his hand into

his jacket pocket and pulled out a small optical disc. "Well now, take a look at this. This is what they were probably looking for on the scientist!"

"That poor man thought that he wasn't going to make it," said Julia. "Thomas, what is the scientist's name?"

"Dr. Lee, Richard Lee." said Thomas.

Ray gasped. "I know him. His wife died of leukemia last summer. No children. I'm not even sure who we'd inform if we can't find him." Anticipating the question, Ray turned to Thomas. "Dr. Lee leads the group that's close to finding a promising new treatment for a number of different cancers – specifically leukemia. Stem cell programming and replication technology."

"Why would he want to take sensitive research to the surface?" asked Thomas? "It would have terminated his contracts, and landed him in prison. Why would he jeopardize his hard work like that?" Ray and Julia looked at each other nervously, then back at Thomas. "What?" asked Thomas. "What are you not telling me this time?"

Julia sighed. "We found something. Something amazing. Some of the data looked like it may have been useful for Dr. Lee's research. So, we—"

"So I sent some of it to Dr. Lee," interrupted Ray, "Only to discover in the next few days what that data really meant. We made a mistake bringing another scientist onto the project."

"Well, what did it mean?" asked Thomas. "What was so important that Dr. Lee was willing to risk everything to get ahold of it?" By now, Thomas was so intrigued by the idea of a major discovery that he'd almost forgotten about the mayhem of the west wing, and everything that seemed wrong with his old friend Agent Forsythe.

"I'm sorry, Agent Thomas. We just can't risk you being compromised – and for your own safety and the safety of your boy, you probably shouldn't know," said Julia. "It's possible that people have already died as a result of what we did. Dr. Lee is a skilled geneticist, but not very good at discretion. Can I see that disc?" She held out her hand toward Thomas. Her normally joyful countenance was now stern and troubled.

Thomas hesitated, then gave it to her. His forced smile didn't come close to hiding the annoyance he harbored. "I don't like this, you guys. We've been friends for a long time. If you've found something, you really should let me know so I can provide the security you need."

"Thomas," said Ray, "Think of your boy. The Investor Consortium has got to know that you know nothing, or you'll lose everything."

"Fine," said Thomas reluctantly. "I trust you guys know what you're doing."

Julia placed the disc under a reader. Data leaped onto a nearby display. Patterns swept across the screen from multiple directions, and more patterns emerged within others, forming what seemed to be a double helix.

"That's enough!" said Ray. He took the disc and threw it into a portable incinerator which instantly reduced it to fine white powder. He looked at his wife who was still stunned and gazing at the now blank screen. "Jules, we don't know who else may have seen this. How did Dr. Lee get that much data? I only gave him a sampling."

"Ray, the data unpacked itself," said Julia. "You only gave him the sequence that I isolated, but somehow it still contained a lot more data."

"Who do you think Dr. Lee would have wanted to

contact on the surface?" asked Thomas. "Why would they have cared so much about that data?" He was going to ask more questions, but then realized the futility of his efforts.

"Agent Thomas," said Ray, "We need you to monitor all of Dr. Lee's team and virtual team members on the surface. He probably had at least a few confidants on his team that might also have copies of that data. We need to know who they are and, if possible, confiscate what they have. We need to contain this."

Despite his frustration, Thomas decided not to push more questions. Okay fine, he thought. Maybe it's better that I not know. "Ok, so, here's a reasonable question: how am I supposed to get back to the surface?" asked Thomas. "All of the escape pods have been activated, and the west wing airlock is obviously not accessible."

Ray smiled at Julia. "You'll have to drown in that solution we've been developing. Once you do, we can transport you into the surface monitoring station."

"No no no, that's not ready. You said so yourself!" snapped Thomas.

"We made some modifications to the fluid density and the ventilator," said Julia. She paused and looked at him thoughtfully.

"What?" asked Thomas.

"It won't be pleasant," said Julia, "And you'll have to really push yourself to expel the material from your lungs when you get to the other end."

"Wonderful," said Thomas. "Whatever, I can take it."

"Follow me," said Julia, smiling. "I'll get you ready." She turned and started toward the exit.

"Wait," said Thomas, "Won't you guys be taking the west wing back online?"

"No," said Ray impatiently. He turned and madly started to tap on his display. "Jules will brief you on the details on the way to the transport tube."

"When you do bring it online, you're going to need me here for support," said Thomas. He wasn't sure what unnerved him more, the idea of drowning in tubes and being shot into oblivion, or leaving the Miras unprotected. "This doesn't sound like a very good plan."

"Marc and Liz will soon be on their way here. They bring their own security," said Ray.

"But...," said Thomas.

"But nothing," blurted Ray. "The protocols I've designed will ensure that Marc and Liz are safe when they arrive at the west wing. Agent Thomas, find out what those investors are looking for specifically. We need you to work from the top down. We've got our work cut out for us here. Also, notify Susan of our situation and protect her from the IC. Tell her that we've executed Plan B."

"Umm, I know that it's none of my business," said Thomas, "But I thought that your daughter wanted nothing to do with you guys."

Raymond smiled. "Well, you're right of course," he turned and looked at Thomas, "It's none of your business."

"Whatever," said Thomas. He was used to dealing with Ray when he was grumpy. Not that I can blame him, he thought.

Thomas walked into his son's room. "Hey daddy!" he said.

"Hey Tommy. Whatcha doing?"

"Train track," said Tommy as he moved a toy train around a large and complicated track. "This is my train.

That one is yours."

Thomas didn't know what to say. He hadn't spent enough time with his son in the last few weeks. Ray and Jules have been awesome babysitters, but nothing replaces a boy's parents, thought Thomas. "Your mother would be proud."

"What was mommy like?" asked the boy, continuing to move a small train engine around the track. "Was she funny like you?"

Thomas dreaded these questions, and only made him miss his wife even more. "She was much funnier," he said, forcing a smile.

"Where did she go?" asked Tommy. This time he stopped playing and looked up at his father.

I came here to say bye to the boy, and now I have to answer these questions, thought Thomas. He sighed loudly. "She went to a happier place where she wouldn't be sick anymore. Listen, Tommy–"

"Will I see her again?" interrupted the boy. Before he could try to answer that question, he asked another. "Wanna play with me?"

Thomas sighed and scratched his head while his heart beat hard inside his chest. "Listen, Tommy, I have to go do a job for Mr. and Mrs. Mira," he said quietly. "I will meet you on the surface when the Miras are done here. They'll take good care of you."

Tommy jumped up and ran to his father, embracing him with a huge hug. "When we get to the surface, I want to go swimming!" he said.

"Deal let's do it," said Thomas, chuckling at the irony of them already being at the bottom of the Atlantic. Thomas picked up his son and turned around. Jules was standing at the door with a large smile, but Thomas could also see her sadness.

"Little Tommy will be safe here." said Jules.

"Thanks, I appreciate that." Agent Thomas smiled and sighed deeply. "Tommy, be good for the Miras. I'll see you again soon."

"I will. I love you, daddy," said Tommy. He gave his father another hug.

Thomas put him down and turned to Jules. "Ok, Mrs. Mira. Lead the way."

They walked down a long corridor. The further they walked, the more cluttered the hallway was with boxes and supplies. Jules moved some of the boxes aside with her foot and tapped a code on a nondescript part of the wall. Immediately, a section of the wall opened to reveal a spiral metal staircase descending into darkness.

"Where does that go?" asked Thomas. "Why the secret passage?"

"We couldn't risk this area being detected," said Jules. "Funding for liquid ventilation technology was cut two years ago, and the IC prohibits research work on unfunded projects."

"Of course," said Thomas, refusing to hold back his sarcasm. "Wouldn't want hundreds of people miles below the ocean to be able to breathe fluid in case of an emergency." He straightened and glared at Julia, not sure to whom else he could aim his frustration. "The Investor Consortium used to be open to that sort of enabling innovation. Now, they just want to manipulate and twist everything to their advantage – and trapping hundreds of scientists deep down in the depths of the SeaLab program is one way to do that."

"You're preaching to the choir, Agent Thomas," said Julia. 'And you're correct, except that we come down here willingly. We don't feel trapped."

"Well, I do," said Thomas. "I don't know how so many of you guys can skip so many consecutive vacations to the surface."

"We love what we do," said Julia. "And we still find ways to conduct our research on our own terms." She walked into the opening and motioned for Thomas to follow.

After a long, mostly dark descent downward, the heat dramatically increased to the point that Thomas had to unbutton his uniform shirt. Sweat rolled down his face. "I suppose you wouldn't want the ventilation system to work too well down here," said Thomas. "Might draw too much attention."

"Precisely!" said Julia. She paused nervously. "I should probably tell you that we mean not to go back online. We're taking SeaLab IV down permanently."

"What?" asked Thomas. "How? The Plan B protocol never..." He stopped and raised his finger accusingly at Jules. She looked surprised and stepped back. "My son is here, and you and Ray! How on earth do you plan to get Tommy and yourselves out of this place?"

"Tommy is safer down here, and you know that," said Julia. "You need to assess the situation on the surface. That's the best way to protect your boy."

"Sounds like you've learned some IC manipulation techniques." said Thomas.

"We never meant for any of this to happen, Thomas," said Julia. "We're doing the best we can, given the situation."

"Do Marc and Liz know about any of this?" asked Thomas. "Do they know what kind of predicament they're joining in on down here?"

"We can't tell them," said Jules, "Ray feels like it would be too great a risk — mostly to them."

"Why?" asked Thomas. "Because the IC might decide to shut things down? You're already going to do that, so what's the point?"

"You know I can't tell you why," said Jules. "Just trust me." She held out a syringe and without warning, jabbed it into Thomas' arm. "This is a muscle relaxer. It will also slow your breathing."

"A little warning would have been nice." said Thomas.

"What good would that have done?" asked Julia.

Thomas smiled. "Good point," he put his hand on Jules' shoulder. "I have your word that Tommy will be ok, right?"

"You have our word," said Jules. "And you'll be ok as well."

"Ok, I'm ready," said Thomas with a somewhat slurred voice. Apparently the muscle relaxers are kicking in, this is fun, he thought."

"Listen, Ray and I are really sorry for all of this," said Jules. She placed a mask over his face and tapped a few buttons on the side which caused it to suction on tight. The muscle relaxer had taken enough of an effect that he couldn't immediately react. "This ventilator will guide a fluid feeder into your lungs. It will hurt a bit, but not for very long. Try to relax. This thing will take the CO_2 away fast enough to keep you alive."

Thomas took a deep breath, rolled his eyes, then closed them. He tried to speak, but for obvious reasons, stopped trying.

"We'll be looking for the beacon signal from Miami through the restricted security network bands," said Julia. "Good luck!" After securing Thomas to a special restraint fastened to the wall, she tapped something on a control panel, and the floor slid away beneath Thomas's feet.

Thomas looked at Julia and nodded just before he disappeared into the blackness below.

CHAPTER TWO

Seraphim

SEALAB IV SURFACE MONITORING FACILITY –
SOUTHERN FLORIDA

"They what?" asked Marcus Mira. "They actually called it plan B? That name was just a joke."

"Well, it stuck. Apparently your dad didn't have a better code name for that whacked-out emergency protocol," said his wife, Liz. "Let's get down there on the next transport. Won't be difficult getting past security if they know we're going down to help out with rescue and recovery efforts."

Marcus, scratching his head, brought up a three-dimensional model of the entire under-sea complex on a small tablet. "If the plan B protocol worked as designed, there wouldn't be anyone left down there to care, and it will take hours for those escape capsules to surface."

"Yeah, they can't ascend too fast, or they'll all get narced — five miles is a long way down," said Liz. "How long before the surface station is alerted?"

"When my parents decide to alert them, I guess," said Marc. "But they will have to give some timeframe after a few hours as to when the transport line will be operational again. To the surface station, it just looks like they're doing routine maintenance — no one will be worried."

"Marc," said Liz, "Why are you dodging the question?"

Marc sighed and reluctantly turned away from his display. "Okay, fine. I'm just nervous. My folks are five miles underneath the Atlantic and they've just initiated the most drastic security drill anyone has ever designed for a SeaLab facility, and we don't know why."

"And we can't know why," said Liz, "Because the protocol also severs all standard communication lines. So, how are we supposed to know if it's even safe to go down there?"

"The instructions are clear," said Marc, "We're to be the first ones down there — before anyone else has a chance to break in unopposed."

"But, how do we know what prompted your parents to execute plan B?" asked Liz. She raised her voice and stared with concern at Marc. "Yes, we're pretty well trained for this contingency, but I'd really like to know at least a little bit about what we'd be running into down there."

Marc knew that Liz could see right through him, and therefore could see that he was also doubting the whole plan B contingency his parents had created to protect the station from being commandeered by hostiles. "Anyone left behind wouldn't pose a threat. They'd be cold and low on oxygen," said Marc. "Plan B would have disabled the entire west wing, all four levels, but not the airlock itself. The east wing would barely know anything had happened, and the causeway separating the two wings would be locked down. Hopefully, the west wing was completely evacuated. All facilities there will be temporarily shut down, including electricity and oxygen. It's not destroyed, but anyone who may have decided to stay behind would not last too long."

"Yeah, I know," said Liz. She sighed loudly. "That's why we have to get down there to turn the station back on. Let's just hope those poor folks got out ok. After all, they would have believed that there was a hull breach and would need to escape or they'd be in big trouble." Marcus seemed to be lost in thought as he stared at the tablet. "Are you ok, Marc?"

"Yeah, I'm fine," said Marc after a long pause. "Can't wait to hear about what warranted executing plan B."

"I'm sure your parents had a good reason. Something must have gone dreadfully wrong for them to do that," said Liz.

"Yeah right," said Marc, "Either my mom's paranoia took over or my dad just wanted to clear everyone out on the west side to protect his latest batch of research findings."

"Or both," said Liz, smiling. "Either way, we should get packed for the trip we both hoped would never come."

"The only thing I'm not quite sure of are the IC's own independent monitoring systems," said Marc. "For us, it would take some effort once we get down there to assess the situation. We don't know how long it would take the IC to do the same."

"The Investor Consortium's monitoring systems were designed by your parents, and we already know that Plan B correctly severed distress communications to the surface," said Liz. "Otherwise, we would have heard something already from the Surface Monitoring Station.

"I have the administrative access codes," said Marc. "Let's pack up and hurry down there, flip the lights back on, and find out what's happened."

"You make it sound like a trip to the park," said Liz, smiling nervously. "Kinda wish we actually were going to the park, rather than that stifling, deep-sea coffin."

The afternoon sun drifted high over the Florida sky, and the air carried a strong scent of salt water. After some last minute preparations, Marc paused to take in a few more deep breaths of the ocean air as Liz walked back into the room. "Are you ready?" he asked, shoving some last-minute items into a small pack. "Our shuttle leaves in twenty minutes."

"Always in a rush when you get stressed," Liz sighed then smiled patiently, "Try and relax. I'm sure your folks are fine."

"It's been too long, and we haven't heard a peep for three months. It's not like them," said Marc. "And–"

"–And they haven't answered any of our messages," interrupted Liz. "Yeah, I know. I'm worried too, but we do know that they read them."

"It's not good enough," said Marc. "Something is wrong down there. They've been in the east wing too long. West wing is where all the activity is, where you've gotta keep your ear to the ground, and they have actively avoided that wing entirely."

"They have Agent Thomas to keep them briefed." said Liz.

"He got transferred only days ago to the west wing, and until then, he was spending most of his time on the east wing," said Marc. "Not sure how well he could have been keeping an eye on things."

"I guess we can't count on Thomas to handle everything down there," said Liz. "Listen, I'm ready if you are. It will take a good five hours to get down there safely. If Plan B was really executed an hour ago, that would give us around two hours once we get there–"

"–to flip the air back on and assess the situation before anyone left behind would run out of med-kit air tank reserves," interrupted Marc. He glanced at Liz, who was scowling back at him. "Sorry, didn't mean to cut you off."

Liz's face relaxed and she smiled. "Whatever. Let's get going then."

The transport station was just down the road. After a brief security check, they would enter a transport vehicle on a magnetic rail that would take them five miles to the bottom of the Puerto Rico trench. This trip will be worth the trouble, thought Liz, as long as it settles Marc down. He's starting to drive me nuts. As they drove to the station, she looked out the window. The sun was shining onto the ocean, and the beach was littered with activity. Families playing in the sand, eating shaved ice, and enjoying life. She longed for a family, but their attempts had all resulted in failure. She frowned and turned her gaze ahead as the station slowly appeared on the horizon before them. The shuttle, grappling a single rail, left the southern Florida shoreline and jutted for more than seventy miles out onto the surface of the Atlantic Ocean. It would only be a handful of minutes before they'd reach the transport and start their long journey five miles down to SeaLab IV which was firmly attached to the wall of the trench, not far from the bottom. For Liz, the Florida shoreline fading into the distance behind them was bitter-sweet. Half of her longed to build a family in a neighborhood of normal families on the surface, and not spend the majority of her life deep under the ocean or out in space. Maybe, then, she thought, life in a normal environment would rub-off onto she and Marc. On the other hand, Liz's other half wanted to be re-immersed in her work and, for at least a short time, forget her longings.

As their shuttle pulled up alongside the station, the conveyor slid to the side, loading them onto the transport. As they passed through the loading dock, they were all scanned as part of the security protocols that had been put in place by the Investor Consortium only months before.

"Mr and Mrs. Mira," said the security officer, "Looks like you have the transport to yourselves today. Good luck down there! Hopefully, you guys get whatever the problem is down there fixed."

"That's our job!" said Marc, almost with too much enthusiasm. Liz elbowed him. "The station will be open again in no time."

"Hey, it's no big deal to me," said the officer. "I get paid by the hour. Have a good trip."

Liz looked at Marc and smiled. He smiled back and reached for her hand, which she grasped firmly. She looked all around as the doors of the transport closed. Good, thought Liz. None of the staff seemed to have been alerted to the incident at SeaLab IV. Marc and Liz looked at each other and smiled nervously. The five-hour trip to SeaLab IV was Liz's least favorite part, which is ironic considering her choice of the field of marine biology.

Marc tightened his grip on Liz's hand, and marveled at what the water pressure per square inch was that far

31

down. At sea level, the human body endures fourteen and a half pounds of pressure per square inch. We can't really tell, because the fluid in our bodies pushes outward equally. However, every thirty-three feet, another fourteen and a half pounds per square inch of pressure is added, and there's no good way for the human body to compensate. He decided to not remind Liz of that fact. She seemed stressed enough – besides, she knew all of that better than he did. Finally, they both sat in their seats and relaxed as the cabin pressurized. They heard hissing sounds all around them as they were encased in form-fitting rigid pods. Breathing masks descended and wrapped around their faces moments before a warm fluid engulfed them. Quickly, Marc and Liz drifted to sleep as the silent, automated transport plunged imperceptibly downward.

For those less familiar with SeaLab IV, the shuttle featured interactive displays with maps of the facility. From such a display, one could learn that SeaLab IV is made up of two wings: west wing and east wing. Like the center of a bow-tie, both wings were connected by a narrower region which housed oxygen and ventilation factories, as well as a host of other sophisticated functions required to sustain life several miles beneath the ocean. The only way in or out of SeaLab IV was located in the far end of the west wing – the west airlock. The east wing was where all of the science and research personnel resided, far away from the hustle and bustle of the west wing.

It was Raymond and Julia Mira who insisted that they have complete control of the east wing so as to maintain the seclusion and the privacy that the scientists required. Those located in the west wing were mostly not scientists, but personnel responsible for administration and security.

Each wing was overseen by a wing administrator, as well as a person appointed to represent the Investor Consortium (again, generally referred to as the IC). That person was referred to as a the investor liaison. The wing administrator for the east wing was Julia Mira and had been so since the contracts were originally signed with the IC. The Mira's contract with the investors required that they maintain operational control of the east wing.

The west wing, referred to by Raymond Mira at times sarcastically as "the wild west", had started to experience an increased frequency of security breaches. These occurrences resulted in tightened security and increased scrutiny of personnel as they periodically departed to the surface and returned again. After awhile, it was deemed unwise for personnel to leave more than a few times a month – especially the scientists and researchers. Over time, trips to the surface were limited to only two a year.

The arrival alarm jarred Marc and Liz from their sleep. Their restraints released, and Marc stood up and stretched. "Well, we're back in SeaLab IV," he said with a yawn. The light around the airlock door pulsed with a deep red glow.

"Looks like the Plan B protocol worked," said Liz. "I'll reactivate the environmental drives so we can breathe in there."

"Sounds like a plan." said Marc.

Liz entered a security code on the wall. The light

turned green after a few moments, and then the large airlock door slid open with a loud persistent hissing sound. Marc looked through the airlock and out into the courtyard leading to the rest of SeaLab's west wing. Only the dim emergency lighting was on, and red lights flashed on every wall. All exits to the rest of the wing were still sealed off and glowing red. "Wow," he said.

"What is it?" asked Liz as she rubbed her eyes.

"Do you hear that?" asked Marc. He stepped closer to the airlock opening.

"Hear what?" asked Liz, slightly annoyed.

"That's just it — nothing. Not a sound," said Marc. "Last time we were here, the place was crawling with lab coat geeks. Never been so quiet around here. Of course, everyone evacuated, but it still feels weird."

"Hey, we're two of those geeks," said Liz. She placed her hand on his shoulder and squeezed slightly. "And you're my favorite geek."

"I love you too, Liz," said Marc distractedly. He stepped through the open airlock and down onto the metallic steps leading to the vacant security station. After entering a code into the console, a steel panel opened to reveal a secured firearm. "Here ya go," said Marc as he picked it up and tossed it to Liz. "You like these things more than me. Consider it an early anniversary present."

Liz caught it effortlessly and chambered a round. She rolled her eyes and slapped Marc on the shoulder. "You need to work on your romantic skills."

"Hey, it looks like we have the entire west wing to ourselves," said Marc. "Besides the unusually chilly temp and thin air, it feels pretty romantic to me."

"Heh, yeah. Like I said." Liz checked the clip and

looked back at Marc. "We need to find you a gun, too. Who knows why your folks flipped the switch on that crazy protocol."

"Yeah, whatever the reason, they thought things over here must have been dangerous enough to go to those lengths," said Marc. "I'll grab the firearm in the control room."

"We need to scan the rest of the wing for stragglers," said Liz. "If there is still anyone here, we've only got a few hours left to get them some air."

Marc and Liz entered the empty and silent control room, which was really the only room they could access from the main courtyard. Once inside, Marc opened another security panel and grabbed the gun inside. Liz ran to the opposite end of the room and unlocked another panel. Inside was a large switch.

"A few hours isn't a whole lot of time to troubleshoot things if this doesn't turn on with the first try." said Marc.

Liz held her breath as she slowly pulled down the master power switch. "C'mon baby, switch on," muttered Liz as she looked nervously back at Marc.

After what seemed like an eternity, but was actually only a handful of seconds, a dull rumble and distinctive hum could be heard around the room. Almost immediately, the controls leaped to life, and the air seemed to crackle. "Yes!" said Marc. "Nice work! I'll start those scans."

Liz walked back out into the courtyard. The temperature was already rising, and the lighting was now fully operational. Most importantly, no more flashing red lights. She took in a deep sterile breath of air, and it seemed to make her dizzy. She stumbled toward the nearest seat in the middle of the large round room and sat down. She shook her head and smiled. Well, that was stupid, she thought. Always takes a bit to acclimatize to the air down here. Almost five miles down – hard to believe. She stood back up and slipped her gun into the back of her trousers. Liz looked around the room at the three doors leading out of the courtyard. They were still closed, but now glowed green. The hair on the back of her neck stood up, and she started to feel queasy. "Marc, how we doing on those scans?" she yelled.

Marc stepped out of the door leading to the control room. "Better come have a look at this," he said. His face was slightly paled.

She ran back into the room, and Marc was again tapping on displays all over the room. "What is it?" she asked.

"This can't be right," said Marc. "None of the escape capsules launched. Not one of them were activated."

"Let me see," said Liz. She walked over to another wall and tapped on a few of the other displays. "That's weird. Where's the video feed for the capsule bays? How could they all be down?"

"Oh, wow." gasped Marc.

"What is it?" asked Liz.

"The cameras were designed only for internal conditions," said Marc. "If I'm reading the error codes correctly, all of the capsule bays were flooded. If that's the case, the extreme pressure would have certainly obliterated the cameras."

"Flooded?" gasped Liz. "Where are all the people? There are over three hundred stationed on this wing the last time I checked."

"I've scanned the entire wing, and the results are coming back now," said Marc. "The station only has emergency med kits with oxygen in personal quarters and common areas, and there's only about a hundred of them."

"Plan B protocol wasn't supposed to flood the capsule bays, was it?" asked Liz.

"No way!" said Marc. "I have no idea how that could have happened. I tried opening a line to the East Wing, but plan B severed all ties between the two wings. The only way to the other wing is manually through the causeway." He stepped away from the display in front of him and looked at Liz. "Are all the exits out in the courtyard still closed?"

"Yeah, they are. Closed and locked," said Liz. "They're supposed to be locked, right?"

"Plan B should have kept them locked," said Marc. He ejected the clip of his gun. "Oh great, only ten rounds. How much do you have?"

"Full clip." said Liz. "Why do you ask?"

"I'm picking up movement near the common area on the other side of the west wing," said Marc. "Not sure what it is. I'll have to tweak the scanner to get more information."

"Sure would have been great to get a little more intel before coming down here." said Liz.

"My folks would have told us more if they could have." said Marc.

"I'm talking about your parents," said Liz. "No warning, no details."

Marc gritted his teeth. "Yeah, my dad's itchy trigger finger strikes again." A binging sound started to come from one of the displays. "Liz, we've got a really weak reading in the security section next door. And…,"

"And what?" asked Liz. She looked at the display. "What are those four things over there on the other side of the station?"

"I don't know. I thought that they might be anomalous readings, but then they just moved again," said Marc. "It's intermittent, and there's no heat signature. Weird."

"Robotic equipment?" asked Liz. "Where are they located?"

"All four are located around the causeway that leads to the East Wing," said Marc. "I'll access the video feeds for the causeway and see if we can get a peek at them." He switched on the feed, and they both gasped.

"Who the heck are they, and why are they trying to torch their way into the East Wing?" asked Liz.

"Never seen body suits like that, all white," said Marc. "They're intruders. I think we found the troublemakers."

"I only see two of them," said Liz. "You said there were four, right? Where'd the other two go?"

Marc turned back to the other display and grimaced. "They're almost to the courtyard. You suited up?"

"I'm always suited up," said Liz. "I'll keep an eye on the courtyard and make sure nothing tries to get through any of the doors."

Ray turned around excitedly. "Marc and Liz have activated the west wing, but the courtyard is still in lock-down. I'm running a scan so we can get a better look, and possibly open a line to them."

"I don't like this at all," said Jules. "We don't know what kind of mess we might have left over there for them to clean up. We should have warned them somehow."

"What?" said Ray. "And also risk warning the intruders – whoever they are – over in the west wing?"

"Yeah, I know," said Jules. "Good point."

"I enabled Marc and Liz's codes at the causeway," said Ray. "They'll be okay. They just need to get to the causeway, and once they're in the east wing, we can execute the remainder of plan B."

"And what then?" asked Jules. "SeaLab IV will go dark for good?"

"Yes, and see what intel we can get from Agent Thomas," said Ray, grimly. He turned back to his display.

"I'll go make sure little Tommy's alright." said Jules.

Ray felt the weight of the situation in the west wing on his shoulders. What was Dr. Lee planning to do with that data? he thought. And, who was interrogating him? Ray felt certain that Forsythe was not behind it. This was bigger than the IC. The investors would never do anything to compromise the security of their research. "Be careful, kids," he whispered.

The courtyard was eerily silent. No station staff, no busy traffic through the central crossroads of west wing, and none of the typical music or white noise played over the com system. The now fully-operational lighting system afforded a false sense of security as every hallway and common area was now in full view. There was literally nowhere to hide.

Liz turned to Marc. "Plan?" she asked. "Are there still just the two coming our way?"

"Yes," said Marc, "The other two are still trying to break into the causeway. I can only hope my folks know what to do once we get there."

"First, let's apprehend these two," said Liz. "Their movements are strange, yet professional." A lump started to form in her throat. "Who knows what havoc they've caused beside the mess they left in the capsule bays."

"Then we've gotta get over there and verify the status of those escape pods." said Marc.

The main room of the courtyard was shaped like a bat wing; not a single flat wall anywhere but in a few of the central passages. The control center afforded a complete view of the courtyard and the three doors leading to the rest of the station. The door to West Wing North-A was on the left, and the door to West Wing South-A was on the right. The door in the center led to a large walkway that cut straight through to the common area.

"Still have their position?" asked Liz.

"I know that they are there," said Marc, "But I can no longer see them on the sensors. Somehow the video feed doesn't show them at all."

"Refraction suits?" asked Liz.

Marc sighed. "Maybe, let's assume the worst." He drew his sidearm and chambered a round. "My bet is that they're waiting somewhere for us on the other side of the center door."

"And if they're not there, we can make a run for the common area," said Liz. "From there, we can bypass the North-B and South-B sections."

"Good," said Marc, "After we check the bays, I want to

stop by the administrative offices before we go for the causeway and see if we can find out what happened over there."

"That's pretty risky. I say we make a run for the causeway and skip the rest," said Liz. "We're outnumbered two to one, and that's only counting the goons we were able to detect on the motion sensors."

"We have to try," said Marc. "When the rest of plan B is executed, there won't be a west wing anymore, and we need to try and figure out what happened here before it's gone."

"Whatever," said Liz. "I'm not liking this at all."

Marc and Liz both drew their guns and approached the center door. Marc entered the security code, and after a short delay, the door opened with a loud hiss. The lit hallway extended for a great distance before them. Marc held out a portable sensor. "Liz, now." She fired a handful of rounds in a methodical pattern down the hallway as Marc closely analyzed the sensor display. "Nothing," said Marc. "No movement. Either they're not there or we're dealing with some really cool customers."

"Feels like a trap," whispered Liz as they walked through the door and into the large hallway. The door at the other end was still closed. "I think they're waiting for us in the common area up ahead."

"Well, I'm still not getting a reading on them," said Marc. "Last time I got a blip, it was in the common area beyond that door."

"Can they open that door?" asked Liz as she kept her aim on the far end if the hallway.

"They can open all the other doors, it's just the three leading to the courtyard behind us that are locked down."

said Marc.

"Except for the center door that we opened for them," said Liz. The color left her face as she turned to look behind. "Oh no."

The hiss of the other two doors opening in the courtyard was unmistakable. One of the intruders had somehow slipped past them in the hallway and managed to hack the codes for the other two doors from the courtyard. "Liz, I'm getting three blips now in the courtyard," whispered Marc, "Two coming our direction, and the third is headed for the control center."

"Are you ready for this?" asked Liz.

Marc nodded. He put the sensor back into his pocket and holstered his gun. He extended two fingers and pointed down, then around in a circle. Liz pursed her lips and did the same. Here we go, she thought. Her eyes closed. She understood Marc's plan – she would take down the two intruders coming their way, and Marc would break for the control center and intercept the third. It was a play the intruders were least likely to anticipate, especially since they were invisible and had the upper hand.

Liz suppressed a wave of panic back down her throat like a dry, jagged pill. She took a deep breath and dove backward into a roll. As she sprung from the floor, she kicked upward. The kick pierced empty air, but she continued to rise toward the wall. Immediately, she felt the crackle in the air of gunfire. Keep moving, she thought. I must keep moving. Two, then three more rounds hummed by her head. Judging from their origin, she now had a pretty good idea of where one of the intruders stood. Liz leapt from a wall and dove back down toward the floor. As she spun around, one foot found its mark, and when her other foot came around, it sent the intruder to the floor. She sprang toward her opponent, wrapped her legs around his neck, and flipped him upside-down. His resistance abruptly ended when the bones in the intruder's neck snapped. Immediately, she raised his torso up in front of her just as several more rounds from another unseen opponent found their mark in the intruder's already deceased body. She felt around his head, arms, and neck. When her fingers found what seemed to be a tube or cluster of wires, she yanked violently. A loud hum echoed in the hallway, then silence. Instantly, the intruder became visible. He was completely clad in a pearly-white body suit. She sneered and looked down the hallway. The other intruder wasn't attacking.

Liz placed the palm of her hand on the floor. Her carefully tuned senses could tell that the other intruder had turned and was running to get to Marc and join with the third intruder back in the courtyard. I'm just going to have to risk there only being three of them, she thought. She whistled twice – a signal to Marc that he now had two opponents. She relaxed her leg grip on the dead body and sprang up into a sprint back toward the courtyard. Liz felt numbness all over her body, and a dull ache in one of her arms and legs. No matter, she thought, and within a few seconds she bolted back into the courtyard and whistled again, this time longer. Banging and the sound of breaking glass came from the control room. As Liz ran toward the room, a sharp pain from the side knocked her to the ground. She threw her shoulder to the side and rolled so she landed face up. "Marc, hit the water!" she yelled.

Liz turned just in time to see an uncloaked and badly beaten intruder, also in a white body suit, fly from the control room and hit the wall. He laid motionlessly on the floor. Marc hit a sensor on the wall, and water started to rain down from sprinklers all over the courtyard. Marc quickly grabbed the handgun from the fallen intruder and ran in Liz's direction. Marc and Liz both saw the shape of a person walking toward them through the water droplets. Before Marc could squeeze off a round, the intruder leapt to the side, and then dropped into a roll toward Liz. She leapt to her feet, but the intruder grabbed one of her feet and slammed her back to the floor where he pinned her by the neck with one hand. As he raised the other to strike, the sound of gunfire rang through the air and he fell dead on top of her.

"Good call on the sprinklers!" Yelled Marc as he continued to aim his gun around the room. "Are you okay?"

"Yeah, I think so," grunted Liz. She slowly stood up but was unable to straighten one leg. Blood mixed with water stained the tile floor with a pale red color. Blood also ran from her arm. "I took a round in my leg, and my arm was grazed. See anyone else?"

"I don't think so." said Marc.

"What did they want in the control room?" asked Liz. She winced and leaned against a curved wall.

"I didn't take the time to find out," said Marc. He grabbed Liz's good arm and with his help, they went back through the center doorway and down through the passageway toward the common area that led toward the other side of the west wing.

"I don't remember this place being so big." said Liz.

"Everything seems bigger with a bullet in your leg," said Marc, forcing a smile. "Need to get you over to the east wing and get you patched up."

"There's one more intruder, Marc," said Liz. "We're not done."

Marc pulled the sensor out of his back pocket and turned around a few times. "He seems to be hanging out in the west wing admin's office," said Marc. "His last position was at the causeway entrance just beyond the office.

"Probably wants to ambush us," said Liz. "Marc, these guys are really good. Where did they come from? I wonder who trained them, and what about those cloaking suits?"

"Last time I heard mention of light bending technology was from a research company called Seraphim," said Marc. "Remember that controversial effort to cloak security drones and place them all over in urban centers?"

"Yeah. I seem to recall that Seraphim went out of business," said Liz. "Government shut them down."

"Well, the government also shut down the SeaLab project," said Marc, "Yet, here we are."

"That was a US Navy program, not a private security company," said Liz. "Not sure that's a good example of what happened with Seraphim."

"Do you always have to be so argumentative?" asked Marc.

"No, I'm sorry," said Liz. She turned and sneered at Marc. "Maybe the cheery, happy me will come back after we get this massive bullet out of my leg!"

Marc smiled and helped Liz into the common area. It was a large room that separated the two halves of the west wing. Dining areas and chairs took up much of the room in the middle, and a variety of closed-up food establishments lined the walls all the way around the room. The main exit from the common area was straight ahead, and there was a door to the left and a door to the right – in that respect, similar to the courtyard. They could still hear the sprinklers spraying water, and the fire alarm ring away behind them.

"We made quite a mess back there," said Liz. She smiled, then winced in pain. "Can we please sit down for a minute?"

"The intruder has moved," said Marc with a hush. "He's in the corridor straight ahead of us."

"What do we do?" asked Liz. Her face was losing color, and Marc knew that she wouldn't be able to fight.

"Sprinklers," said Marc. He ran to a security station between two food stands, broke the plastic barrier, and triggered the fire alarm. Immediately, the alarm sounded and numerous sprinklers showered down upon them.

"Oh, good idea." said Liz as she started to lay her head down on the table.

"No, you don't!" said Marc. He placed his gun on the table and tore a piece of fabric from his shirt. More blood started to pour onto to the floor as he tied the fabric around her leg.

Liz's vision started to blur as she gazed ahead at the three doors leading to the rest of the station. So far to go, she thought. She shook her head quickly, grabbed Marc's gun, and fired straight toward the center door.

Marc swung around in time to see the outline of the fourth intruder fall to a heap onto the floor. "Nice shot!" said Marc.

"I always was a better marksman," Liz said as she dropped the gun on the metal table with a clang. "I don't feel very good."

"You're going into shock," said Marc. "I'll get you out of here." Marc picked up Liz and carried her through the second corridor which opened up into the administrative offices for the west wing. Once there, he saw how the intruders had tried to cut through the large steel causeway door with a torch. It was the only thing keeping the intruders from entering the east wing.

Marc laid Liz, soaking wet and shivering, down onto a couch and covered her up with a blanket. "I'll be right back." He said as he walked into the wing director's office. Marc gasped when he saw the body of Agent Forsythe laying in a pool of blood just inside the door. He checked Forsythe's pulse in vain and cursed. "Why? What happened here?" he said, frustrated. On the other side of the room was the body of an older scientist, still tied to a turned over metal chair. A large fatal gash spread across his neck, but his death was evidently not instant. A phone was on the floor, not far from one of his lifeless hands. Marc picked it up and noticed a hastily-tapped message:

must protect data keep from seraph I'm. Sndf gettt helpdpll

Marc stared at the message, and back down at the lifeless scientist. All around the room, dark suit pants and coats lay in clumps on the floor. Hmm, four sets of clothing, he thought. Four intruders. That's how they got in — they posed as investor liaisons from the IC. Marc looked back out into the lobby and anger washed over him. He grabbed the scientist's badge and walked out of the room.

"Okay, Liz. Let's get you some help!" said Marc as he entered a code for the large steel door leading to the causeway. Someone's going to pay for what they've done, he thought. Even if it takes years. Marc lovingly wrapped Liz up into a few more blankets and carried her into the dimly-lit causeway.

CHAPTER THREE
Plan B

Ray and Jules ran into the courtyard of east wing just as Marc stumbled out of the causeway, almost dropping Liz. "She's lost a lot of blood," said Marc, trying to catch his breath, "She's going into shock."

Jules ran up to Marc. "I've got her!" she said sternly.

Marc smiled and sighed heavily, but his relief quickly turned to anger. "What were you two thinking?" he hissed. "Liz and I were attacked — we could have been killed!"

Ray stepped back and paled. "Attacked? What do you mean? Anyone who chose to stay behind would not have been able to-"

"-Dad, you made a mistake. Just admit it," interrupted Marc, 'Do you have any idea who was after us back there?"

"I... I guess I don't know," stammered Ray, scratching his head.

"There were four of them, as far as we could tell," said Marc. "They were pretty much invisible and much better trained than your average IC agent — not to mention that they were fully conscious. If we hadn't surprised them, we'd both be dead."

Jules laid Liz down on a couch and checked her vitals. "She'll be just fine, Marc." Jules turned and glared at Ray. "Which is more than I can say for your father."

"What?" said Ray. "You were encouraging me to initiate plan B."

"Yes, that's right," said Jules, "But I also wanted us to keep a com-line open to them in case of unforeseen circumstances. You were concerned that it could be hacked, so you omitted it from the protocol."

"And I was right," said Ray defiantly, "That com-line could have been hacked." Ray took a deep breath and scratched his head. "I'm so sorry, kids," he said. "I thought that I had every contingency covered in the plan B protocol."

"Who were they? How could they be invisible?" asked Marc. "And, why did you execute plan B?" The questions flowed from his mouth like a string of bullets laced with anger.

"Well, a company named Seraphim developed a fabric that could bend light, but it wasn't even close to being ready for a practical application," said Ray. He looked thoughtfully at Marc, and then shamefully at the floor. "But you already know that."

"Yes, I already know that," said Marc tersely. "What I really want to know is why you executed plan B."

Ray glanced at Jules, who really hadn't stopped glaring at him. "Ok. Fine. You're right, I acted hastily." said Ray. "And I failed to adequately brief you, but we didn't know you kids would be in such danger."

"Dad, why plan B?" asked Marc, raising his voice. "What's going on?"

Ray looked nervously at Jules. "We had a breakthrough, and within hours we were compromised," said Ray. "An associate of ours went missing in the west wing, and he had a copy of some of our data. It would seem that he was trying to get to the surface with it."

"And you thought that he'd just waltz out onto the surface with it?" asked Marc. "A security team would surely have apprehended him once they detected the unauthorized storage device."

"Agent Forsythe had a choke-hold on west wing security, which was a really good thing, until we found out that he'd been compromised," said Ray. "Thomas discovered that he was no longer to be trusted. Marc, we had to lock things down, and we thought that plan B would also clear out the place and subdue anyone who wanted to stick around."

"I stopped by Forsythe's office. His dead body was laying on the floor," said Marc, gravely.

"Forsythe, dead?" gasped Ray. "Good heavens, I wonder what he got himself into."

"He always seemed very boy scout to me," said Marc. "As far as I could tell, four individuals posing as IC officials killed him, and then turned the place upside down. I believe that the same four individuals attacked us. They were strong, fast, and didn't seem to have been weakened by the lack of air." He looked over to Liz who was starting to move her head. Marc smiled, exhaled deeply, and looked back at Ray. "Dad, I'm sorry. You did the right thing."

"Did you happen to see a scientist among the victims?"

asked Jules.

"Yes," said Marc, "Also in Forsythe's office. The name on the badge was Dr. Lee. His body was still bound to an overturned chair."

Jules looked at Ray. "Oh no, that's him," she said. "Dr. Lee was the colleague of ours who tried to smuggle the data to the surface — at least, that's our assumption."

"He left a vague text message on his device," said Marc. "It was short, something about protecting the data from seraphim. I thought that maybe he was referring to Seraphim Research, the company who developed the cloaking technology."

"I developed that technology," said Ray. "Those government-funded goons just productized it." He paused and stared back toward the causeway. "We need more answers. Seraphim went under a long time ago — and good riddance to them if you ask me!"

"Well, Agent Forsythe was a good man, and a good friend. So sad," said Jules. "With all that happened, I hope that the rest of the people surfaced ok. We couldn't monitor the west wing escape capsule bays from the east wing."

"Flooded," said Liz as she tried to sit up. Jules nodded and she laid back down. "The capsule bays were all flooded — at least, that's our best guess. The remotes were down, so we couldn't check to see if any of the escape capsules successfully launched."

"Impossible," blurted Ray. "Of course they launched. How would they not launch?" He stumbled and sat down in a metal chair. "I hope those people got out ok. You didn't see anyone at all down there, right?" Ray started to pale. "What on earth happened over there?"

"We were hoping that you could tell us," said Marc. "The place was vacant, except for the four cloaked creeps that attacked us. We just assumed that everyone else was able to evacuate. The only way we can verify that for sure is to go to the bays and check the sensors ourselves... unless there's a better way."

"There were no other life signs," said Liz. Wincing in pain, she struggled to sit up, and when Jules tried to stop her, Liz waved her away. "I'm fine, thank you Julia."

"No, you're not," said Julia. "Need to finish removing this thing," Liz grunted as Julia finished removing the bullet slug from her thigh. "You're all bandaged up, but you've lost some blood. Gonna have to stay down for a bit."

"Thanks, Julia." said Liz.

"I don't understand," said Ray. "There was no other way out for them than by escape capsule, and the main airlock to the surface transport would have been disabled. The escape capsules are fool-proof."

"Dad, I ran full-spectrum bio and thermal scans and nothing turned up," said Marc. "If any of the personnel were left behind in the west wing, we would have detected them."

"That doesn't make any sense," said Ray. "Between the east and west wings, there are over three hundred fifty people."

"Also," said Marc, hesitating, "The escape capsule bays on both sides of west wing were completely dark on the monitors. Couldn't see a thing."

"Extreme pressure force would have destroyed the cameras. Ironically, it seems that they were never designed to be submerged," said Ray. "What about the seismic sensor logs?"

"No readings, and the logs had been cleared," said Marc. "Something happened in those bays that someone really didn't want recorded in any way."

"Somehow the scanners must have missed all of those people," said Jules. "Or the logs were tampered with. What's the latest status report from the surface monitoring station?"

"All systems normal, but transport is suspended for maintenance," said Ray. "Just the way plan B protocol was designed to make the situation appear." Ray started to look concerned. "We have to go over to the west wing."

"We have to find out for ourselves what happened to all those people," said Jules. "For all we know, they're being held in the containment areas and somehow cloaked like those guys you ran into. Whatever the case, we must not complete the plan B sequence until we know for sure. We have to go check the west wing ourselves."

"We're not going back there," blurted Marc. "Obviously you have no idea how dangerous those intruders are. We took care of four, but there may be more of them."

"Marc, we have to try," said Ray. "Your mother's right. We have to be sure there's not anyone there needing help."

"Jules, what did you mean by completing plan B?" asked Liz.

"We'll talk about that after we get back," said Ray. "Liz, you need to stay here and monitor our position."

"I thought you couldn't monitor anything in the west wing from here." said Marc.

"You'll be able to monitor us with these," said Jules. She

handed a thick rubber wristband to each of them and brought up a display. "Those bands will scan up to forty meters in every direction based on your position."

Little Tommy walked casually into the examination room where they all sat around Liz who was still laying down on a bed. "Hey lady, are you ok?"

"Tommy, you remember Liz and Marc, right?" asked Jules.

"Yeah," said Tommy. He looked confused as he looked at Ray and Jules. "Are we going on a walk? I wanna go on a walk."

"Sweety," said Jules, "We need to go to the west wing for a little while. Stay here with Liz and take care of her, ok? Do what she says."

"Yes Mrs. Mira," said Tommy. He looked up at Liz and smiled. "Want some Cheetos and juice?"

Liz loved kids but didn't quite know how to interact with them. She looked at Jules, who just shrugged and laughed.

"Yes. Tommy. Liz would love some juice and Cheetos," said Jules.

"Liz, listen sharp and stand by," said Marc. "We're gonna go check the north and south escape pod bays first."

"Actually," said Ray, "First, we'll stop by the administrative offices. That's the easiest place to find any network tampering."

Ray, Jules, and Marc approached the causeway entrance. "Liz, keep eyes on our position and pay special attention to motion," said Marc.

"Copy that," said Liz over the radio in her best trucker voice. "I'll just be hanging back here with little Tommy.

Try to come back in one piece, please."

Ray smiled and looked at Marc. "Tough girl, never seems to lose her sense of humor." Marc gazed at Liz as she blew him a kiss before the door closed.

As the causeway door opened before them, Ray tossed a flash grenade through the opening. The loud bang and flash caused them all to flinch and stagger backward.

"Liz, did you detect any movement?"

"No movement," said Liz over the radio after a short pause, "The causeway seems to be clear." After repeating the same exercise at the other end of the long hallway, they stepped carefully into the west wing courtyard. Everything was just as Marc and Liz had left it.

Ray and Jules ran to Forsythe's office and gasped. "Oh, this is horrible. Blood everywhere," said Jules.

Ray seemed to ignore the blood and bodies altogether as he hastily hacked into the west wing security network. "Nothing here," said Ray as he turned away from the display on the desk. "Forsythe's logs have been cleared. It's gonna take me a bit to hack into the remainder of the west wing branch. Hopefully, there's some remnant of security footage that can shed light on what happened here."

"Mom and me will go check out the capsule bays," said Marc. "Let's keep the radio chatter to a minimum. We don't want to tip anyone off who may still be hiding out over here."

"When I'm done here," said Ray, "I'll join you." His attention by now was completely fixed on the display as it lit up in response to his commands.

Jules and Marc ran back toward the common area and stopped just before the entrance. "Whoa, sprinklers are still going," said Marc. The entrance to the escape capsule bays was located a few junctions beyond the north and south common area exits. "We still in the clear, Liz?"

"No signs as far as I can tell," replied Liz over the radio. "Be careful anyway."

Marc smiled and looked at Jules. "Well, Liz hasn't picked up any movement." He paused and stared out into the same common area where Liz shot the last intruder.

"You alright, Marc?" asked Jules.

"Yeah, I'm fine I guess," said Marc. "Too many unanswered questions. Something here doesn't feel right."

"Well, considering what you and Liz experienced in here, I don't blame you." Jules could tell that Marc was still angry. She looked down and saw that his fists were clenched.

"I wasn't ready," said Marc. His hands relaxed at his sides and he turned to Jules. "Mom, they took us by surprise. I need to find out who they were, and who sent them."

"One step at a time," said Jules. "Let's keep going. We've got to make sure everyone else got away, and we don't leave any survivors behind."

"Behind? Aren't we just going to turn the west wing back on?" asked Marc. "Can't we do that, and then check for survivors?"

"Marc, dear," said Jules, "A full execution of the plan B protocol initiates a permanent shutdown of the entire station. West and east wing." She smiled nervously at Marc. "We couldn't switch the station back on even if we wanted to. That was part of the design. If we could, then someone else could find a way."

"Unbelievable," blurted Marc. "The entire station is permanently shut down?"

"Well, almost all of it," said Jules, smirking slyly. "Now, let's get this done so we can get out of here. This place freaks me out — like a home after it's been burglarized." Jules stepped out into the common area and sprinted toward the north door.

"This just keeps getting worse and worse," Marc muttered to himself as he followed Jules into the spacious, dimly-lit room. "Liz, dad, we're going now to check out the north bay."

After overriding the first security door leading to the north bay, Jules and Marc entered the darkened access hall which led to the main entrance doors to the bay.

"Stop!" boomed Ray's voice over the radio. "Don't even try and get close to the bay doors. Do you hear a hissing sound?"

"Yes, actually. Where are you Ray?" asked Jules.

"I'm at the south bay," said Ray. "Probably close to where you guys are, but on the south side. Just back away from the door... Marcus don't let your mother any closer..." Ray's voice shook and trailed off.

"Are you guys okay?" asked Liz over the radio. "What's going on?"

"Ray, did you find something?" asked Jules as she continued to walk toward the large doors. There were small portholes at eye-level every few feet, but they were all covered. "The hissing is getting louder."

"Is there a leak?" asked Marc, but the radio was silent. "Dad? Are you alright?"

Finally, Ray answered. "They're all dead over here, Marcus," he said after a long pause. "Nothing but bodies floating around in the bay on this side. I don't know how many. It's too dark."

"No way!" yelled Marc. He ran toward the display on the far side of the room. "It appears that none of the capsules were activated," he said. "What about your side, Ray?'

"Same," said Ray after a pause. "Listen, I hacked into the main west wing branch and was able to restore a few of the last video feeds. It showed everyone packing into the bays, and before they could activate the escape capsules, the doors sealed behind them and then the bays flooded."

Since Ray was able to re-enable the controls to the bays, Marc tapped some commands into the display, and the emergency steel covers over the porthole windows slid away. At first, all they could see was darkness, but then the faint outlines of bodies drifting around in their unforgiving watery graves.

Jules dropped to her knees. "No." she muttered. "Why?' She turned to Marc and held back the urge to cry out in anguish. "How could anyone be capable of doing such a horrible thing to all those people? These weren't just scientists and workers. Civilians and children were also down here!"

Marc gritted his teeth. "Mom, we have to go," he said. "The bulkhead wasn't designed to take full-on exterior stress for a long period of time." He walked close to one of the portholes, and a pale image of a face hit the other side of the window. The mouth was gaping open, and the eyes were wide open and bloodshot. Marc winced and stumbled backward.

"Marc's correct," said Ray, "The bay doors have been a ticking time-bomb since the bays were flooded. There's nothing we can do for those people. They're gone."

"Why would anyone do this?" asked Marc. "I'm starting to see why you were so paranoid."

"Marcus," said Ray quietly, "I sent all of those people to their deaths when I initiated plan B."

"No, Ray, it's not your fault," said Liz over the radio. "You didn't know–"

"–You're right, I didn't know about the intruders, and I should have known more before doing something as drastic as that," interrupted Ray. He sighed loudly. "I'm going to make this right somehow, but for now, let's get back to the causeway. I'll meet you there. We need to execute the rest of plan B."

SOMEWHERE IN THE SEALAB IV SURFACE MONITORING FACILITY, MIAMI

Agent Thomas sat up, shivering and soaking wet. His chest felt as if someone was standing on him. When he tried to stand up, he felt queasy and lost his balance and tumbled to the floor. Wow, weird, he thought. He didn't feel like he had to breath, but when the aching in his chest intensified, he couldn't resist inhaling. As he tried to inhale, his diaphragm started to spasm. He tried to cry out, but no sound was made. Without any warning, he started to cough uncontrollably, and fluid streamed from his nose and mouth, followed by vomit.

Thomas, in pain and his eyes burning, laid down in the large half-tube again and dozed off. When he awoke, this time he yawned and his stomach felt a lot better. After taking a deep breath, his ears popped and stung. It wasn't until the air flowed back into his Eustachian tubes that Thomas realized that he'd been temporarily deafened.

Sounds all around him rushed into his ears like a loud cold wind, causing him to stand up in alarm.

"Well, that really sucked," he said, coughing. Thomas looked around the dimly-lit room. Where am I? he thought. Jules spent so long instructing me on what to expect in the fluid tube, that she never bothered to tell me where I'd end up. Just great. He closed his eyes and tried to remember if she had told him anything about his destination, but her words were all a blur. All he remembered was choking on the fluid, panicking, and flying through a dark tube going who knows how fast. He'd heard about the Mira's fabled emergency escape, but never really gave it much thought. Now, he felt sorry for not having paid better attention. Usually, he dismissed Ray and Julia Mira's rambling as science babble and just nodded.

Thomas stepped carefully out of the tube and stretched. He felt a warm breeze in the room and heard the rumble of what seemed to be a ventilation system. This place is familiar, he thought. Wait a minute. He walked around the small dimly-lit room and felt the walls for a light switch. Instead, what he found was a button, which he pressed almost without even thinking. The room shook slightly and the rumbling sound got louder. "What the...?" muttered Thomas as he stumbled back against the wall. The room seemed to move upward. And just as he turned to get a closer look at the button he pressed, the motion stopped, and what seemed like elevator doors opened in front of him. He turned back around and the tunnel was no longer there, just solid wall. Wow, that's a weird elevator, he thought. After cautiously walking out of the elevator into a larger and darker room, he looked back just in time to see the elevator doors quietly disappear behind some large panels. Without the light from the elevator, the room was now even darker.

Thomas felt around the walls and this time he found a light switch. He flipped on the lights and saw that he was in a large vacant commercial kitchen. "I know where this is," said Thomas. "It's the kitchen back at the surface monitoring facility." He looked around incredulously. "How on earth did I get to southern Florida so fast?" He looked at his watch and saw that it had only been about an hour since he had left SeaLab. He smiled and shook his head. Those old folks never cease to amaze me, he thought.

It was after-hours, and only a minimal number of employees were still at the facility. Thomas found some janitorial clothing and changed out of his wet clothes. I always thought that it would be fun to be a janitor, he thought. Might be a nice break from private security. He smiled, grabbed a broom, and casually stepped out into a large hallway.

"Excuse me," said a man in a shirt and tie. "I'm glad I ran into you. I spilled my coffee over here. Can you clean it up?"

Thomas held back the urge to tell the guy to clean it up himself, forced a smile, and quickly blurted, "Right away sir." No one up here is gonna recognize me, he thought. I was always down at the SeaLab station. Being a janitor might be a good long-term disguise. He twirled the broom around like a staff and whistled as he walked back to the janitorial closet.

Thomas entered the control center with a mop in hand. "Ok fellas, sorry for the delay," he said casually. "Where's the spill?"

"Geez, finally," said one of the three men monitoring random readings on a myriad of displays. "Right over here." He glanced at Thomas, back at a display, and then again at Thomas. This time he analyzed him more thoroughly. "Haven't seen you before. When did you start?"

"It's just been a few months," said Thomas. "Probably haven't seen me 'cause I been takin' care of the two annexes next door."

"Uh huh," said the man as he looked skeptically at Thomas, "Just be sure and wear your badge tomorrow. I'll let it slide this time."

"Thanks," said Thomas. He cleaned up and started to leave the room, but then stopped. "Hey, how's the station doing down there in that trench? I heard that's where it is."

"Yeah, that's right," said one of the other men in the room. "It's down there all right, and that's about as much information as we're allowed to share."

"Oh, yeah, sure," said Thomas, really trying to get more into character. "I can dig it, fellas." Knowing exactly what to look for, Thomas scanned the displays around the room, and once he found what he needed, he left the room. "Have a great evening."

"Yeah yeah." said one of the other men as he continued to stay focused on his display.

Thomas casually walked back down a long empty hallway. After returning the mop and bucket, he made his way to a large room lined with lockers. He smiled and shook his head in dismay. Wow, that was stupid, he thought. I should have grabbed my extra security badge before trying to get intel. He reached into his locker and clipped a small badge onto the lapel of his janitor uniform. After passing through the security station, he entered a small annex and closed a large steel door behind him.

"Ok, time to get a signal to the Miras," whispered Thomas. He picked up a crowbar from a utility closet and pried open an access panel. Quickly, he pulled a small disk from his pocket and placed it against a conduit. It pulsed red and then within a few seconds started to pulse a green color. Thomas smiled and closed the panel. "That should do it," he turned and was surprised to see a man in a dark suit standing right behind him.

"A little late for a conduit cleaning, isn't it?" asked the man in the suit.

Thomas tensed, then forced himself to relax. "I'm supposed to check for mice. Heard they were multiplying over here," he said. Thomas fought the urge to swallow. Kind of like the urge you feel to hit the brakes after approaching or passing a cop on the freeway. It would be a clear sign of guilt. "I was trying to finish up before my shift ended."

"What were you really doing in there?" asked the man. "What did you put on that conduit?"

"A device that creates a high-pitch sound that drives the little buggers away," said Thomas. "Works every time."

The man in the suit frowned. "You can go now."

Thomas didn't know whether to be relieved or alarmed. As he walked past the man in the suit, he could hear him walk the opposite direction toward the access panel. Just can't leave well enough alone, can you, suit man? thought Thomas. He turned around in time to see the man in the suit nod to someone, but Thomas couldn't see anyone else there.

The man in the suit turned swiftly back toward Thomas and sneered as he reopened the panel, "I believe that your device is faulty and needs to be inspected." he said.

"That's not necessary," said Thomas, "Just had it tested."

The man in the suit ignored Thomas as he turned back around to open the panel. At the same time, the sound of rounds being chambered in unseen guns was heard. Thomas looked around the small shadowy room but couldn't see anyone. Oh, ok. Here we go, he thought. Thomas took a swift breath in and his arms and legs tingled. Adrenaline coursed through his veins on command as he dropped and lunged toward the man. The suited man's effort to dodge Thomas failed as Thomas shot his fingertips into the man's right knee, instantly dropping him to the ground. Silent shots were fired from another unseen person, but as Thomas twisted and pulled the suited man over, he became Thomas's shield. The man in the suit slumped over onto the floor as Thomas grabbed his gun. He leapt up and rolled, expertly firing multiple rounds into the air in the direction of the gunfire he had heard in the shadows. I have to ensure that they don't disable the beacon, he thought. Thomas then did the unthinkable, turning away from the door and darting back toward the access panel which now seemed to be opening on its own. "What the..." blurted Thomas. Can't see them, therefore, I may as well be blind, he thought. Thomas closed his eyes, then dropped and rolled erratically. As he approached a wall, he leapt off of it into the air. As he landed, he hit something – not a wall or a pillar, but another person. Keeping his eyes closed, he forced his auditory senses into overdrive. He heard and then felt something fly in his direction. Thomas grabbed the person's arm and twisted around, bending his opponent's arm behind him. When he felt the shoulder joint pop, he twisted what felt like a wrist. With blinding speed, he turned the gun in his opponent's hand around and fired, dropping him to the floor. Almost without thinking, Thomas then turned his opponent's limp hand around and fired in the direction of another sound, resulting in another seemingly invisible body hitting the ground.

Thomas, breathing heavily, released the gun and his opponent's wrist, which dropped lifeless to the floor. Thomas's limbs shook with burning pain as he opened his eyes. Only the suited man's body was visible several feet away. So, there two others, he thought. Thomas cautiously turned and felt around with his foot until it made contact with something on the floor. It felt like a body, but he couldn't actually see anything there. He crouched down and felt the object. It was definitely the form of a man, an invisible man. Thomas felt something like a watch on his wrist. When he pressed the surface of the watch, the body of his opponent appeared. Thomas leapt up in astonishment and turned in the direction of the other attacker. After pressing on the other person's watch-like device, he also appeared. They were both wearing white body suits. "Wow," said Thomas. He heard a dripping sound on the metallic floor and started to feel dizzy. As he looked down, he saw that droplets of blood were falling from his own arm. He took a deep breath, which caused him to wince in pain and cough. His left arm and right leg started to throb, and his chest ached.

Oh wonderful, thought Thomas. A shot to the arm and another to the leg. "Oh crap... that's just wonderful," he muttered. As the adrenaline wore off, Thomas's entire body ached. He pushed himself away from the wall and approached the panel. After moving the beacon to the back side of the conduit, he closed the access panel and this time bolted shut the door leading to the room.

I've gotta get outta here, thought Thomas.

CHAPTER FOUR

Disclosure

CIA BRANCH OFFICE, SOMEWHERE IN CALIFORNIA

A young and recently promoted operative paced back and forth, grumbling. His assignment had shifted months before to oversee and investigate unusual events involving Investor Consortium interests. What this meant was that he had become chief SeaLab baby sitter. That also made him a primary CIA operative in charge of IC oversight.

His mind reeled with a growing list of recent troubling events at various SeaLab facilities: strange attacks in California and Texas surface monitoring stations, an unexplained maintenance shut down of SeaLab IV in the Atlantic, and now another incident reported at the surface monitoring facility in Miami. The incident in Miami was especially troubling to the operative.

Someone broke into the facility from the main service gate, he thought. Why did the tracks go cold from there? Control room personnel mentioned seeing a new janitor, but now he's nowhere to be found. Who was he? He wasn't from the IC, since he left a trail of dead IC officers... or were they even IC officers? There were too many unanswered questions – and no one had anything close to an answer. Of course, no one has answers, he would often think to himself. I'm the one who's supposed to find the answers.

"Agent Vinton," said a slender marine holding out a sat phone, "They want to talk to you."

"Who is it, lieutenant?" answered Agent Vinton, slightly annoyed. The day had been long and difficult for everyone in their unit, and nerves were starting to fray. "They? Who is they?" asked Vinton impatiently. "You've really got to stop using the word 'they'."

"Sorry, sir. It's the local Investor Consortium branch," whispered the lieutenant. "They asked for you by name."

"Of course, they did," said Vinton. "They probably know more by now of our operation than we do. Better pack things up. This isn't going to be pretty."

"Yes, sir." said the marine, smiling slightly.

Vinton cleared his throat and grabbed the phone. "This is Agent Vinton," he barked. "I really don't have time now to provide a report. We're trying to wrap up an operation here." Vinton paused, then gritted his teeth. "I see," he said, "I-I understand. We'll do what we can." He switched off the sat phone and tossed it back to the marine, who carefully caught the expensive piece of telecommunications hardware.

"What did they say?" asked the lieutenant. "Another wild goose running around on fire that needs to be put out?"

"We're to divert all resources to the surface monitoring

station for SeaLab IV," said Vinton. "They said that it's probably not a big deal, but then I received orders to conduct a full inquiry when we arrive."

"Another inquiry? Why?" asked the lieutenant. "We just got done doing those in San Diego, and then another in Corpus Christi. We spend more time filling out interrogation reports than anything else."

"Yes, I know. And now we have another to do in Miami," said Vinton impatiently, "Let's move it. We have our orders."

A chorus of personnel around Vinton said "Yes sir!" and got to work with preparations to relocate their mobile triage operation to Miami.

"Miami, of all places." grumbled Vinton under his breath as he stormed out of the room.

SOUTHERN FLORIDA, SOUTH OF THE SEALAB IV MONITORING FACILITY

The sun was just starting to break over the trees. Agent Thomas, speeding down a lonely road toward the Everglades in an old utility truck, unrolled the window and raised his left elbow to rest it on the opening. He gasped involuntary in pain and swore, slamming his right fist into the dash of the truck. Doing that caused even more pain in his right arm. After swerving back and forth on the road, he steadied the wheel and forced a deep breath. "Pull it together, Thomas!" he yelled to himself. His body felt numb, making him forget how badly he'd been injured by the highly-trained spooks he ran into at the surface monitoring station. Where did those guys come from? he asked himself over and over. Who were they? They were definitely not Investor Consortium agents. Thomas started to realize that he really could have died back there. Escaping SeaLab IV at the bottom of the ocean, his escape from the station, and finding this truck to get away seemed like a surreal blur of events. What remained clearly burned in his mind was the image if his son, Tommy Jr., and the last words he heard from him: "Love you daddy." In his mind, he could still see his small face looking up and smiling. At least he was in a safe place, five miles beneath the Atlantic. Tears started to well up in his eyes as he slammed the gas pedal down.

Agent Thomas was an expert at tracking, but even better at not being tracked. He grimaced in pain as he tightened a tourniquet on his arm. The bullet had only grazed his arm, but it still made a nasty, bloody, fleshy mess. The surface monitoring facility overlooking Card Sound was now far behind him. He felt bad for hot-wiring a utility truck, but it was better than being tracked down by security, dogs, and heaven forbid any more of those cloaked spooks he ran into.

As he entered the everglades, Thomas knew that the turnoff for Key Largo was not that far off. Thomas fought the overwhelming urge to drift asleep as his vision started to blur. "Wake up, Thomas!" he shouted to himself. After slapping himself in the face, he shook his head, sat up, and veered off the side of the road. Gonna have to walk from here. Just as he opened the door, he could hear sirens in the distance. "Ah crap," muttered Thomas. He slammed the door shut and checked his clip. Empty. Agent Thomas, round two, he thought. He ran with a slight limp off the side of the highway, and out into the wilderness. Rivers and streams were everywhere, but he had to run for awhile to reach any foliage that would provide enough cover for his next move – a move that he'd done before, and was not at all looking forward to doing again.

Finally, Thomas reached a humid and muddy embankment. Not far behind he could hear his pursuers close in. Ahead and down the slope before him, he could see marshes, more dense areas of swamp trees, and a few rivers running parallel to each other, connecting at points until they disappeared into the mist. Well, at least alligators are reasonable, he thought. Without another second of hesitation, he sprinted ahead straight toward the nearest river bank. It would have to be a wider part of the river, and the embankment would need to overlook deeper, less disturbed water. He removed his torn long sleeve shirt as he ran, and dove into the water, estimating that his pursuers weren't far behind. Thomas didn't have much time to think. With the end of a shirt sleeve wound around each of his hands, he swam straight down to the bottom and then back in toward the embankment — where alligators were likely to keep the cold dead bodies of their prey. As Thomas approached the dark underwater cavity, an alligator emerged. It must have been surprised to see another potential victim just waltz into his dark, watery meat locker. Thomas threw an expertly timed elbow straight down onto the monster's head and then swam directly over it. Before the beast could turn around, Thomas swiftly wrapped his arms around its neck from behind and tied its mouth shut with the sleeves of his shirt. The aches and piercing pains of his wounds were soon enough masked by another surge of adrenaline as he felt toward the alligator's face and pressed his thumbs mercilessly into its eyes. The alligator instantly went into a frenzy of death rolls as it tried to free itself and get in front of its strange attacker. Thomas held on, locking his arms around its neck and straddling its back. His lungs ached, and he started to feel numb, but as the monster rolled, Thomas's head broke the surface of the water long enough for him to catch a breath. On the next roll, he could see that he was near the opposite embankment, and he could hear gun shots. One of the unfortunate pursuers it seemed had already been taken by another alligator, and more were coming. On another roll, Thomas untied his bloody shirt from the alligator's mouth and shot his heel into the back of its head, buying him a precious few seconds to push away from his bewildered foe. Thomas's stained and torn shirt was still hanging off of the alligator's jaw as it turned toward the others on the embankment opposite of Thomas. While they were distracted, he ran deeper into the swamp.

"Are you kidding?" yelled one of the pursuers. "He's gone! Look at his shirt! His body's down under there somewhere. No way he got away from that gator."

"We have our orders," blurted another officer between heavy breaths. "We need to bring back the body for identification."

"Seriously? Identify what?" asked the first, looking and pointing at the spot where one of their team members had just been taken by another alligator. "The lunatic we chased here was suicidal. Look what happened to Roberts."

The senior officer rolled his eyes and stepped toward the water, but the other officer stopped him. "Let go of me," snapped the senior officer. "We're not going back empty handed."

"At least we'd be going back with our hands," said the junior officer. "Listen, I know this area, and I know what these animals are capable of doing to a man who steps any closer to that water. Would be freakin' suicide to go any further, and HQ will understand that." He removed his hat and ran his hands through his sweaty hair. "They've gotta understand. Chances are, there's no body left to recover."

Thomas continued to run through the swamp. His legs felt as if they had hundred-pound weights attached to them, but he wouldn't stop until he reached the other side of the ravine. He remembered seeing signs for a tour charter somewhere ahead where he could steal a swamp boat. Once he was able to reach Key Largo, he hoped that he could put this part of his assignment behind him.

"Thomas did it! The conduit beacon worked!" said Jules. "We're getting the signal now."

"Yes! Way to go, Thomas," said Ray. He turned to Marc and Liz. "That means no news about the mess down here was relayed to the monitoring station. As far as they know, we're offline temporarily for maintenance."

"That will only buy us three weeks," said Marc. "After that, the surface monitoring station will send a team down to override the airlock."

"Yeah, and we already did that," said Liz. "Once another team get's the transport back online and comes down, they'll see that the front door is wide open. The Investor Consortium will freak out–"

"–The IC is not our concern," interrupted Jules. "What

we need to be concerned with is how soon Thomas can find out who's responsible for the deaths of over three hundred people down here – the entire staff from west and east wings! Until then, we can't go anywhere. Of the four of us that were left here, Thomas was the only person capable of living through our emergency escape tube. We had no other choice."

"So, what exactly is Agent Thomas supposed to be doing up there now that he's sent us his message?" asked Liz.

"Jules sent Thomas up to the surface to assess the situation and conduct an investigation," said Ray. "We needed to know that we hadn't stirred any bees nests on the surface. It would seem that is the case."

"As part of his investigation, Thomas will be heading to Rhode Island." said Jules.

"What's in Rhode Island?" asked Liz.

"My sister, Susan," said Marc. He smiled and turned to Jules. "She's not exactly going to roll out the red carpet for Thomas."

"No, I suppose not," said Jules. "But she'll nevertheless be under Thomas's protection in case the IC – or whomever else – decides to drop by."

"Seems like a risky plan sending him up there in that tube," said Liz. "I thought you hadn't found the right solution balance in the fluid."

"You're right," said Jules, "But we did make some improvements."

"Good grief," said Marc. "I hope risking Thomas's life was worth it."

"Don't worry, dear," said Jules. "Thomas knows what he's doing."

"For heaven's sake, he has a family," said Liz. "How much does little Tommy know about all of this?"

"Liz," said Jules, "Remember that over three hundred people died, an unexplained attack on west wing security occurred that implicates the IC in a whole cluster of covert and illegal activity, and an entire SeaLab station is on the brink of termination. We had no choice, and Thomas knew that."

"Guys, when are you going to tell us what you're trying so hard to protect?" asked Marc after an uncomfortably long pause. "What findings have you made down here that could possibly explain the IC's actions, and why initiate plan B?"

Jules looked nervously at her husband and back at Marc. "We had to bring you two down here without raising any suspicion. After we saw how Agent Forsythe had changed, we had to go on the defensive."

"So, Dr. Lee, your friend who was killed in Forsythe's office, was meeting with someone for a handoff?" asked Marc.

"Yes," said Jules. "That's what we think Dr. Lee was doing."

"But, a handoff of what?" asked Liz. "What stolen data of yours could he possibly have had that justifies any of this?"

Ray sighed loudly and looked at Jules. "Maybe it's time."

"Time for what?" asked Liz.

"Time to explain what we found." said Jules.

"Well, three months ago," said Ray, "we successfully set up a deep sea relay—"

"Dad, skip the blow-by-blow account," interrupted

Marc. "Just tell us what you guys found."

"Fine," said Ray. He looked nervously at Julia. "Our neutrino harvester started receiving some strange readings. Upon further investigation, we found embedded in the massive data stream a schematic of human DNA."

Liz stared incredulously at Marc and then glared at Ray. "DNA... in a neutrino field? Do you have any idea how crazy that sounds? That's insane!"

"Liz!" snapped Marc. "Yes, it sounds crazy, but you don't need to be rude."

Liz glared at Marc. "No, not this time, Marc!" said Liz. Her emotions started to boil as she clenched her fists. "This was supposed to be a romantic little routine trip to SeaLab IV to visit your folks – two scientific hermit crabs at the bottom of the Atlantic Ocean. We have been chased, attacked, shot, beaten, and narrowly escaped with our lives."

Marc's arms dropped to his side, and he sighed. "Liz, I'm really sorry–"

"I'm not done!" said Liz. "Over three hundred people are dead, and we knew many of them, Marc. Some had kids down here, and now they're all gone. Their loved ones on the surface deserve an explanation."

The room was silent, except for the hum of the lighting and the shuffling of feet. Neither Marc, Jules nor Ray dared say anything. For the first time, they could hear little Tommy playing in the other room. Liz started to sob.

"Liz, I'm really sorry," said Marc. "No one could have known any of this would happen." He walked over and placed an arm lovingly around Liz.

Neither Ray nor Jules could think of anything to say. Just as Ray was about to finally say something, Liz blurted, "I'm pregnant."

"What?" said Marc. "How? When?"

"I know it's hard to believe," said Liz in a lower voice, "But I wanted to be sure this time before telling you. I wasn't sure I could handle another... failure."

Almost involuntarily, they all converged into a group hug in the middle of the room. "May I ask then," said Jules, "How far along you are?"

"Fifteen weeks," said Liz, "None of my pregnancies have lasted past two months. This is the first." She looked up at Marc and beamed a smile.

Marc smiled back, but then his expression showed concern. "You've been through quite a bit down here, Liz. We need to get you checked out!" he said. "Mom, we have an ultrasound machine down here, right?"

"The baby is fine," said Liz. "I wanted to find the perfect time to tell all of you, but then all this happened, and–"

"No need to explain, Liz!" said Ray.

Liz took a deep breath. "Now," she said, glaring at Ray and Jules, "Would you both please provide a clear and rational reason why you decided to initiate plan B? What about your precious research was so important, that I almost had to lose my baby to save it?"

Ray looked at Jules and shrugged. "Well?" he asked.

"Don't you well me," said Jules. "You know as well as I do what's there."

"What's where?" asked Marc. "You found Atlantis? The cure to cancer? Jimmy Hoffa? Elvis?" Marc tried to contain his frustration.

Ray wasn't amused. "Follow me, both of you," he said. They walked to the main laboratory on the other side of the east wing. As they entered the lab, the lights turned on and displays on the walls leaped to life. Stainless steel tables were neatly lined up on one side of the room. Liz looked skeptically at Marc.

"Ok, why are we here?" asked Marc. "Can't you guys just tell us?"

"Dear, we already tried that," answered Jules, slightly annoyed. "And for the record, the implication that Ray or I would idly initiate something like plan B is somewhat offensive."

"Alright," said Liz, "I'm sorry. I overreacted."

"For good reason, my dear," said Ray. "You and Marc deserve an explanation, but if you really want one, you'll have to keep an open mind."

"Uh-huh," said Liz. "What did you find? And don't say DNA in a neutrino field."

"Actually, the neutrino particles in the field are in the shape of DNA – a double helix." said Ray.

Liz took a deep breath, exhaled loudly, and sat down in a chair. Her face was red with anger as she looked at Marc. She then glared at Ray. "First of all, there's no way to manipulate neutrino fields. Second, who cares about DNA? We've sequenced it already."

"Ok, time out guys," said Marc, "I'm not a physicist. What the heck do neutrinos have to do with DNA?"

Ray and Jules looked at each other, apparently not quite sure how to help Marc. They looked at Liz and gestured toward Marc.

"Umm, Marc. Ask Ray and Jules," said Liz. "Just because I minored in physics doesn't mean I have any idea what they're talking about!"

"You know that neutrinos are particles smaller than

atoms, right? In particle accelerators, we smash protons into each other, and what results are the particles that make up those protons," said Jules.

"Yes, we know what neutrinos are," said Liz. "That's nothing new."

Ray exhaled loudly and brought up a display. After tapping a bunch of commands, the lights dimmed, and a round metallic console emerged from the floor in the center of the room. "That, kids, is the world's first functioning neutrino harvester."

"Who cares," said Marc, immediately regretting his lack of patience. "Sorry, go on."

Ray cleared his throat. "Our planet is continuously showered by trillions of those neutrinos every second. They have nearly no mass at all. Hundreds of millions of those suckers are flying through all of us and everything else at light speed right now."

"Geez, dad," said Marc. "I'm trying to be patient here. I know what neutrinos are. What do they have to do with DNA, and what does any of this have to do with what happened today?"

"Ray, just show them the paper," said Jules. "Might be better that way."

Ray glared at Jules. "Fine, but an explanation beforehand would have been better," he said. He tapped some more commands, and another console emerged from the ceiling, directly over the console in the floor. Immediately, a pillar of light appeared between the console in the ceiling, and the console on the floor, like two spotlights pointed directly at each other.

Everyone stepped back, but Liz brought up her arm to guard her eyes. "Ray, can you take that thing down a notch or two?"

"Sorry, I still have to zoom in quite a bit," said Ray. As he did so, the solid pillar of light started to look more like a column of bright lines all parallel to each other at an angle. As Ray zoomed in even more, the space between the lines increased.

"So, what is that?" asked Marc.

"Just wait a second," said Jules, smiling wryly. "He'll show you."

"I have to record some of this so that I can play it back at a much slower speed," said Ray. "At the speed of light, the particles all just look like lines that never end."

Marc looked at Liz and shrugged, but Liz stepped closer. Her eyes were wide with amazement. "Are you recording a segment of the path of neutrinos in the neutrino field?"

Ray smiled. "Here, this should be clearer." He tapped some more commands, and the lines went away. What they now saw was a cloud of bright, tiny dots slowly moving in a diagonal direction from the top to the bottom. "What you're looking at is a recording of the flow of subatomic particles – called neutrinos. It's kinda like looking through a side car window on the freeway, and watching all the cars go by."

"And we can see those particles, because you're using a holographic projection to simulate the particles?" asked Liz.

"Yes, that's right." said Jules.

"Oh, ok," said Marc. "That makes perfect sense... except that I still have no idea what all this has to do with anything."

"Right, I understand," said Ray, as he turned back to

his display and tapped even more commands. The cloud of slowly-moving dots disappeared and again the bright dense group of lines reappeared.

Marc stepped closer, hesitated, and waved his hands through the projection. The lines weren't disturbed. "So, again we're looking at a live representation of the traffic of neutrinos flying by at light speed," said Marc, "And we're looking at that traffic flying by as if through a straw?"

"Yes, that's right. You're an observer in a car on the freeway at night, and you're looking through a straw at all the lights of the cars going by," said Ray. "A rough analogy, but it works."

"This is your discovery?" asked Marc. "A machine that allows us to see with our own eyes the constant flow of trillions of teeny-tiny neutrino particles flying through us from the sun?"

"Well...," said Ray.

"Well, that's amazing," interrupted Marc, "But why would the IC or anyone else kill so many people for that? Wouldn't the IC just swoop in and take credit for it? Why would you resort to plan B?"

"He's not done, Marcus!" said Jules. She only called him Marcus when he was in trouble.

"Fine," said Marc. "I'm listening." He stood back and defiantly folded his arms.

Ray tapped some more commands, and a cloud of particles seemed to freeze in place. "Ok, so I've captured some particles there," said Ray. "Actually more than you can see at this zoom level." Ray filtered out the bright lines so that all they could see was the cloud of particles.

"To be clear, Ray has control now of a group of those neutrino particles," said Jules. "He's going to arrange them into atoms, and then arrange those atoms into molecules."

"What?" asked Liz. "How?"

Ray ignored the question and zoomed out until they could see the entire cloud. By that point, it looked less like a cloud of bright dots, and more like a bright blob hovering in the air.

Again, Marc swiped his hand through the light projection. "Still just a light show, dad," he said.

"Marc, let him finish." said Liz.

Ray tapped more commands, and the blob started to rearrange itself into a framework of distinct shapes.

"It looks like liquid sugar crystallizing, but at high-speed." said Marc.

"Exactly!" said Ray, who didn't turn away from the display "Sugar crystallization just happens because it's the easiest way for the sugar molecules to attach to each other as the water evaporates," said Ray. "What I'm doing here is accelerating the same sort of process, but with cellulose molecules."

"Paper?" asked Marc. "Why are you using neutrinos to build paper molecules?" Just as Marc finished asking the question, the reality hit him of what Ray was doing. "Wait a second. How are you doing that?"

"I'm not actually doing anything yet, Marc," said Ray. "All I'm doing is modeling a matrix of cellulose molecules, like when you go to the beach and form a bunch of sand into the shape of something, like the shape of a shark, or whatever."

"Oh, ok," said Marc. "Those bright dots are like a bunch of sand. Got it."

"Fascinating that you can even manipulate those

massless particles to begin with," said Liz as she gazed at the model before her of brilliant dots of light. "You can move sand around because the grains of sand have mass, but neutrinos are massless."

"Actually, they do have mass," said Jules, "Just not much – in fact so little, that those particles can fly right through us and we don't feel it. Every second of every day, they are flying through us at light speed."

By now, Ray had formed what looked like a sheet of paper out of numberless bright dots. "Well, there's a model of a sheet of paper," he said proudly.

"I agree with Liz," said Marc. "That's pretty amazing, but what good is it? It's easier to just draw a sheet of paper with a pen... on a sheet of paper."

"But we're not just drawing stuff, Marc. Watch this," said Ray. He tapped some more commands and then stopped. "This last part took me awhile to figure out." He tapped the command, and the brilliant model of the sheet of paper became an actual sheet of paper, which replaced the bright dots. The paper slowly floated back and forth to the floor and laid at Liz's feet.

The room was silent.

"What just happened?" asked Marc. "What I think just happened, didn't really happen. Did it?"

"Marc," said Liz, "Your dad just created a sheet of paper from neutrinos."

"No way," said Marc. "How is that even possible? What did you discover to allow you to do that, dad? How did you do that?"

"Ok, so, we have your attention now." said Jules.

"Yes, you have our attention." said Liz.

"I need a drink." said Marc.

"I need to recalibrate the neutrino harvester," said Ray. "It will be a few minutes, then I can try and answer your questions."

"Marc, Liz," said Jules, placing some drinks on the workbench and sitting next to them, "Ray and I thought that we lost Digger, our most sophisticated submersible, about nine months ago."

"We certainly would have noticed that incident show up in the activity reports on the surface." said Liz.

"We never reported it, and there's no way we were going to try and contact you guys to tell you," said Jules. "You see, within a few weeks, we found it... or rather, it found us."

"What do you mean, it found you?" asked Marc.

"Ray had fitted Digger with a miniature neutrino harvester – the device we use to view, record, and capture neutrinos," said Jules. "He had also programmed Digger with an international morse code transceiver. We activated a morse code beacon here on the station, and Digger responded."

"So, the submersible contacted you via morse code." said Marc.

"Yes," said Jules, "But just long enough for us to remotely engage and connect Digger's on-board neutrino harvester with the main harvester here in the lab."

"Long enough before what?" asked Marc. "Were you able to retrieve Digger?"

"No, it fell through a crevasse about ten more miles." said Jules.

"Down?" asked Marc. "It fell down ten more miles?"

Ray walked back in and started tapping more commands into his display, and the light projection turned back on, producing the same bright pillar of light that they saw before. "I had to recalibrate a few things. Like Jules probably explained, Digger fell several miles further from the bottom of the Milwaukee Trench and seemed to settle on something solid. We soon after lost the ability to communicate with it via morse code. All we could do is zero in on its on-board neutrino harvester!"

"So, Digger's harvester serves as a signal booster for the one here in the lab." said Marc.

"That's right," said Ray. "We're hoping that Digger doesn't fall any further, or get damaged to the point that it ceases to function. Frankly, I'm surprised it's still working that far down. We want to record as much data from the neutrino stream as possible before that happens."

"Wait, what do you want to record?" asked Liz. "It's just a bunch of random neutrinos bombarding the earth, right?"

Ray and Jules looked at each other and smiled. "No, actually. Turns out that it's not entirely random," said Ray. He tapped a short command, and the pillar of light zoomed into a strange-looking bundle of lines amidst the rest of the lines that were perfectly parallel.

"What's that?" asked Liz. "That cluster seems different than everything around it.

"Yes," said Jules. "We were crushed when we thought that we lost Digger. It was Ray's idea to use our morse code receiver to try and pick up on the automatic distress signal we knew that Digger would be transmitting. When we found Digger, we were able to activate, link to, and track Digger's neutrino harvester. When Digger fell even deeper, that was the only link we had."

"Sounds like you could use the neutrino field to

communicate with Digger no matter how deep it falls." said Marc.

"We were worried about Digger's machinery failing under that much heat and pressure that far down," said Ray, "Not whether or not we could continue to keep contact with Digger's harvester."

"Right, of course. Fifteen miles into the earth is an incredible depth," said Marc.

"So, when we linked up with Digger's harvester, we noticed that the new vector we plotted happened to line up with the center of the planet."

"What?" asked Liz. "I don't follow."

Jules pulled out her tablet and drew a circle. "This is our planet." She drew a dot close to the edge of the circle. "This dot represents our position right now on the earth." Jules then drew another dot a bit further from the edge of the circle, not far from the first dot. "This second dot represents Digger's position about ten miles further down." Jules then drew a straight line through the two dots, and it cut straight through the center of the circle. "Digger's new position enabled us to dial into a different part of the neutrino field that we had never seen before, and we found something."

"What did you find?" asked Marc.

"Look here," said Ray, pointing to the holographic display of light in the center of the room. "I'll zoom in on that different-looking group of strands, and filter out all of those straight parallel lines of light." As he did that, they could plainly see that the bright dots formed a seemingly unending chain of DNA.

"DNA?" asked Liz. "Why did you guys form the sand on the beach into the shape of a double-helix?"

"Liz, we didn't model what you're seeing there." said Jules.

"Certainly not!" said Ray. "It took me three weeks just to model the molecules for a sheet of paper. If you think I was able to model a strand of DNA, you're giving me way too much credit!"

"Ok, yeah, sorry," said Marc. "But, if you didn't model that, who did?"

"I don't know," said Ray. "It's like wandering along the beach, and stumbling upon a sand sculpture of, I don't know, a life-size sculpture of the Notre Dame Cathedral! Of course, our first question was... who built this!"

"Can you zoom in a bit?" asked Liz.

Ray tapped some commands, and the display of bright dots changed so that the dots spread apart, but more dots appeared. "As you zoom in, you can see more detail within. It's really pretty breathtaking."

"That's human DNA," said Liz. "If I'm not mistaken, that's a portion of the DNA in the fourth chromosome."

"Geez, Liz," said Marc. "I think I'll take your word for it."

"I'm no physicist, but I am a biologist," said Liz. "That's definitely human DNA."

"You're right, Liz," said Ray. "We farmed out a lot of this data to Dr. Lee. He was stunned. Said it was prototypical DNA."

Marc gasped. "Are you suggesting that is the DNA from which all other DNA is encoded? That's crazy."

"Marc," said Ray, "I found within this information, a controller gene to manipulate the drag on particles... you know, to give particles mass."

"What?" asked Marc. "Liz, can you translate for me?"

"I can tell you what he's saying," said Liz. "Not that I understand how it's possible. Ray says that he found a part of this DNA model–"

"–That someone somehow created using those neutrino particles." interrupted Marc.

"Yes, that's right," said Liz. "Anyway, part of that model has a gene that, when combined with another model–"

"–Like a matrix of paper molecules." interrupted Ray.

"Will change the mass of that model, so that it becomes tangible... so you can feel it." said Liz.

"Yes, I know what tangible means," said Marc. "So, let me get this straight: Ray discovered an endless beach, and on that vast sandy beach, someone had pushed a ton of sand together to form an intricate sculpture of human DNA molecules. But that's not all. Ray also discovered that a part of that gigantic impossibly-difficult sand sculpture of human DNA included a gene that, when combined with another sand sculpture on the beach, turns that simpler sculpture into the real thing." said Marc, almost in one breath. "And by real thing, I mean, not made of sand – like that sheet of paper you just created from nothing!"

"Actually, neutrinos have mass, so they're not technically nothing." said Jules.

"Marc, your analogy is rough and crude, but good." said Ray.

"The question remains," said Liz, "How did you know what gene in that incredibly-long strand of DNA would enable you to manipulate the change of mass?"

Ray smiled. "I'll zoom in closer to the DNA model, and you'll see." He zoomed in, and there seemed to be indicators next to certain parts of the strand. "There are a couple hundred marked genes, as far as we've been able to tell. We just took the first gene with one of those markers and popped the hood on it. Who knows what the next one can do!"

"Holy crap," gasped Liz. "Oh my...," She raised her arms and buried her fingers in her hair as she paced around the lab, mumbling to herself. "Somehow, Ray, you guys stumbled upon the architectural plans for human beings. Let's say we're talking about a house. Someone could say: Hey, look! There should be another light switch in this room or another window in that room! When we're born, we get half of our forty-six chromosomes from our father and the other half from our mother. So, we completely rely on the DNA we get from our parents to get us by. We can only hope that we don't get a gene that increases our chances of getting Down syndrome, cystic fibrosis, or a predisposition for diabetes or cancer. If we do, then, sorry. Too bad. Gotta fight through it."

"Yeah, and with this human DNA template, a person could hold it up to the DNA of a cancer patient, and figure out what genetic thing needs to be fixed to cure the cancer," said Marc. "Isn't that right?"

"Yes, possibly." said Jules.

"Or possibly even breed a person to be able to create or manipulate matter itself," said Ray. "All that person would have to do is make sure that the right gene is flipped on."

"I feel kinda sick," said Liz. "This is way out of the park, Ray."

Ray scratched his head and looked to Jules. "Ok, we need to decide what to do. We either abandon the research, deeming it to be too dangerous for anyone to have. Or, we record as much as we can and preserve it until we know what to do with it — while preventing the Investor Consortium, Seraphim, or anyone else from obtaining any of it."

"Well, we preserve the research, of course," said Jules. Liz was about to protest, but stopped herself. Instead, she stared blankly at the wall.

"I agree with mom," said Marc. "If you were able to discover that information, someone else would be bound to find it as well. Better that we know about it than for anyone else we know to get their hands on it."

"And," blurted Liz, "The lives lost to save this information is too great a price to pay to just abandon it all now."

"This is madness, Ray," said Jules. "Why we'd even consider trashing the whole thing is beyond me. We have made this discovery for a purpose. We are ready for it, otherwise we would not have discovered it."

"For what purpose? There are many who would disagree with you, mom," said Marc.

"Those who would disagree are swayed too much by fear," said Jules. A fire burned in her eyes that he had not seen for a long time. "I believe that everything happens for a reason, and at the time when it is supposed to happen. I take the road of faith. Just think of how much progress science would ever make if it were driven by fear. True science is driven by faith."

"Yeah, but how can you be so sure of there being a purpose to your discovery?" asked Liz. "That implies that someone or something else authored that purpose."

"Well, mankind hasn't managed to destroy itself, and the planet is still habitable, despite all of the paranoia and pessimism of the early twenty-first century," said Jules. "Even with all of the pollution, the planet has adapted and so have we. Everything happens in this world for a reason – even if we don't understand the reason."

"So, what's the plan then?" asked Marc. "Where do we go from here? I don't even know what to think right now."

Ray stood up and smiled. "We capture and preserve as much data from the neutrino stream as we can, we tuck it away, we return to the surface and then continue the research. My hope is that a future generation can find the reason for it all."

"That's all?" asked Liz. "What about everyone else? Don't you think mankind has a right to learn what we've learned?"

"When you make the most fantastic discovery, a lot of people want a piece of it," said Ray, "Even if they don't know what to do with it. No, there are too many people who would abuse our research."

"This is just so huge," said Marc, "The master template for human DNA. It's like we finally dug our way far enough down into the cardboard box of styrofoam peanuts to finally find the user manual for mankind."

"It's more than that," said Ray. "Someone modeled our DNA schematic. No one on earth could have done that."

"So, that's the purpose? God?" asked Liz. "Really?"

"Clarke's third law states: Any sufficiently advanced technology is indistinguishable from magic," said Ray. "I would add a fourth: Any sufficiently advanced intelligence is indistinguishable from God."

"So... God," said Liz. "That's your hypothesis?"

"Well, how about The Creator?" asked Jules. "Does that sound better to you?"

"What about aliens? What about human beings from the future?" asked Liz. "Why do you discount those possibilities? Why must some people jump to the conclusion of it being God?"

"Why must some people exclude the possibility of God?" asked Jules. "Besides, an alien is just intelligent life not from our world." Jules smiled and looked into Liz's eyes, placing a hand on her abdomen. "We have the capability to reproduce, but that doesn't mean we also have the ability to create. If not us, then who? If we found out who, would we not regard them as a God?"

"A matter of semantics, I suppose," said Liz. She rolled her eyes and sat down in a hard metal chair. The arm of the chair felt cold and lifeless, but her mind was warm with activity, and her heart raced. "Gotta get my breath," she said, her chest heaving. Can't believe my world-renowned scientist in-laws are lecturing me on theology, she thought.

"Mom, dad," said Marc after a long pause. "I think we're all agreed. Do what you have to do to complete the plan B protocol. We have to preserve your research, but we also can't risk the IC, Seraphim, or really anyone else getting their hands on it." Marc looked down at the sheet of paper sitting on the table that Ray had created, and he shuddered at the thought of what else someone could do with that power.

Several hours later, as much supplies and equipment as could be salvaged from the west and east wings were carried to the far end of the east wing.

"What part of the station will remain after the rest is detached?" asked Liz, still panting from her limping walk back to the lab.

Marc looked at Liz and smiled. "You seem to be healing up pretty quickly," he said, "Probably should take it easy though, don't you think?" Marc sighed as he set down the last load of plastic boxes onto a metal table.

"I'm ok. I had to take a walk and blow off some steam," said Liz. "Gotta keep moving, or else I'll go crazy down here. Not sure what's stressing me out more, the thought of the IC getting ahold if your folk's research, or spending another few months down here."

"Gives us some time to make plans, and learn about what they found," said Marc. "Right?"

Liz smiled and rolled her eyes. "Yeah, ok. Sure, Mr. Silver Lining man," she said. "Now, you gonna answer my question?"

"Right," said Marc, looking at his tablet and then around the room. "After we go through the causeway from the west wing, you pass through the common area, and then the east wing administrative offices. After that, you go straight and then through an airlock," said Marc. "My mom said that once you go through that airlock, you're in the safe zone – that's what she calls it, anyway."

"And you never knew about that part of plan B?" asked Liz.

"Nope, not that much," said Marc. "Mom and dad were still developing the protocol long after I was involved."

"Tommy's gone to bed," said Jules. "Now would be a good time to do this."

"I really hope you guys know what you're doing," said

Liz. 'Did Thomas know about your plan to trash the station?"

"Liz, dear. That part was Thomas's idea!" said Jules. She pulled some sort of key out that hung from a necklace around her neck and handed it to Ray. He pulled out a similar key and fit them together. The end of the resulting object started to glow green. When Ray inserted the object into a nondescript slot in the main control console, some new controls appeared, also glowing with a green light. Ray turned to his display and tapped a few commands. Large amounts of data scrolled across the display, and at the end of the hallway, the airlock closed and locked shut with a loud hiss. Ray turned to the others. "Ready?" He entered a final command, and the room jolted. The holographic display in the center of the room went dark, and the lighting flickered and dimmed. They could hear a roaring sound, and then silence. "Well, that is that,' said Ray. "Welcome to SeaLab XII."

"Twelve?" said Liz. "What if the Investor Consortium decides to build another station? They'll name it SeaLab XII."

"The IC has pulled funding," said Jules. "The press release should be out in a few days. The destruction of SeaLab IV and the deaths of everyone aboard will only pour fuel on that political fire. They'll want to channel funds immediately to the new space station. Eyes are again looking to the stars. SeaLab XI over in the Pacific's Mariana Trench will be the last SeaLab station to be built, and no one will ever learn what became of this station."

Marc frowned. "The press release will also state that Ray and Julia Mira died on this station."

"That's right," said Ray. "But not you, Liz or Tommy. We already hacked the station's activity logs at the surface monitoring facility in Miami to show that you guys never arrived. As far as the IC is concerned, you're on vacation at an undisclosed location."

"Not too far from the truth, right? Although, this hasn't been much of a vacation," said Liz. She looked at Ray and forced a smile. "It was nice of you to not kill us, along with you and Jules."

"Well, we like to help out where we can." said Ray, sarcastically.

"Speaking of that, how do we plan to eventually return to the surface?" asked Marc. "The tube?"

"Yes, the tube," said Jules. "It worked for Thomas. It will work for us as well. In a few months, I'll have all of the kinks worked out." She smiled and picked up a mug as she and Ray started for the door. "Can we get you guys a drink, or something to eat?"

"A few months?" asked Liz. "We're stuck here for... months?"

"No thanks, mom. I think I lost my appetite," said Marc.

"Me too," said Liz. "We're just gonna hang out here... for a few months, that is." She walked over to Ray's display, and then to the console in the middle of the room. After typing a few commands, the pillar of light again zoomed into the cluster of particles that made up the endless chain of DNA. She turned to Ray. "Is it okay if I take another look?"

Ray smiled. "Yes, of course. The recording of the patterns is taking place, regardless of what we do here. Just know that I put a lock on the other marked genes in that model." he said. "Also, be careful what matter you compose. Stick to standard, stable molecules... not that you'll be here long enough to build anything dangerous."

Ray and Jules went to sleep, but hours later, Marc and Liz were still looking at the model of human DNA in the neutrino field. It was made of an amazing number of bright dots, and as they zoomed in, even more bright dots became visible.

"Pretty amazing," said Liz. "I could look at this for hours.'

"Um, Liz," said Marc, "We have been looking at it for hours. It just keeps going and going."

"It's repeating," said Liz. "Once you get to the forty-sixth chromosome, it just repeats all over again with the first."

"Wait, go back and zoom in some more."

"Ok, why? Did you see something?"

"Yeah. Zoom in some more," said Marc. "See where one ends and the other begins? There's something round in there."

Liz craned her head forward. "I see it, hold on." She zoomed in and rotated the model around slightly. "It looks like a ball." She zoomed in even more on a cluster of bright dots that formed a sphere. When she kept zooming in, they could see the sphere in more detail.

"It looks like a planet," said Marc. "A planet with one continent."

"Yeah, I wonder what that means." said Liz.

"Doesn't look like our planet," said Marc. "Or maybe

it's a representation of our planet before the continents spread apart?"

"I think there's something inside the sphere," said Liz. She zoomed in even further and stopped. Liz and Marc both walked closer to the pillar bright dots in the center of the room to get a closer look.

"Is that what I think it is?" asked Marc. "Looks like an XX and an XY?"

"Female and male." said Liz.

"So, whoever constructed this model, knew our alphabet," said Marc.

"No," said Liz, "Not necessarily. Those are probably representations of the human sex chromosomes. All chromosomes look like X's, including sex chromosomes, except one. The male sex chromosome looks like a Y because it's missing one-half of one of it's two arms."

"Ok, I guess that just raises more questions, doesn't it?" asked Marc.

"Yes, it does. So many more questions," said Liz as she tapped more commands into the display.

"I'm really tired," said Marc. "Let's go to bed."

"I'm going to stay up and look at those other marked genes in the model," said Liz. She looked at Marc mischievously "I was able to see Ray's password, so I have access to the whole thing."

"I'm not sure he'd like you fiddling with that," said Marc. "Be careful." He yawned. "Let me know if you find anything."

"I will," said Liz, without breaking her stare on Ray's display. "Get some sleep, Marc. If Tommy wakes up, I'll take care of him."

After Marc left the room, Liz placed her hand over her

belly. Hopefully, this one makes it, she thought as she glared at the model of DNA. Time to figure out how to keep a baby.

CHAPTER FIVE

Night Sky

Thomas' contacts in Key Largo paid off – not that they would ever know he had been there. All they would find in the morning was an empty slip where a small fifteen-foot boat had been moored. Thomas swallowed his remorse as he thought about how he had stolen the boat from people who had trusted him – but he had no choice. The boat wasn't licensed, and therefore couldn't be tracked, and he knew they wouldn't report the theft. They'd just buy a new one. It was the perfect opportunity and he couldn't pass it up.

The situation is different now, thought Thomas. I have to get to Newport, or the Investor Consortium will start to mercilessly pick apart the entire Mira family. They're counting on me. His orders were simple: get to Newport, Rhode Island and warn their daughter, Susan, and provide assistance and security as needed. She was the

100

only other Mira family member unaccounted for, and the IC would most certainly detain her if they could. The IC would stop at nothing to control any major finding coming out of their precious SeaLab program – even if it meant that people had to disappear. It had happened before and would certainly happen again. "Not under my watch," grumbled Agent Thomas. "Not again, and certainly not to the Mira family." They had saved his life many times and were now also keeping his boy safe. He owed them big time, not that they would ever hold that over his head. They were good people.

Two days and several "borrowed" tanks of gasoline later, Thomas finally saw the lights of Virginia Beach in the distance through a light, night-time fog. Remorse again pained him as he strapped a makeshift pack to his back, threw a large anchor overboard, and dismantled the hull so that it started to take on water. "Good-bye, friend," muttered Thomas to the slowly sinking boat just before he dove into the cold Atlantic water. It would normally take him an hour or so to swim that far to shore, but injuries to one arm and one leg caused massive muscle spasms that forced him to stop and rest until he could continue. Thankfully, by now his body had become numb to the pain, and the antibiotics he found the day before should have fought off any infection he was sure he'd been exposed to in the Everglades. That seemed like months ago, but had only been a few days. Thomas recited passages from the book of Isaiah in the Bible that he'd memorized in seminary years before. He'd forgotten much of what he'd learned in those days before enlisting, but somehow he had never forgotten some key parts of passages from Isaiah. They had helped to carry him through the most strenuous exercises in the past, and would do so again. As he felt strength leave his arms or legs, he would just keep reciting verse after verse in his mind, and through sheer focus and will-power, he would get through. Before long, Thomas clawed his way to shore. He rolled over and stared up at the night sky through unusually blurry vision. Much of the fog, it seemed, had drifted away, revealing a slim crescent of a moon wreathed in an entourage of stars. His eyes narrowed, then closed as his chest heaved one massive breath after another. Just as his breathing started to slow, he scrambled to his side and sprang to his hands and knees just as a stream vomit violently exited his mouth. Thomas stayed on his hands and knees until he started to shake. Gotta get up, he thought. Gotta keep going. He stood up clumsily and stumbled forward into the dark outskirts of some inlet near Virginia Beach. One more day thought Thomas. That's all – then I can take a breather.

After walking for a few hours, he approached a truck stop next to a nearby gas station. He looked around at the license plates on each of the vehicles, made note of the type of vehicles, and tried to assess which might be the best mode of transport. Thankfully, not many people were around, and those he did see appeared to be too busy to take notice of him. Good enough, he thought. I'm not gonna steal anything this time — too tired to drive anyway. Thomas spotted a pickup truck at the far end of the parking lot with Delaware plates. He needed to get to Newport, but finding a Rhode Island plate would have been a long shot. After climbing into the back of the old pickup, he waited patiently. The hardest part was avoiding sleep. Finally, Thomas heard footsteps approach the truck just as he slid under a tarp in the bed. He heard the jingle of car keys as the person paused before opening the driver-side door. Thomas held his breath until he heard the door shut. The engine roared to life after a bit of effort. After leaving the station, the truck sped down the main road, making several turns before entering a major freeway. Thomas peered out from under the thick tarp and stared upward so that he could see the numberless stars that littered the sky overhead. He smiled as he thought of bits and pieces of a passage from Isaiah. Something about lifting your eyes up on high, and beholding who hath created the stars, that bringeth out their host by number. He calleth them all by names by the greatness of his might, for that he is strong in power; not one faileth.

Thomas wasn't particularly religious, but for some reason just remembering part of that passage gave him hope. He heaved a sigh of relief to see that they were, in fact, driving deep into Delaware to the north – that is if his reading of the night sky was accurate. So far, his pursuers had failed, but he knew better than to underestimate the IC. Also, there were those invisible guys, and the one in the suit who he thought was a harmless IC agent. He was no IC agent, thought Thomas. Too well trained. And the others, where had they come from? Did they come from the IC? Some sort of special task force? If so, why? Had the word gotten out that quickly about whatever discoveries the Miras had made? He'd remembered the Miras talking about light-refracting fabric. Maybe that's what those spooks were using. I don't know. Just gotta keep my head down, he thought.

After fighting for so long, Thomas relented and finally

drifted to sleep.

The sun shined in through the windows lining one side of the bank, warming the room. Sue stretched and yawned. She was grateful to get to the bank early enough in the day before it got busy — which also meant that there would be less of a chance that she'd run into anyone she knew. She was not in the mood for small talk.

"How can I help you this morning?" asked a polite and unusually bubbly teller.

"I need the name on my accounts changed." said Sue.

"Oh, ok." The teller fumbled through a file and finally pulled out a form. "Please fill this out."

Sue took the form with dread. I hate forms, she thought. She looked up and forced a smile. "Any chance I can just tell you what my last name is, and what I need it changed to?"

"Um, sure," replied the teller reluctantly, "I can try to do that. I'll need an old form of identification, and a new one." Sue handed two cards to the teller, who took them cheerfully. She looked them over carefully and peered at Sue. "So, you're changing your last name from Mira to Stephens."

"Yes, that's correct," said Sue impatiently. "How long will this take?"

"Should take ten business days to process." said the teller cheerfully.

"Thanks." said Sue.

"You're welcome, Ms. Stephens!" said the teller.

"Mrs. Stephens," corrected Sue tersely. "I'm married.

Stephens is my married name. Therefore, you may call me Mrs. Stephens."

"I'm sorry. Please forgive me, Mrs. Stephens," said the teller, trying to maintain her eerie cheerfulness. "Let me take this back to my supervisor just to make sure there's nothing more we need from you."

"That would be great," said Sue. She tapped her fingertips rhythmically on the faux-wood countertop, not trying too hard to conceal her impatience. She couldn't wait any longer to get rid of her maiden name. Some of her friends had encouraged her to hyphenate, or just keep her name, but she wanted to be rid of it. Things had gotten so weird with her parents and brother, Marc. They were getting way too sucked into that SeaLab program, and now the infamous IC had their fingers all over it. Well, not me! she thought. I'm going to have a normal life — with kids and a house in a normal neighborhood. No constant moving around and fearing that the IC would jump in at any moment and tear apart my life.

Friends had been hard to come by for Sue, especially as a child of SeaLab researchers. She was constantly gone and could never do much with friends. Most of the friends she had made in Newport were now gone, having grown up in or around the area and had always wanted to move away someday. Sue didn't blame them at all, but now she felt more alone. She had opted to stick around in Newport since it was already so far away from her past. She never regretted staying, since only a few months after making her decision to stay, she found the man she would marry. "I wish Frank were here," she muttered. "He'd find a way to speed all of this up." She had figured out pretty quick after meeting him that he was far better in the people-skills department.

"Mrs. Stephens?" asked the teller.

Sue spun around to see that the teller had somehow returned without her hearing it. The teller stood there with a dumb grin. "That's all we need."

"Thanks." said Sue.

Before Sue could walk away, the teller continued. "Just got married, then?"

Sue sighed patiently. "Four months ago."

"Don't like the old maiden name, eh?" asked the teller.

Sue exhaled loudly, rolled her eyes, and forced a smile. "Just wanted to move on to the new name. I have my own reasons."

Again, the teller spoke. "Well, I think that's just wonderful. I'm getting married in two weeks!" she said with a silly overflow of glee. "See?" she said as she held out her hand. A big diamond sat upon her finger.

Sue relaxed and smiled. "I remember when my husband asked me to marry him. It was such an impulsive thing. We had just met a few months prior, but it felt so right."

"Oh. That's nice," said the teller. She paused and cleared her throat. "I was going to ask you how hard it was to change your driver's license, social security card, and all that to your new name."

"So far, not too hard," said Sue. She turned and again walked toward the exit.

"Well, thanks Ms. Mira," said the teller. "I guess I get to be one of the last people to call you that – as far as this bank is concerned, anyway."

Sue stopped but didn't turn around. She clenched her jaw and sneered. "Yeah, I guess you're right. My accounts will show the name change in ten days, right?" she asked impatiently.

"Yes, we will get that change processed as soon as possible." said the teller cheerfully as Sue made the last few steps toward the door.

Well, that's it, thought Sue. Finally, I can put the Mira family mess behind me and start a new life.

As the door to the bank silently closed, the teller's cheerful veneer melted away. Another customer approached the teller, but she put out an away sign and walked into the back room, ignoring the customer's angry protests. She placed a finger to her ear and waited. "Yes," she said. "Yes sir. I found Susan Mira."

Once the pickup truck stopped again in Delaware, Thomas slipped away and caught a late bus to Newport. The benefit of riding late in the evening was that there were fewer people around, but he knew that would also make him easier to spot. No one's around to find me, he thought. Not yet, anyway. Finally, the bus arrived at Newport. He staggered off the bus and onto a barren sidewalk just outside of downtown. It had now been several days, and he was dirty, smelly, sweaty, bloody, and pale. He had worked too hard to shake his pursuers off of his trail, and he was sure now that he had lost them. This will all be worth it, thought Thomas, if I can find Susan Mira before the Investor Consortium or Seraphim made their move. The most unnerving thing for him was not knowing well enough who his pursuers were, and what they wanted. Thomas was not used to being on the defensive for so long.

Darkness descended upon Newport as the sun disappeared behind the hills to the west, Thomas made his way to the wharf, which was the first place to lose daylight. He had been to Newport before, so he knew his way around. Thomas, starting to feel weaker and nauseated, decided to start his search near the city administrative buildings up the hill. Surely there would be a doctor's office or medical center there that he could use. After walking for several city blocks, fatigue started to take its toll. His vision started to blur, and his arm started to pulse with pain. He unwrapped a covering around his arm and noticed that the skin was red and swollen. "Infected," he said under his breath. "That's just great." Thomas gritted his teeth and scanned the area, but there were only small shops and residences. He walked another block away from the main street and found a run-down strip mall which seemed to have an outpatient clinic. Next to that was a vacant storefront, and next to that facing a street heading down toward the wharf was an outdoor supply and souvenir shop. After numerous attempts to break into the clinic, his vision started to blur and dizziness almost overtook him. I've gotta get inside, he thought. I need help. From the back of the strip mall, he could see that the storefront and souvenir shop were connected. Maybe from the inside of the shop, I can get into that clinic. Thomas broke the window of a sturdy door leading to the shop and entered what looked like a vacant section of the large, two-story strip mall. The dusty room was dark and smelly, like workers had left food to rot in a nearby wastebasket. Thomas didn't care about the smell and sat down on an overturned bucket. His vision started to blur again as sharp pains shot through his head. His arm pulsed with pain and was hot to the touch, and now he couldn't straighten or bend one of his legs. "Pretty messed up, alright," was the last thing he remembered saying before falling to sleep on the floor.

What seemed to be only a few minutes later was actually several hours. Early morning sunshine shone in through the cracks between plywood nailed up to cover the nearby windows. Thomas propped himself up and coughed uncontrollably. Even in his injured and somewhat delirious state, he could sense that someone was standing behind him.

"What on earth do you think you're doing here?" asked a man with a thick Latino accent. He chambered a round in his large shotgun and aimed it directly at Thomas' back.

"I need help," said Thomas, grunting in pain as he slowly stood up in the poorly lit room. "I need to get a hold of a friend of mine. She lives somewhere here in Newport. Can you help me?"

"Looks like she isn't a really good friend." said the man with the shotgun.

"We haven't talked for awhile," said Thomas. His face was sheet white and blood dripped from his hand. He turned around and steadied himself against a wall.

The man with the gun stepped backward. "You're on private property," he said, continuing to keep aim on Thomas "Where are you from?"

"I'm Thomas, and where I'm from is my business." Thomas started again to cough. "What's your name?"

"You can call me Gustavo," said the man. "You're in bad shape, amigo. Let's get you fixed up... you get attacked by a tiger or something?"

"Alligator," said Thomas. "Actually, I attacked it. Long story."

Gustavo paused for a moment and nodded his head. "Yeah, I'll bet." He slung the shotgun over his shoulder and lifted Thomas up carefully. Thomas grunted in pain as they hobbled through a door and down a long hallway toward the souvenir shop. "You're body's shutting down due to an infection of some sort," said Gustavo. He noticed the gunshot wounds and tried not to react.

"I'll be ok, just need some more antibiotics and new bandages." said Thomas.

Gustavo cleared off a long table and helped Thomas lay down. "You want me to do this, or you?"

"If you could, that would be great." grunted Thomas.

While Gustavo treated Thomas, he hesitated, then decided to ask another question. "So, who is it that you're looking for?"

"Just a friend. Again, my own business," said Thomas. He sat up and rolled his head from side to side, making popping sounds in his neck. "Well, that was fun," he said. "Thanks." He looked around and saw some dusty coveralls folded up on a shelf. "Can I borrow those?"

"Si, that's ok," said Gustavo as he tossed them to Thomas. "Don't want your friend alarmed by the blood stains."

After zipping up the tattered janitorial coveralls, Thomas wiped his face with his sleeve, then ran his fingers through his hair and looked toward the back door. "I need to go now."

"Amigo, you're still bleeding," said Gustavo, tossing him a bottle of water. "You're not ready for nothing."

"I made a promise. The blood will clot," said Thomas as he drank the water in a single gulp.

"Make good on your promise," said Gustavo. He looked Thomas up and down thoughtfully, and then stared him in the eyes. "You seem like a good guy. You can come back here if things don't go well with your friend."

Thomas smirked, turned around, and limped out the door and into the alleyway behind the building.

Gustavo waited a few minutes, put on his coat, grabbed a rifle and some binoculars, and started to follow Thomas. Ok amigo, he thought, you piqued my curiosity.

On his way to the library, Thomas noted the nearby middle school. His father had worked as a school teacher for his whole life. He was grateful for parents who valued education and taught him well. I'd like to maybe be a teacher someday, thought Thomas. When all of this blows over – if it ever blows over.

"Is there any charge for using the displays over there?" asked Thomas.

The librarian sneered, looked Thomas up and down, and pushed a tablet across the counter toward him – as if she was sliding a steak to a tiger. "No. Just fill out this form, press your thumb there, and then we'll print out a library pass for you," she said quietly. "Only takes a few minutes."

"Thanks," muttered Thomas, trying to be just as quiet. No one else seemed to take notice of him as he completed the form. Once he had access to the library network, he hacked the city registry. It didn't take him long to locate a woman named Susan Mira, but it took a little more time to connect the dots to discover that she had recently changed her name to Susan Stephens. Thomas scribbled an address on his hand as he quietly left the library.

The morning clouds were starting to part to reveal a clear blue sky above, while the overnight fog clung to the ground and lingered mostly around the wharf, but also up the hill and between the trees into the older suburbs. Thomas started to sweat as he walked west from the town center toward one such suburb. The homes were older and squarish. Trying to hide a limp, he stayed out of sight as much as possible by strategically choosing certain sidewalks. He made note of every person he passed, every individual he spotted through any window he could see as he walked by, and every rustle in every tree around him. What he didn't see, however, was approaching from behind. The road narrowed and curved to an old cul-de-sac. The fog thickened as did the foliage and trees. Thomas paid no attention other than to fold up his collar to shield himself from the cooler breeze. Warm in the sun one minute, cold in the foggy shade the next, he thought. Suddenly I somehow miss the constant warmth of Florida. He smiled and chuckled to himself. Never mind. There's no way I'm going back there.

A slight breeze whipped through the fog, causing its wisps to curl in strange directions. The fog moved also for an unseen individual just a few hundred feet behind Thomas as he trudged forward. Thomas, so focused on the address, neglected to look behind. He surely would have seen the disturbance in the fog. Instantly Thomas stopped and cocked his head sideways. He thought he heard footsteps. As he continued to walk forward, his pursuer stayed still. What he heard next alarmed him. A round chambered, he thought. I could swear I heard a rifle round chambered. The hair stood up on his arms and the back of his neck and he froze. I'm stuck, he thought as the blood left his face. I'm so close, and now they catch up to me. Thomas's shoulders hung with despair as he slowly turned around to face his invisible pursuer – but not entirely invisible. He could barely make out the shape of a slender figure in a firing position amidst the swirling fog. As a breeze picked up, the fog started to dissipate, and so did the faint outline of that individual. Thomas raised his arms and folded his hands behind his neck. He looked down and closed his eyes, hoping that it would be a quick and painless death.

A few seconds passed, and a muffled crack of rifle fire pierced the air. A shock passed through Thomas's body from his head down to his feet, along with a rush of adrenalin. His fingers and toes tingled, and as he looked up.

As Thomas lowered his hands and turned around, Gustavo emerged from behind a small group of young trees. "Hey amigo!" he said as he cracked a huge smile. A rifle with a large scope and silencer was slung over his shoulder.

Thomas exhaled loudly and laughed. "You were keeping an eye on me." His smiled turned to a stern grim stare. "Thanks. I owe you big time."

"Glad I didn't bring a knife to a gunfight, right?" said Gustavo.

Thomas turned quickly toward the house that matched the address he was seeking, and then turned back toward

Gustavo, who was already picking up on what Thomas wanted. As they both hid behind a grouping of trees, they watched as a small car emerged from the detached garage of the house and drove by them.

"It was a dude," whispered Gustavo. "Isn't your friend a she? Maybe now's a good time to pay her the visit you wanted so badly."

Gustavo started to step toward the road when Thomas jerked him back. "Wait. Not sure it's such a good idea to approach her now. It's gotta be more natural." They both saw a woman emerge from the house and walk to a mailbox. Before walking back into the house, she paused and turned to look in their direction. Thomas involuntarily held his breath. Finally, she closed the front door, and Thomas heard Gustavo exhale. "I'm going to be here for a long time, probably years – at least as long as she's here. I need to make sure she's protected." He remembered the picture Jules had shown him of their daughter Susan. That was definitely her.

"You her bodyguard or something?" asked Gustavo.

"Yes, well, kind of, said Thomas awkwardly, and trying not to say too much. "I work for her parents. They are SeaLab scientists, and the Investor Consortium – or who knows who else – might come after her. I made a promise."

"I understand," said Gustavo gravely. "Let's start by taking care of the body of your cloaked pursuer over there on the sidewalk."

"Wait. How'd you know what to look for?" asked Thomas. "That was a nice shot. I was sure I was dead."

"I've been around the block, amigo," said Gustavo. "Long before you were born, probably. A year ago I encountered those cloaked ones. They were patrolling my village back in Argentina. People were disappearing." Gustavo looked Thomas up and down. "You seem to have your own history with the cloaked ones, eh?"

"Yeah. That's right," said Thomas.

"Was that before or after you attacked the alligator?" joked Gustavo, slapping Thomas on the back. Thomas winced in pain and glared back at him. "Sorry amigo!"

"Let s get that body outta here," said Thomas carefully emerging from the trees and onto the sidewalk. "Looks like we re all clear."

"It's over here," said Gustavo, bending down to feel what looked like air. "Some sort of light-refracting fabric. Pretty high-tech."

"Yeah, not high-tech enough I guess," said Thomas. "Last time I encountered them, they were accompanied by what seemed to be an IC agent. I want to keep the suit this time, maybe find out how it works. This tech is illegal and it wouldn't surprise me if the IC is running covert ops under the table with this stuff for their own purposes."

"There was a company developing this technology," said Gustavo, "But they were shut down by the IC. It started with an S and sounded like styrofoam."

"Seraphim," said Thomas. "Means angels, I think."

"Not an appropriate name, if you ask me." said Gustavo, crossing himself.

"Angels of death, I suppose," said Thomas. "Either way, they should have been shut down."

"Wel, in the meantime, the offer's still open, amigo," said Gustavo. "Stay at my place until you find your own. Any enemy of the cloaked ones and the IC is a friend of mine."

"No, Gustavo, no," said Thomas shaking his head. "I've gotten you into enough trouble here."

Gustavo's face grew stern and a frown formed. "Thomas, you owe me, and I say you're staying with me – at least until your wounds heal," he said as he held out his hand.

Thomas smiled and shook Gustavo's hand. "Deal. Thanks amigo."

CIA BRANCH OFFICE, MIAMI

"Agent Vinton," said the lieutenant, "The security personnel were unable to apprehend the individual who broke into the monitoring facility in Miami. They say that he was eaten by an alligator."

"What?" blurted Vinton. "How?"

"Also, they lost one of their officers to another alligator." said the lieutenant.

"Cretins!" blurted Vinton as he threw a ceramic mug full of coffee across the room, shattering it. The room quieted. "That's it? Did they happen to get a body?"

"No, they deemed the situation to be too dangerous," said the lieutenant. "There's more. A report of a break-in at Key Largo and the Surface Monitoring Station scanners picked up something briefly off the coast of Key Biscayne to the north." He paused and looked back over the latest reports on the display.

"Well, now, that's something we can work with," said Vinton sounding a bit more patient. "I wanna tie this one off. I can't stand Miami."

"Yes sir," answered the lieutenant, holding a finger to his ear. "More reports coming in now from Virginia

Beach. Locals reported strange activity between there and a nearby gas station."

"Virginia?" said Vinton. "That's quite a boat ride from Key Biscayne."

"Agreed, sir," said the lieutenant. "Our men experienced some difficulty with the locals who claimed to see a man, soaking wet, wandering around that gas station parking lot."

"What do you mean, difficulties?" asked Vinton.

"When they went back to question them again, one was dead, and the other two didn't even remember being questioned." said the lieutenant.

"Any surveillance camera footage?" asked Vinton.

"I asked," said the lieutenant, "But when they checked it out, it was blank."

"Like, maybe it was scrubbed?" asked Vinton.

"Yes sir. So it would seem."

"Similar patterns in San Diego and Corpus Christie," mumbled Vinton. "Who is shadowing us?" Vinton wondered if the IC were covering their tracks, and if so, why.

"Shadowing us, sir?" asked the lieutenant.

"Nothing." said Vinton.

The lieutenant shifted uncomfortably. "We know that there were a few vehicles there with Delaware plates, some sort of work crew driving through," he said. "Chances are that he hopped a ride to the north. I recommend we look toward Delaware."

"Thank you, lieutenant," said Vinton. "Call Langley and see if we can commandeer the branch offices in Providence and also Shreveport. The northeast is the new hotspot. Nothing happens there without me knowing about it. Staff up, network out, dig down, and let's get some new locals up there. We need new agents who know that area like the back of their hand. Recruit anyone with a clean record and with a military or intelligence background."

The lieutenant hastily tapped the instructions into his device and looked up at Vinton. "Is that all, sir?"

"Lieutenant, I want Rhode Island, Massachusetts, and Delaware saturated with intelligence gathering assets," said Agent Vinton. "Am I clear?"

The lieutenant stood at attention. "Yes sir!"

"Ok people!" said Vinton, pacing around the small room. "We're heading to Providence. Pack up. We leave at sixteen hundred hours."

And not soon enough, he thought.

CHAPTER SIX

Complete

A month had passed since Agent Thomas left to the surface, and two weeks since Liz was no longer pregnant. Another miscarriage, she thought. Over and over in her mind she wondered what she could have done differently. She blamed herself. She blamed the whole situation. The only person Liz couldn't blame was Marc. He was part of her, and she was a part of him. She shook her head in vain, as if to shake the repeated thoughts of despair from her mind.

"Another headache?" asked Marc. He sat down next to her and held out a sandwich.

"I'm fine." she said, continuing to stare at the display.

"Please, Liz," said Marc. "You need to eat. You've hardly eaten anything for the past two days."

"I'm not hungry, and I don't have a headache." said Liz.

Marc sighed. He kissed her cheek and put the plate down on the table. "I'll leave this here in case you change your mind."

As Marc stood up to leave, Liz grabbed his arm. "Thanks," she said quietly. "It wasn't your fault, Marc."

"I feel like it was," said Marc. "I could have shielded you better. I should have."

"Marc, come on. It wasn't your fault," said Liz. "We could not have known what we were getting ourselves into. It's my fault that I didn't even tell you that I was pregnant." She looked carefully at Marc who stared past her blankly at the wall.

"If I had known, maybe it could have been different." said Marc.

Liz hung her head. "I don't think so."

Marc stood up swiftly and walked toward the door. Liz could tell he was upset. "Marc," she said.

"What," said Marc without turning around. His fists were clenched. "Why can't we have kids? Are we broken?" he said abruptly.

"I have something to tell you," said Liz. "You're not going to like it."

"What is it?" asked Marc quietly, trying not to get angry.

"Look," she said, turning the display toward Marc. "I've been analyzing and comparing the patterns in that second chromosome on the left, and on the first chromosome on the right."

Marc leaned closer to the display, and then sat down in a chair next to her. "So mine is which one?"

"The one on the right," said Liz. "Mine is the one on the left."

"Klein-Veldt Disease?" asked Marc. "We both have it?"

"That would explain our batting record so far, and also those seemingly identical genetic aberrations," said Liz.

"Klein-Veldt encodes a mutated gene preventing the child's heart from developing a strong atria-ventricular node."

"So, unless we can figure out a way to get the fetus fitted with a pacemaker, we can't have kids," said Marc. He slammed his fist down on the desk, rocking the plate with the sandwich on it. Liz looked at him thoughtfully and placed her hand on his. Marc's frown revealed frustration he'd been bottling up for a long time. "I'm sorry, Liz," he said. "I'm so sorry."

"So, we're both broken," said Liz. "I'm sorry, too. So much for wonderful surprises and romantic deep-sea getaways." She picked up the sandwich and took a large bite.

Marc smiled. "I love you, Liz. I'm sorry I got upset."

"I'm sorry for shutting you out. I wanted to be mad at someone. I wanted an explanation." said Liz. She turned back toward the display. "Let me show you something." As her fingers danced across the keyboard, the display switched to show a complex arrangement of structures. When she zoomed out, a double-helix became visible.

"Is this what I think it is?" asked Mark.

"Yeah. It took me a week to parse it out from all the other neutrino noise," said Liz. "What you see is just the human DNA template data from your parent's lab."

"Do they know about this?" asked Marc. My dad was pretty specific about not copying anything..."

"Do you want children, or not?" asked Liz. Her eyes seemed to have a fire behind them.

Marc knew immediately that this was one of those questions you should say yes to – even if you disagreed. "Of course I want children. We both do, but my dad specifically told us to not access that data without his permission."

"Relax," said Liz. "He's just paranoid. You know that. Besides, we are five miles under an ocean, with absolutely no network connections to anything but ourselves."

"Ok, fine," said Marc. "Tell me what you're thinking."

Liz smiled. "I can't tell you, but I can show you," she said as her hands again danced over the keyboard. The display shifted back to their own DNA sequences, but this time, with the DNA template data layered beneath theirs. "See that?"

Marc again leaned closer to the display. "So, that's the correct sequence on the right for me, and the correct sequence there on the left is for you?" he asked. "What's your point, Liz?"

"My point is that we now know what to fix so that we can have kids." said Liz.

"Ok, but, we don't have the ability to change or rewrite our own DNA," said Marc. "We'd have to synthesize actual DNA from each of our instances of DNA, using that new template as a guide."

"Yes, that's right," said Liz with a thin grin. "Remember that sheet of paper? Your dad developed a controller for the Higgs field using the DNA template. Using that controller, we could theoretically synthesize new human DNA."

"He also said that a living sample would be quite a bit more complex," said Marc. "There's a huge difference between a matrix of cellulose molecules, and living human tissue."

"Yes, of course," said Liz. "But our DNA and the information from the template could handle that complexity for us. Thanks to your dad's discovery of the controller, I think it's possible."

"I appreciate your enthusiasm, Liz, but I'm not sure you're thinking straight about this," said Marc. "It took my dad weeks just to figure out that Higgs controller thing, the thing that gives mass to those floaty bright particles and creates real sheets of paper."

Liz smiled. "Yes, the Higgs controller. You're right, he did a lot of the work for us," said Liz.

"To do what you're suggesting might take months, if not years," said Marc. "Isn't that right?"

"We can't exactly go anywhere and we seem to have a lot of time on our hands down here," said Liz, "And your dad doesn't have my genetics background." She smiled and looked back at her display. "I'm thinking that it might take me weeks or months – not years."

Marc smiled and shook his head nervously. "I hope you know what you're doing." He leaned over and kissed her forehead. "Let me know if I can help out at all."

"Mmm-hmm." said Liz, already lost in her work.

The station – or what remained of it – was still large enough so that if one wandered, one could easily get lost. Jules, having helped to design the station, wished that she could go somewhere and actually get lost. She yearned for the surface. It had been too long since she felt sand between her toes or squinted in the bright summer sun of southern Florida. The video feeds of the deep-sea landscape around the west side helped, but since everything was always so dark that far down, the only visible sign of anything was the occasional phosphorescent creature swimming by. There was another painful reason why she hated being there more and more each day. As she stared out into the dark expansive void, she thought of the rest of SeaLab IV that was no longer there. It was now the watery tomb for hundreds of associates and friends.

Ray yawned and stood to stretch. "Hey there Jules. Yearning for the beach, too?"

To Julia, her husband's voice was a balm. She smiled as she continued to look at the video feed stretched across the wall. "Liz took the bait, Ray," said Jules without turning around.

"Well, that's good," said Ray. "Only from the specified location we discussed, correct?"

"Yes, that's right," said Jules. "That way, if the kids ever get caught with that data, they'll disappear behind some sort of steel reinforced concrete compound in the desert."

"Better than the alternative," said Ray. "If they were caught with anything else we found – including the Seraphim files – they'd be terminated without any questions."

"Yeah yeah yeah. I get all of that," said Jules. "But we can help them, at least. Right?"

"If the IC ever gets ahold of them, they won't do any harm, to them," said Ray. "The IC would see them as having smuggled data from us. The IC would want them to help them get to us. It's insurance."

"Hmm, didn't think about that." Jules turned around. Tears streamed down her face. "What have we done to our family, Ray?" asked Jules.

"We made the discovery of the millennium," said Ray, gravely. "That's what we did. Better for us to have discovered all of that before the IC."

"We can't stay down here forever," said Jules, "Nor do I care to. We need to finish capturing all of that data."

"No worries. Only one hundred eighty thousand petabytes of data to go," said Ray. "Should take nine more months."

"I hope your plan works, Ray," said Jules. "You've really taken cloud storage to the next level."

"Yeah. As long as the sun keeps shining, our neutrino infrastructure should provide an endless amount of storage," said Ray. "And thanks to that template, we know how to write to that storage network."

"The trick will be to devise a way to easily access and navigate that information." said Jules.

"You're right," said Ray. "That certainly is the trick." He folded his arms and smiled deviously at Jules.

Her expression of concern melted to anger. "So, that's what this is all about? That's why you wanted Liz to be able to access the DNA template and those mysterious marked genes?" she asked. "You're going to need a native DNA-encoded prototype to access the information, and you're using Marc and Liz to create it."

"Well, we're too old. Can you think of another way?" asked Ray. "How else do you expect anyone to be able to access and retrieve information from that neutrino stream? The only neutrino harvester in existence is down here, and I'll be darned if anyone else ever gets their hands on it. Can you imagine what would happen if the IC got their hands on it?"

"Well, you always wondered how you could possibly leave a worthy legacy for the kids. However, Marc and Liz will never forgive you for your deception," said Jules. "We're talking about a living person, Ray."

"Marc will understand," said Ray. "Liz won't."

"What about Susan?" asked Jules.

"We need to make sure she stays protected. She knows too much about SeaLab and plan B. She also knows too much about the neutrino harvester." said Ray.

"That's what worries me," said Jules. "If the IC or Seraphim ever got ahold of her..."

Ray nodded with regret. "If Agent Thomas can't protect her, we've all got much bigger problems!"

The rain poured down relentlessly in Newport. Months had gone by, and Agent Thomas was still learning to tolerate the locals. It was quite a different place than he had ever lived, but it grew on him – like rust or moss. Despite his aversion to the open seas, he took up sailing, supposing that the best way to get over the past was to take it head on. His heart ached for his boy, but he didn't worry about him. He knew that little Tommy would be safe with the Miras.

Gustavo and Thomas formed a two-man team. Together, they had a system set up in town to keep an eye on the IC and any government operations in the area. Thomas also kept a keen eye on the Stephens. The Mira's daughter would not be harmed; he and Gustavo would make sure of that.

"How's the new job going, Thomas?" asked Gustavo as he downed a taco. Amazingly, none of the food fell out of his mouth as he spoke. "Still laughing about your choice of profession. You could have chosen to do anything with skills like yours, amigo."

"Being a janitor at the school will keep me in the middle of the chatter, and no one will ever know I'm listening," said Thomas, smiling. "Besides, it's therapeutic to clean stuff up."

Gustavo laughed. "Very clever. Not sure I would have thought of that. I think I'll stick to my cutlery and souvenir shop."

"Well, I hope you do," said Thomas. "The town needs more responsible business owners like you around here. Also, you've been a great landlord."

"Have been?" asked Gustavo. He frowned and put down his half-eaten taco. "You talk like you're leaving. Found a place?"

"Well, you've been great, but I need a place closer to the Stephens," said Thomas. "I need to keep a better eye on them. There's a room in the back of the school and the superintendent and faculty have been so impressed with me that they'd like me to stay there. Rent is really reasonable too."

"But, I don't even charge you rent!" said Gustavo. He feigned offense but then cracked a huge smile. "I'm so happy for you, amigo!"

"It'll be good for you to keep an eye on activity from this end of town since you're closer to the wharf," said Thomas. "Ever since we intercepted that cloaked spook months ago, I've been worried that there would be more people coming after Sue."

"Yeah, she was the most lethal bank teller I'd ever encountered." said Gustavo.

"She was prepared and she took me by surprise," said Thomas. "I could have taken her myself if–"

"–You're a stubborn gringo, amigo," interrupted Gustavo. "If I hadn't followed you, we wouldn't be talking right now."

"Yeah yeah yeah. I know," said Thomas, smiling. "Well, it's been months, and no word from the Miras."

"When do you think they'll return to the surface?" asked Gustavo. "Ever since the media outlets' announcement of SeaLab IV's so-called fatal reactor meltdown, everyone has assumed that you and the Miras died along with everyone else."

"Well, Ray and Jules Mira would not have shut down SeaLab IV and faked its destruction unless they intended to stay down there for a long time – maybe years," said Thomas. "I just wonder when I'll see Tommy Jr. again."

"You must miss your boy dreadfully." said Gustavo.

Thomas frowned. "Yes, I do. At least I know that down there, he's safe. If he were up here with me, I'd worry about him all the time. If the IC ever got ahold of him, I don't know what I'd do."

"You'd have to destroy the IC, I suppose," said Gustavo, smiling and grabbing another taco. "I would help you do it, too. Either way, I've got a bug on the inside of the IC that will let me know the moment there's any news from the surface monitoring station for SeaLab IV ...or whatever the Miras are calling that place now."

"The IC is very patient, and the Seraphim operation that seems to be infiltrating the IC seems to be even more patient than the IC itself," said Thomas. "If Seraphim really is as influential as it seems, they could really do some damage."

"If everything you've told me is correct, then we are ahead of Seraphim," said Gustavo. "We know who they want."

"That's why I need to move to the school," said Thomas. "You've been very gracious to share your home with me. Thanks. I don't know how I could ever repay you."

"I'm glad I could help," said Gustavo. "Besides, you can never repay me. Just let me be involved when it's time to slam some cloaked ones!"

"We've still got our weekly pub time. We'll use that to catch up in person," said Thomas.

"When do you plan to move into your room at the school?" asked Gustavo.

"Tonight." said Thomas as he grabbed a taco.

Weeks turned to months. Marc and Liz had grown more at peace with the idea of being in SeaLab long-term. At the same time, Jules had grown more and more restless. It was all Ray could do to keep her distracted. While he planned the next rover survey into the deep-sea cliffs, she worked to recalibrate the gas levels in the breathable fluid for the transport tubes – the same one Thomas had used to get to the surface.

"A couple more weeks and I may actually get this thing to work within safe parameters." said Jules, wiping the sweat from her forehead.

"And then I suppose you'd like to test it on yourself?" asked Ray. "I don't think so. We'll use the probes. It will take longer, but won't kill anyone."

"Okay, fine." said Jules.

Marc strutted into the room, and his parents stopped and stared at him. "Are you alright?" asked Jules.

"I'm fine," said Marc as he grabbed a bag of chips and a drink and sat down, "Just fine."

"How's Liz doing?" asked Jules. "I went to see if she needed anything, and she just kept looking at her display. She just tap-tap-tapped away."

"Yeah, she's been pretty busy doing ...her thing," said Marc, hesitating as he remembered how he and Liz had agreed to not tell his parents about the reason for their infertility, or about her experiment. "She finds a lot of solace in her research. She's also not been feeling well. Really picky with food."

Ray looked at Jules and smiled. "What's she researching?"

"She's been trying to find the reason why we couldn't have children," said Marc. "That's all." He tried to conceal a smile as he started to fill his mouth with potato chips.

"Sorry she's not feeling well, dear," said Jules. "Is she pregnant again?"

Marc coughed and almost spit out the food in his mouth. "How'd you know? I was going to surprise you!"

"Can't get anything past your mother," said Ray. "You of all people should know better."

Marc smiled and laughed, but inside felt a bit anxious at the thought that maybe they were aware that Liz had accessed his dad's data. "I suppose you're right. I asked Liz if she wanted anything to eat, and she said not to ask her that," said Marc. "I was starving, so I thought I'd come to see if you wanted to eat lunch together."

"How far along is she?" asked Jules. "Probably still the first trimester, right?"

"Yeah, still early," said Marc. He smiled, gave his parents a hug, and walked out of the room.

"Well, that was weird." said Ray.

"Well, it's pretty obvious that they feel like their application of the DNA template was successful," said Jules. "Otherwise, he'd be acting more cautiously optimistic. You know, dreading the next potential miscarriage."

"Jules, it also means that they may have successfully synthesized DNA," said Ray. He smiled and started for the door. "It's time we had a look at their progress."

"Ray!" shouted Jules. "Remember what you said. We have to stay out of it."

Ray, as if stunned, froze in the doorway. "Yes, of course.'

Jules stood up and put an arm around Ray. "In a way, you've already passed on your legacy. Take satisfaction in that, and also that you may soon be a grandpa."

Ray turned to her and smiled. "It also means that we have to get out of here soon. This is no place to raise a child, and the time is now ticking," he said. "How soon can we use the tube?"

"I'll have it ready in a week or so," said Jules. "I'm gonna go congratulate Liz... but I'll be sure not to act too excited.'

"Mr. T," said the elderly woman, "Please sign here and here."

Thomas was still getting used to his new alias "Mr. T". He wasn't sure if it was paranoia – since Thomas was such a common name – or if he thought it might be one more little thing to throw off anyone trying to find him. Either way, he was grateful to the old ladies in the office to give him such a glowing recommendation to the school district for his work.

"Mr. T?" asked the woman, getting somewhat impatient. She leaned over the front desk even closer to Thomas as smiled.

Thomas tried to ignore the woman's advances. He knew that most of the widows in the office of the old middle school liked him, but he acted like he didn't notice. His charm had now landed him in an old apartment in the back of the school near the facilities offices. It had been the perfect place to keep an eye on the Stephens. Frank, Sue's husband, would come into the school to do repairs. He was a nice guy, but there was something about him that seemed off.

The woman stood back and pursed her lips in frustration. "Mr. T? Mr. T!" she said. "Earth to Mr. T."

"So sorry, Sally," said Thomas. "I guess I was just lost in thought." He looked up and smiled at Sally. "Thanks for the opportunity to renew my lease."

Sally relaxed her annoyance, leaned again toward Thomas, and gazed at him as she fluffed up her hair. "We're glad you chose to stick around!" said Sally. A few of the other ladies giggled from the back room.

Thomas cleared his throat and forced a smile. "Well, if that's, all, I'll be on my way," said Thomas. "Thanks so much!" He walked away before Sally could extend yet another lunch invitation.

Thomas walked back down a long familiar hallway lined with lockers. He imagined what life might have been like had he not accepted his first SeaLab assignment. I didn't have a choice, thought Thomas. The IC would have retaliated. I had to be on assignment even as my wife was fighting cancer. I'm just glad that little Tommy was too young to remember.

After passing two more banks of lockers, he approached the locked double door leading to the facilities area. As he was about to insert the key, he noticed that the door was already unlocked. Thomas frowned and positioned the key between his fingers so it stuck out like a dagger when he clenched his fist. Slowly, he opened the door. The hallway was dark, except for light coming from one of the offices on the right.

"Hello?" called Thomas as he cautiously approached the lobby area just outside of the offices. He walked into the office and saw that one of the displays on the wall was blinking with an alert, and just below on the desk was a small package. Thomas closed the office door and hastily opened the small box. Inside was a familiar game device – the same one that Tommy had been begging him to get before he left the station. Thomas smiled and ran back out of the office into the darkened hallway. He walked back to the front office just as Sally was putting on her coat to leave for lunch.

"Mr. T," she said with a broad flirtatious grin, "Back so soon. Care to join us for lunch?"

"There was a package in my office," said Thomas. "Any idea when it was delivered? Who delivered it?"

"Oh, I'm sorry," said Sally. "I forgot to mention that. It was delivered this morning, and I brought it back to your office while you were out. I apologize for not locking your offices up."

"That's ok." said Mr. T.

Sally looked curiously at the package. "Something special?" she asked. "Who's it from, if you don't mind me asking?"

"Not sure, no return address." said Thomas as he turned and walked back toward his office, still inspecting the package.

"Well, maybe another time for lunch then." said Sally.

Thomas ran back to his office and unlocked his display. He had received an encoded message. He hastily tapped away on the display and the message appeared:

"Facility in standby, we have returned and are ok. Your boy missed you. He is being watched over at Touro Park. Meet him there asap. Escorts present. Stick to plan, more instructions to follow. Thanks! End."

The park was only minutes from the school. Thomas knew that Ray and Jules would know to find him here in Newport, but he wondered how they had managed to get to the surface. His walk turned to a jog when he thought about his dear boy drawing in that "breathable" fluid and getting shot through that tube. As Thomas approached from the sidewalk, he could see his son playing under a tree. Good heavens, he thought to himself. He looks all right. Thomas smiled and before he could call to his son, two men appeared and stood in front of him, blocking his view of Tommy. Their menacing expressions turned to smiles.

"It's an honor to meet you Agent Thomas, sir," said one of the men. "We bring you a message from our employers, but first we must establish your credentials."

"Understood," said Thomas with a sigh. He held out his finger, and the other man held his finger onto a small device. A green light appeared on the device. Thomas then checked both of the men the same way to verify their identities. "Has the boy been tagged as well?"

"Yes sir," said one of the men. "The enzyme marker was introduced into your son's system months ago."

"How did they all get to the surface?" asked Thomas. "The tube? How did the boy handle it?"

"He was sedated, naturally," said one of the men. "Agent Thomas, The Miras are taking no chances going forward. All assets are secured, and the Mira family trust has been established by Marc and Liz. Your assignment is to ensure that your boy becomes fully trained."

"Yes, of course," said Thomas. "What of Seraphim?"

"When your son is ready, his assignment is to pursue Seraphim," said the other man. "The enemy has proven to be patient, well connected and elusive. We stand ready for your command through the regular channels."

"I have Newport secured," said Thomas. He turned and looked into the eyes of the two men. Now that he had been identified, Thomas understood that he was now again in command of all of the Mira's security detail. "You will keep an eye on Marc and Liz, and provide any security they require going forward."

"Understood," said one of the men, saluting. "It is an honor to serve with you again, Agent Thomas."

"Call me Mr. T," he said, smiling, "Thank you for safely delivering my son."

"Yes sir," said the two men. "The Miras send their regards."

Thomas nodded, then walked past the men to approach his son.

Tommy smiled up at him. "Dad! I missed you!"

Thomas embraced his son, and tears flowed down his

face. "I missed you too, son!" he said. Thomas looked around to thank the other agents, but they were already gone. He smiled as he walked with Tommy back to the school. On the way, Thomas replayed in his mind what the agents had said, and something puzzled him. What did they mean when they said that Marc and Liz have established the Mira family trust? he thought. Whatever it meant, Thomas felt more determined than ever to fulfill his duty to the Mira family.

UNDISCLOSED LOCATION, WEST COAST OF PUERTO RICO

The warm sea air filled Liz's lungs. Sure is nice to be surface-side again, she thought, and it's nice to know that little Tommy finally got his daddy back! She closed her eyes as she continued to face north. In her mind, she pictured the southeastern Florida coast. Somehow, the northern coast of Puerto Rico just felt so much more comfortable.

"Enjoying the warm breeze?" asked Jules. She had walked out to the balcony and was standing quietly beside Liz.

Liz, trying not to act surprised, wondered how long she had been standing there. "It's so beautiful here, and so peaceful." She opened her eyes and turned to Jules. "So, how long has this place been in your family, Jules?" she asked.

"Three generations," answered Jules. "We would always come here for reunions. I have so many memories of this villa from my childhood."

"I always wanted to visit Puerto Rico." said Liz.

"Well, here you are," said Jules. She hesitated in an awkward silence.

Just as Jules was about to say something more, Ray walked in carrying some boxes. "We thought that this would be a great place to keep an eye on things," said Ray. It seemed as if he and Marc had been bringing boxes in from trucks all day. Ray paused and wiped the sweat from his aged face with a rag. "We need to keep an eye on that trench."

Marc walked in fully laden with more boxes, which he set down as soon as he could. He looked at Liz and smiled. "Hey sweetie, how's everything going?"

"The baby is asleep in the other room," said Liz. She beamed with joy. The baby was a healthy boy. Nothing seemed out of the ordinary with him, and at times, Liz and Marc even forgot about the unusual circumstances surrounding his birth.

Ray and Julia left the room, and Marc sat down next to Liz. She remembered how she longed for a normal life and family. She remembered seeing those other families playing with their children at parks and walking down the streets of southern Florida before they entered that shuttle to descend down to SeaLab IV. She would never go there again – or to what was left of it. Never ever, she thought.

"You know, Marc," said Liz, pausing, "We're going to need our own space to raise our baby."

Marc smiled and looked at Liz. "I've already got a few spots we can go look at in Rincón. That way we still have an ocean view," he said.

Without warning, Liz threw her arms around him. "I love you."

"I love you too, Liz." said Marc.

CHAPTER SEVEN

Threnody

CIA BRANCH OFFICE, PROVIDENCE, RHODE ISLAND

"I'm not sure you understand the situation here," said Vinton into a sat phone. "I really don't have time to investigate the scene in Georgia. I've got my hands full here in the northeast!" Vinton paused and frowned. "Yes sir. Yes sir. Understood." he said. Vinton switched off the phone and exhaled loudly as he looked at several displays on the wall while he ran his fingers through his tousled hair. It had been four years, and one SeaLab station after another had fallen just like SeaLab IV. Thankfully, in those cases, most of the research and all of the staff were saved. A few of the stations were lost permanently; while they seemed to be on permanent maintenance mode. The IC had learned to conceal and continue their illegal SeaLab projects right under the nose of the public. The media was sure that the world was just seeing a decline in the SeaLab program, and that was also the message that they repeated endlessly on the networks.

Agent Vinton knew better. He knew that Mars Expeditions I and II were flawed and would probably be postponed. It seemed that the public eye was again reaching for the stars. Either way, public sentiment seemed to be single-handedly directing his list of priorities, no matter how badly that sentiment conflicted with the truth. Vinton sat down abruptly in his office chair and continued a message, when a tall broad-shouldered man entered the room.

"Frank Stephens, reporting as ordered, sir." he said abruptly. He wore a suit but saluted like a marine.

Almost immediately, Vinton wanted him on the team. He had studied Frank Stephen's military service record – two silver stars and a navy cross. He felt like he knew all he needed to know, and just had to actually meet him. "At ease, and have a seat, Mr. Stephens," he said.

"Yes sir," said Frank. He sat down and straightened his tie.

"I need a project leader from central intelligence in my squadron," said Vinton. "Are you the right man for the job?"

"Yes sir," said Frank. "I mean, yes sir, Mr. Vinton."

Vinton stood and smiled, holding out his hand. "Call me Agent Vinton, Mr. Stephens," he paused then smiled. "Agent Stephens, you will make a great addition to the team."

"Thank you, Agent Vinton," said Frank. "It will be an honor to serve in this capacity."

"I trust your cover is intact with all of your associations," said Vinton. He peered into Frank's eyes, and he stared right back.

"Yes sir, Agent Vinton," said Frank. "I am four years married and have triplets on the way, sir."

Vinton was already aware. It was the only factor that ever really raised serious questions in the covert recruitment process: Family. "That will complicate matters, and make life difficult for you and your wife and children," said Vinton. "Your agreement makes that clear, but I feel it necessary to remind you anyway."

"Yes sir, I understand the risks," said Frank. "I also understand my priorities."

"Very good, Agent Stephens," said Vinton. "I expect you to report for initial briefings at o-six hundred hours, Monday."

"Thank you, Agent Vinton," said Frank. "I won't let our country down."

"Such as it is." muttered Vinton, almost involuntarily.

"Sir?" asked Frank, a bit surprised at Vinton's candidness.

"Just wait until Monday for the briefing," said Vinton. "You're dismissed."

Thomas, by now known around Newport and at the school as "Mr. T", had learned to keep a keen eye on all of the comings and goings around town – especially those having to do with the Stephens family. Thomas had become more familiar with Frank Stephens, who seemed to be a successful general contractor and repairman. Because Thomas knew Frank was really CIA, and that there was no love lost between the CIA and the IC, he relaxed his guard on the Stephens family more and more.

Besides, it had been a long time since the incident on the way to Susan Stephen's home, and there had been no subsequent Seraphim or IC related events locally. However, strange occurrences nationally and internationally were on the rise, and the media networks were in a constant frenzy over missing persons, strange mass blackouts, buildings or areas being mysteriously destroyed. The rate of strange events seemed so great, that they started to become a normal segment on the news, over time falling further and further down the list. Instead, news of developments in the space program dominated the headlines. Mars Expedition I had to be called back to Earth. It seemed that humans needed to be close to the planet to survive, and Mars Expedition II was already making promises it probably couldn't keep. The regular stream of corrupt politics and Investor Consortium antics were taking their toll on Thomas, who was already pretty cynical.

Despite all of the chaos in the media, it was his young boy Tommy who captured most of Thomas's attention.

More and more, young Tommy asked "Dad, why do we live at the school? Why can't we live in a normal home?"

Well, he's almost twelve years old, thought Thomas. It's to be expected. One day, Tommy came home from school (which in and of itself was strange, since he had to walk a quarter mile to and from his elementary school, even though he lived in a school) and asked a question that his father was totally unprepared to answer.

"Can I go live with grandma and grandpa in Virginia?" asked Tommy. "I hate it here. I hate living at this school. Next year I'd be going here for school, and it would be way too weird to also live here."

Thomas struggled to find an answer. Initially, he felt like telling Tommy to suck it up and be thankful for all that he'd been taught. After all, under his training, his son had managed to learn four different martial arts and a broad array of various types of tactical training. He had also gained an education that far exceeded high school levels. "Son, you're right. Maybe it's about time you live with your mom's folks and got out of here."

Tommy's face relaxed, and a smile emerged. "Really?"

"Yeah, I'll get ahold of them and see what we can do," said Thomas. "Just remember the promises you've made. Remember what I've taught you."

"Yeah, I know, dad," said Tommy. "I'll be back with you every summer. Deal?"

"Sounds like a deal, alright," said Thomas, trying to look satisfied with the terms. Someday, young Tommy will need to put his skills into practice, he thought, he just doesn't know it yet. Thomas had been briefed by the Miras as to the basics of their discoveries, and he would do all he could to make sure that those discoveries didn't fall into the wrong hands. With his training and the Mira's near-limitless resources, he was sure they would be able to keep their discoveries contained. He wondered if Marc and Liz would be able to take the reigns once they were too old to manage themselves, and Sue couldn't be less interested in having anything to do with the rest of the Mira family.

The future seemed to rest on Marc and Liz's shoulders – wherever they were these days.

* * *

Marc and Liz settled into their new home in a quiet village on the western shores of Puerto Rico. Their young boy, Callum, seemed quite normal, but also very smart. As the years passed by, Marc and Liz's anxiety about his genetic abnormalities seemed to fade more and more away. He was normal, and that was that. They believed that if they treated him normally, that he would be normal.

"He's just four, Liz," said Marc. "I don't think it's a good idea to enroll him in that accelerated program. It's preschool, for heaven's sake."

"Yeah, but, what if he gets bored?" asked Liz.

"Bored with graham crackers and Legos?" answered Marc.

Liz rolled her eyes. "You know as well as I do what they teach in that class. He's already learned three languages, and his teacher has already recorded his calculus scores. He's going to be noticed."

"They what?" asked Marc. "They promised us that they wouldn't record his scores on the national registry."

"Well, what did you think they'd do? Look at his scores. Marc, Callum needs something more." said Liz. "We need to consider options other than the standard schooling around here."

"I don't want him to be an outcast," said Marc. "He deserves a normal life."

"What's a normal life?" asked Callum as he walked into the room. His dark hair was cleanly cut, and he looked up innocently at his parents.

"Callum, I, I mean we, your mother and me,"

stammered Marc, "We just want you to be happy."

Callum looked down at the floor and back up with a smile. "I want the other kids to be happy, too. Teacher Annie told us about an orphanage. Those are kids without mommies and daddies."

The idea hit Marc and Liz like a lightning bolt. "Callum, you're a genius!" said Marc. He lifted the young boy up and swung him around. After he put him down, Callum smiled and ran off to play. Marc looked longingly at Liz and smiled. "Well?"

"The idea had already crossed my mind," said Liz with a sigh. She smiled. "The adoption laws have really opened up on the island. It shouldn't be hard for us to adopt."

"Nothing more normal than a sibling, right?" said Marc.

The next day, Marc and Liz visited the local adoption agency. "We're ok submitting forms, right?" asked Liz.

"Yeah, it's like we were never at SeaLab IV. Mom and dad made the records reflect that," said Marc. "We're ok."

"Ok." said Liz. "Just something doesn't seem right."

"Buenos Dias," said the receptionist. "Here to adopt?"

"Yes, we'd like to adopt as soon as possible!" said Liz enthusiastically. "Like today, if possible."

"Let me get someone to help you," said the receptionist nervously. "We always have children we are wanting to place quickly."

It was several minutes later when Marc and Liz found themselves in a tidy, yet run-down office. "I have your profiles on my display here," said a social worker. "Both very well educated. SeaLab trained and certified. Looks like you both have spent a fair amount of time down there at the station that we lost. So tragic. I'll bet you both wish you had posts in the Mars programs." The social worker peered at them over her display.

"Yes." said Liz, at the same time Marc said "No."

The worker paused, "I see." she said as she scribbled some notes on her display. Marc and Liz looked at each other nervously.

"We are very good and loving parents," said Marc. "Our four year old boy is a very smart kid and may join the accelerated program at his preschool."

"Accelerated preschool?" asked the worker skeptically. "I see." Again, she scribbled some notes on her display.

After waiting patiently for the social worker to jot down more notes onto her display for several minutes, she finally looked up. "You're in luck. Your profile suggests a boy close to the age of your first child. We have one such boy. He is also four years old and is native Puerto Rican." The worker paused and looked accusingly at Marc and Liz. "He's a very nice boy."

"Sounds perfect!" said Liz.

Marc nodded enthusiastically. "What's his name?"

"Jacque," said the worker with a smile. "Like Jacque Cousteau... except he's not French."

"When can we meet him?" asked Liz.

The social worker looked Marc and Liz over again and abruptly stood up. "Follow me."

About thirty minutes later, they were standing in an orphanage in San Juan. The young boy, Jacque, was introduced to Marc and Liz. All he had was a small bag and a black and white teddy bear. He wore a T-shirt, shorts, and leather sandals. Because there were no living relatives, the adoption process went very smoothly. It wasn't until they were on their way home that they realized that he didn't speak English, only Spanish.

"That's ok, I can teach him English!" said Callum that evening. "I love having a brother!" It wasn't until later that Callum discovered that Jacque really did understand quite a bit of English, but chose to hide it.

"He's had a hard life, Callum," said his father. "We all need to love Jacque. He's part of our family now."

"Yes daddy." said Callum with a smile.

For months, Ray and Jules worked from the villa to complete the upload of the data from the harvester to their makeshift neutrino storage matrix. The only thing Ray wasn't really sure of was how to quickly retrieve the information back from that matrix. Of course, he would need Marc and Liz's child for that.

"How old do you think the boy needs to be before he could possibly retrieve anything?" asked Ray.

"Geez Ray. His name is Callum!" said Jules. "And, I have no idea. I suppose that when he reaches the age of twelve, his mind will be sufficiently formed. That will be the best time for testing." She glared at Ray. "Remember that he's your grandson, and not an experiment."

"Yes of course I know that, Jules," he growled. "Do you miss them being around?" asked Ray. "I understand that they needed their space, but all the way over in Rincón?"

"You were driving them crazy," said Jules. "It's all work with you." She stopped and thought for a minute while Ray continued to tap on his display. "I think we both drove them away, but you ignored them, except to ask questions relating to your projects."

"And you smothered them," said Ray, looking up from his display. "We're a couple of dysfunctional grandparents, aren't we."

"I suppose," said Jules. "Do you think they're safe over there in Rincón?"

"Well, it's a nice quiet area away from the population center," said Ray. "If you're referring to the IC and Seraphim, I guess we can't know. Is anyone safe from them anymore?"

"You're not helping, Ray." said Jules.

A message popped up on Ray's display. "Well, this news might help!"

"Yeah, I'm looking at it now," said Jules squinting at her tablet. "Ray, we have a new grandson! The kids have adopted a little Puerto Rican boy Callum's age. His name is Jacque."

"How wonderful for Marc and Liz," said Ray excitedly. He smiled mischievously at Jules. "How soon before we can get little Jacque out here and hook him up to some equipment for testing?" asked Ray.

Jules glared at him. "Ha ha ha. Not funny, Ray."

Ray put his arm around Jules and hugged her. "Well, at least I can still make you laugh."

The first few months were rough, but Jacque settled right in. Even though he and Callum were different in many ways, they were still friends.

"Ah, they get along so well," said Marc. "It's like they were meant to be brothers."

"Yeah, they're also so different," said Liz, "Yet so

inseparable."

Jacque, almost from the first day he met Callum, was very protective of him. At first Marc and Liz were worried about his behavior, but over time they realized how much Jacque had lost. He didn't want to lose any more family. Callum also loved the attention.

These were the happiest years yet for the young Miras. Rincón was a sparsely populated area, offering just the level of privacy Marc and Liz desired. In recent months, the activity near Puerto Rico increased as advanced modifications were made to the famous Arecibo radio telescope using new technology discovered by the SeaLab program. The hope was that mankind could listen even more closely to the heavens, as if someone had been trying to reach us from another world, but we just couldn't hear. Of course, the skeptics protested the cost and effort, calling the whole thing vain - like the Mars Expeditions.

Either way, Marc and Liz started to get nervous. They hated the idea of the Investor Consortium converging on their island. "Any signal back yet from Agent Thomas about his investigation?" asked Liz. "Sure would be great to know if your parent's data didn't make it out of SeaLab IV."

"Liz, it's been years, and nothing," said Marc. "You know as well as I do how thorough Thomas is. The survivors of SeaLab IV had either disappeared or were clueless of the Mira's dealings."

"Yeah, I know," said Liz. The sounds of the boys playing in the other room turned her concerned frown to a half-smile. She looked up at Marc. "I'm talking about the possibility of unaccounted-for people. We never could account for all the deceased folks." It was still hard for Liz to raise the subject.

"No way we can be sure," said Marc. "But it does seem like if anyone was to come after us, they would have done it by now."

Liz was silent. Her smile melted back into a frown as she stared blankly at the wall beyond Marc. She nervously tapped her fingertips on the table. "If I was planning to make a move on us, I would have been watching us for years now, you know, to wait for the child to get older."

"Now your sounding paranoid," said Marc. Just as those words left his tongue, he too started to stare blankly past Liz. "Let's move the boys to the basement. Would that make you feel better?"

"I hate feeling trapped," said Liz. "I hate this."

"I've done a full search for anything relating to the old Seraphim corporation, and any of its subsidiaries," said Marc. 'It's as if someone tried extra hard to remove it from any record."

"Yeah, a strange thing to try to do for a publicly-traded company," said Liz. "No clues to a connection with the IC?"

"Well, you know," said Marc with a long sigh. "They're transparent as a concrete wall." Marc walked over to the wall and woke up a display. "The only thing that made me scratch my head was a chain of activity starting from the surface monitoring facility at Key Biscayne. From there, I noticed a few strange events down toward the southern keys."

"Yeah, and then up the northeastern coastline," said Jules. "We already know that was Thomas."

"Right, but, he left no trail," said Marc. "The only way we were able to clue into those reports was by tracking local authority scanners."

"So, what's your point, Marc?" asked Liz. "Are you suggesting that the IC might try and track down Thomas? If so, he knows how to handle them."

"Well, no, I'm not worried about Thomas," said Marc. "I'm just wondering who may have tried to track our activity, since we first left the surface monitoring station. We went off the grid for months. So did Thomas."

"But your folks took care of our trail in the official station record," said Liz. "They are the ones presumed dead, not us."

"That's what worries me, I guess," said Marc. He continued to zoom in and pan around a large map, tapping here and there to bring up bits of news and information. "No one has tried to contact us for questioning. Don't you think at least someone from SeaLab administration or the IC would have at least tried to contact us?"

"You're right," said Liz. "If they tried to, they would have just noticed that our place in Miami was shut down with our extended away security system – very easy for them to hack, of course."

"Where do you suppose they'd go from there to try and find us?"

"This is nuts, Liz," said Marc. "It's been so long. No one's going to track us down. The record states clearly that we locked down, departed for the surface monitoring station, and decided not to take the airlock shuttle down to SeaLab due to some sort of shaft malfunction."

"But where do you suppose they would have guessed we'd be after that?" asked Liz.

"I don't know," said Marc. "An extended vacation?"

Liz looked out the window and smiled. "I suppose that would be the truth. Still, seems like they would have at least deployed the standard feelers for us. They might also wonder why we didn't check in after the incident. They didn't even try to verify that we were ok."

"But, they wouldn't have tried to assess that if they thought we never went down there," said Marc. He stopped tapping, and turned to look at Liz. "Another reason why they haven't tried to contact us could be because they already know we're ok."

"Which implies that they know where we are," said Liz. "If they think there's any chance at all that we have any of your parent's research, then the last thing they'll want to do is spook us."

"Hmm," said Marc, now as nervous as Liz. "Might be too late for that."

"Now, Liz, we've got networks setup in the nearby villages," said Marc. "If there were any inquiries, we would have known by now."

Liz appeared to be relieved. She exhaled loudly, stood up, and stretched. "Well, that was fun, but I really do tire of our weekly paranoia sessions."

"We've gotta stay on our toes," said Marc. "No surprises."

"Marc, someday I want us to be able to live in a suburb back in the states," said Liz with a yawn. She rubbed her eyes. "I need a normal life – maybe we can work that into our cover."

"Sounds good, Liz." said Marc as he shut down his display.

Finally, Marc and Liz were able to sleep, but only after moving their boys to the basement.

* * *

The morning sun shone through the window blinds, causing Marc to stir and then sit up. Gonna reserve a table down the road for breakfast, he thought. Gotta move fast before Liz wakes up if I'm to surprise her. Marc grabbed his tablet and quietly tip-toed to the bathroom. After closing the door to a crack, he tapped the tablet display and dialed their favorite local bistro. "Yes, Buenos Dias," said Marc in a low voice. "I'd like to reserve a table for four. Yes, that's right, for breakfast." He listened patiently for a few moments, and then smiled. The morning manager, Angelo, was an acquaintance of theirs. "Yes, is this Angelo?" asked Marc.

"Si señor," said the man. "I am Angelo, the morning manager. Who is this? Do I know you?"

"Yes, of course. This is Marc. I was wondering if you could seat us in a certain part of the restaurant." said Marc. "Our normal spot. I'd like to surprise my wife and would like to arrange something special."

After a longer than normal pause, Angelo cleared his throat. "Will you please elaborate? I don't know anyone named Marc, and therefore don't know what your normal spot is," said Angelo.

"We were just there two days ago," said Marc. "We all had your breakfast burritos."

"I'm sorry, señor," said Angelo. "Perhaps you spoke with someone else? If you tell me what table you'd like, I can accommodate you."

Marc's heart started to race, and a cold sweat formed all over his body. Something's not right, he thought. How can he not remember? He stared out into the bedroom through the barely opened doorway to see that Liz was still fast asleep. It's nothing, he thought. Darn it Liz, got me all paranoid. "There's a good explanation for this." said Marc, forgetting that he was on a call.

"What was that, señor?" asked Angelo. "Do you want me to reserve that table anyway?"

Marc didn't answer, and immediately ended the call. As he left the bathroom and turned the corner from their bedroom, he felt a steady warm breeze. Marc froze and dropped his tablet on the floor.

"Marcus?" said Liz, just barely waking up. "What was that, sweetie?"

Marc didn't answer but ran down the stairs to the basement.

"Marc?" said Liz. She put on a robe and walked over to pick up the tablet, but stopped when she noticed that their front door was open. She froze as if shocked by an electrical current. Quickly, she noticed that the alarm system was disabled. "Marc!" Liz ran to the front door, but then realized that he had not gone out the front door, but instead had run down the stairs to the basement. Her legs felt heavy and her heart boomed within her chest as she stumbled down the stairs. When she turned the corner, the boys' bedroom door was wide open. Marc stood there holding Jacque. Streams of tears rolled down his face, and Jacque looked terrified.

"J-Jacque was curled up over there, inside the closet," said Marc, struggling to get the words out. "He said that Callum..." Marc stopped, as if out of breath.

"Mommy, Callum floated out of the room." said Jacque, confused and a little dazed.

"Jacque was drugged, but only slightly," said Marc. "No sign of Callum. Front door was open."

Liz turned around and flew up the stairs with almost a single leap. She swallowed her panic as she ran out the front door and ran down the road. As she ran, she unsheathed a blade from her thigh, and within minutes she reached an intersection with a small gas station. Scanning the area, she quickly found a familiar face. Thank heavens, she thought. Maybe he saw something. Maybe he saw Callum.

"Can I help you?" asked the man, stepping back nervously.

"Jose, have you seen my boy Callum?" asked Liz while gasping for air.

He looked quickly at the knife in her hand. "Whoa, who? What's with the knife?"

"Jose, we can't find Callum!" she said. "Our son, Callum!"

"Listen, lady, you look familiar," said the man. "But I don't know how you know my name, and I certainly don't know anything about your boy."

Liz's rage boiled over as she grabbed the man's wrist and dropped him to the ground. With her other hand, she held the blade to his neck. "Now, you listen carefully," she said in his ear. "I don't know what kind of game you're playing. You tell me right now who you saw coming through here, or I'll bleed you out right now." As she finished threatening the man, she realized the futility of the interrogation. Liz loosened her grip on him, and he immediately broke loose and ran toward the station, calling for help. Two other people stopped and stared at her, but said nothing.

"Liz, stop!" said a familiar voice behind her. "We have to be smart about this."

"Marc, they took him," said Liz, starting to sob angrily. "They took him and we knew they would."

"I know it's Seraphim now," said Marc. "They left a calling card." He held out a small canister. "I found it in the boy's room. I found another in the front room, and another in our bedroom – under the bed. It's some sort of a psychochemical agent similar to some of the stuff Seraphim was shut down for producing."

"Marc," said Liz, trying to regain her breath. "Jose didn't know who I was."

"Neither did Angelo at the bistro," said Marc. "Liz, they're gone. Long gone." They both looked back at their car that was still running. Jacque sat in the back seat crying.

Liz ran to the car and hopped in, but Marc also got into the car before she could put it in gear.

"Liz, what are you doing?" he asked.

"I'm gonna go find my boy," said Liz. She glared at Marc. "Are you coming?"

Marc turned the key and the engine shut off. When Liz tried to grab the key back, he grabbed her hand and pinched her wrist, causing her to lose all strength to her arm. When she swung at him, he blocked and disabled her other arm. "Liz, I can't let you just run off like this."

"Marcus!" she yelled. "We need to get our boy back! We have to do something!"

"I'm sorry, mommy," said a small voice from the back seat. "I tried to say something, but my mouth didn't work. I couldn't stay awake," said Jacque. "I'm sorry."

Liz took a deep breath and wiped the tears from her

face. "What did you see, dear?" she asked. "What did the people look like that took Callum?"

"People?" asked Jacque. "Callum floated out of the room. Callum was floating."

"No." whispered Liz. "No, no, no." She remembered the intruders in the SeaLab station. She and Marc suddenly realized what Jacque had seen... and what he hadn't seen.

Hours turned to days, and days accumulated to form weeks. Neither Marc nor Liz wanted to stay in Rincón. There were no witnesses. There was no evidence – at least nothing that anyone would believe. The few acquaintances they had made now barely knew them. Marc and Liz got the news to Ray and Jules, but didn't dare make any unnecessary contact. It wasn't until they were about to leave the island that they got a message from the local post office. Marc picked up the package, and inside were blood-stained pajamas with a typed note:

"The child has unique DNA. That alone will be of use to us. The child is no more – that fact should bring you some closure. Any retaliatory action would be ill-advised."

Marc read the note over and over, and finally pulled off to the side of the road. He gripped the steering wheel as if to rip it from the steering column – his knuckles white with rage. He looked over at the package and relaxed. "This is gonna be really hard on Liz," he said to himself as he pulled back onto the road. He knew that there would definitely be some retaliatory action, but first, he and Liz would have to find a new location for their family. Somehow, they would have to explain all of this to Jacque. Somehow they had to help him understand that it wasn't his fault. Over time, Jacque was taught that Callum was a foster child, and he found his permanent family. Marc and Liz would make sure he never again blamed himself for the tragedy. He would never learn anything about the cloaked intruders that so expertly abducted and murdered their child for his blood. Seraphim had made an error in killing their son. With his life went any chance they'd ever have at understanding and wielding the capabilities of his DNA. The final discoveries made at SeaLab IV would be forever secured, and if Seraphim or the IC returned, Marc and Liz would be ready for them.

It wasn't long before Liz finally got her way: A nice suburb in southern Florida. She and Marc saw no other option but to start a new life. This time, things would be different. They would make friends – a lot of friends. They would try to lead a normal life. They realized that the best security might possibly be a nice healthy network of people around them. Marc and Liz focused on Jacque's needs and wants, and tried to put their old life behind them. They would also be open with their name. "No more secrets!" Liz would often say. That was her retaliation – or so Marc thought. Most of the time, Liz would be happily living her new life. However, Marc always knew when his wife took a few moments alone to cry. He would let her be, unless she called for him, which she sometimes did.

Months became years, and Marc and Liz settled into their new life. They didn't fear Seraphim, the IC, or anyone else. They had taken their child – what else was there to fear? At first, Marc worried that Liz was having a nervous breakdown. She was acting more and more giddy. One day, Marc resolved that he would sit down and plan out a suitable revenge for the organization that had caused their family so much pain. It would be good for Liz to try and focus on the past and try to resolve her pain. Marc also hoped that the exercise would keep her from snapping. Marc planned a romantic evening. Everything would be perfect. After Jacque was in bed, he would reveal the evening he had planned, and then they would plan their take-down of the organization known as Seraphim. Perhaps they could even take down the Investor Consortium. Who knows? he thought. Gotta think big, otherwise, what's the point?

Marc was barely able to hide his smile as he walked back to Liz from Jacque's room. The house was silent, and Liz giggled as she read something on her tablet. When she saw Marc approach, she quickly cleared the screen and looked up at him and smiled. "You have something up your sleeve, don't you my dear?"

Marc sat down, looked at Liz, and released the smile he had locked up for hours. "I have a surprise for you, Liz," he said.

Without hesitation, Liz placed her index finger over his lips. "First, I have a surprise for you," she said. "I'm pregnant."

CHAPTER EIGHT

A New Life

Marc and Liz's plan to formulate a retaliation was suspended with the birth of their new son.

"I've got it!" said Marc. "We'll name him Arec."

Liz smiled. "Let me guess, after Arecibo?"

"Yeah, I guess," said Marc with a cautious grin. "Someday he'll help us find the answers we've been looking for, right?"

Liz paused, then looked at her husband thoughtfully. "He's our son – first and foremost, but yes, I hope that someday he can help explain all of this."

They held each other and smiled. The midday Florida sun shined overhead as they watched Arec play outside in the backyard with Jacque. It had taken time for Jacque to really bond with his new little brother. When Marc explained to little Jacque that Arec would not be leaving the family, he frowned and looked at the ground. What he said in response would never be forgotten.

Jacque looked up at his father and said, "I will protect him."

The words still burned in Marc's memory. At times, Marc wondered how much Jacque had truly remembered of Callum's abduction. Now, years later, Jacque and Arec played in the yard as if nothing had ever happened before they moved to Florida.

"Kids are resilient, aren't they?" asked Liz. "A child's mind is so powerful."

"Yeah, and so seemingly simple," said Marc, pausing to gather his thoughts. "Liz, somehow it feels like things will be alright this time."

"Of course they will be," said Liz as she stood and stretched. "We've got Jacque." Liz smiled and walked back toward the house, pausing slightly to call to the kids: "Dinner in a few minutes, boys!"

"I'll get them inside in a few minutes," said Marc. He watched as Arec ran, and imagined Jacque and Callum at the same age. They were growing up so fast. For Marc, just enough time it seemed had passed so that he could think about Callum without plunging himself into depression. He was afraid that with Liz, the wounds would forever be too new.

Jacque and Arec ran past Marc, and up some stone steps toward the back porch. Jacque ran ahead of Arec, but then Arec stopped abruptly and looked up into his father's eyes. Marc stared back into his. "You hungry, Arec?" he asked. Jacque stopped and waited patiently for his brother near the back door, smiling.

"Yes!" said Arec enthusiastically. Arec took one step in the direction of the house and disappeared.

Every time he does that, thought Marc, it makes my heart leap. Arec would move extraordinarily fast at seemingly random times, and it seemed as if Arec didn't realize what he was doing. The door leading into the house waved in the breeze while Jacque stood there and looked around incredulously.

Jacque gazed back at his father and shrugged. "How does Arec do that?" he asked. "He disappeared again."

Marc grabbed Jacque's hand. "I don't really know," said Marc. Together, they walked into the house.

As they walked inside, Liz was setting the table. "Where's Arec?" she asked. She stopped and looked with concern at Marc. "He did it again, didn't he?" she asked, looking around the room.

"He disappeared again, mom," said Jacque, slightly amused and cracking a smile. Not because he thought Arec would get into trouble, but because he really was intrigued.

"Yeah, he did it again. That's twice this week," said Marc. "Arec, come downstairs and join us for dinner, please!"

"Ok!" yelled a small voice from upstairs.

Liz flinched and dropped a fork on the table when Arec suddenly appeared back at his normal place at the table. "I'm hungry," said Arec, smiling.

Liz was about to discipline Arec, but Marc stopped her. "He's only four, Liz," said Marc. "He doesn't even realize what he did."

"Fine," said Liz. "But that doesn't make me feel any better about it." Finally, Liz would settle down, knowing full-well that she couldn't complain, and knew better than anyone else what types of odd behavior she might expect from the boy. It was always just a matter of when another strange thing would happen.

* * *

The sun set behind the hill to the west of the villa. Ray finished sipping a drink and set it down on a glass table as he and Jules lounged on a patio overlooking the ocean far below. "The boys are really growing up fast, aren't they?" asked Jules as she looked through a stack of recent photos on her tablet. "Sure would be nice to see them more."

"You know we can't do that," said Ray. "The risks, Jules. Remember the risks. We have an agreement."

"Yes, yes, I know," said Jules. "But it's been years! Forget the agreement. We need a new agreement."

Ray scratched his head. "I've got the neutrino cloud completed. Watch this," he said.

"You're changing the subject again, Ray," said Jules. "You've got to stop doing that. We need to talk about it."

"Talk about what?" asked Ray. "The circumstances haven't changed. We know that Liz did it again. She used the DNA template to conceive Arec. We already know that." Ray walked toward a display. "We can watch them from afar, from a safe distance."

"It's just about the experiment to you, isn't it?" asked Jules. "He's your grandson, and we've never even met him. We don't know them. We haven't spent much time with them."

Ray stood abruptly. "Jules, just stop and look," he said. "This is important!" He fired up the display on the wall near the dining room table and tapped a few commands.

Jules sighed loudly. "Fine, look at what?"

Ray tapped a final command on the display, and a stack of paper about ten inches thick materialized onto the table. He looked at Jules and smiled.

"That's it?" asked Jules. "With the amount of data we collected in that stream, we should be swimming in paper." She picked up one of the sheets. "It's blank. They're all blank."

"The paper is just the medium, Jules," said Ray, impatiently. "The densely-packed information embedded in that paper can only be perceived by one who has the ability to interpret the patterns as originally represented in the neutrino stream."

"So, Arec will be able to read this?" asked Jules as she carefully inspected a seemingly blank sheet of paper, holding it up to the light. "What if a sheet gets damaged or lost?"

Ray smiled and involuntarily giggled. "Watch this." He took another sheet of paper and tore it in half. He then took the pieces, dropped them in the sink, and lit them on fire. The page reappeared on the table. Ray looked at Jules. "Well?"

"So, it's like putting your hand in front of a projector, the information continues to project itself, even if it has to replicate more screen upon which to project it," said Jules. "But how?"

"I don't know, Jules," said Ray. "The information persists as long as the neutrino stream continues to project the patterns."

"Ray," Jules said, pausing to sit down, "Who is sending these patterns? Have you made any progress in understanding why that transmission of data even occurred?"

Ray sat down across from her and held her hands. "Jules, the more I analyze the patterns, the more it seems that there are parts representing us – the intended recipient, and someone else."

"Yeah, the planet with a single continent," said Jules. "And the XY. That's us, right? What part of the stream is supposed to represent someone else?"

Ray hesitated, then brought up the display again. "I found this seemingly duplicate pattern three petabytes after the part that we showed the kids. See a difference?"

Jules leaned closer and adjusted her glasses. "That model of a planet looks more like ours, with separate continents." She gasped and looked at Ray. "So, that represents us, and the other model of a planet, the one with a single continent, represents them?"

"My best guess is that this whole thing is some sort of attempt to reach out to us – possibly even a distress signal."

"Well, don't let your imagination get the best of you, my dear Ray," said Jules. "An intelligence with that level of capability likely wouldn't need our help with anything."

Ray rolled his eyes and turned back to the display. "Well, either way, I'm adding a subroutine that will bind the pages. Also, I'd like to get the size down to the thickness of a simple notebook. I just need to improve the compression algorithm."

"Yeah, you'd have to do that if you expect Arec someday to lug that thing around with him," said Jules. "Also, a simple notebook is a good disguise. Remember when the IC came for an inspection, and we had that notebook sitting out with some pretty critical data in it?"

"Yeah," said Ray, chuckling. "They flipped through it and thought that we were planning to build a rocket."

"The notebook needs a name," said Jules. "Let's call it the Rocket Handbook".

"Has a ring to it for sure." said Ray.

Jules' smile faded. She tapped her fingers on the table and looked up at Ray. "What if it falls into the wrong hands?" she asked.

"Yeah, I considered that as well," said Ray. He tapped another command, and the paper disappeared, including the piece Jules was holding. "I maketh, and I taketh away." Ray smiled.

Jules' eyes lit up. "Fine. That is pretty amazing. You're just running an inverse create command on the paper medium, correct?"

"Yes, that's right," said Ray. "But I can only unmake matter I created with the controller."

"Hopefully, when − or if − Arec can read all of that stuff, he can tell us what it means." said Jules.

"Hopefully sooner rather than later." Ray turned off the display, sat back, folded his arms and smiled. "Now, maybe we can discuss the topic of visiting the grandkids."

For years, Agent Vinton − now chief IC investigations liaison − passed much of the Mira investigation to his protege, Agent Frank Stephens. Of course, this played nicely into Frank's plans to keep the Mira investigation from going nowhere. It also made Frank appear at times as if he just wasn't making any progress in his work.

"Agent Vinton," said the lieutenant, "Agent Frank Stephens is on the line."

"Ah, it's about time," said Vinton as he took the phone. "This is Vinton. What are my options?"

Frank and Vinton by now were accustomed to using

coded speech in their conversation – especially over a com line. "The pizza place we tried on the corner is a no-go," said Agent Stephens. "The best bet is on fifth and main in Delaware. The sausage is great, and the crust is fabulous."

"Thanks for the tip," said Vinton. "Time to take the pizza hunt down a notch. Understood?"

"Understood," said Stephens. He hung up and exhaled loudly. "Finally, permission to lay off the Miras for a time," he said. "That should get the agency off of my rear end for now – and hopefully out of Newport". Frank was excited for the career break that practically fell into his lap years before when Vinton hired him, but since then, the CIA and several other agencies started to show signs of pandering to the Investor Consortium. Working for the IC, even indirectly, was something Frank could not stomach. Good thing I joined the project when I did, or Vinton would have made the connection between Sue and the rest of the Miras. If they ever see the fudge-work I did on her records, I'm finished – and so is Sue. With how hard she's tried to hide her relationship with her parents, she'd never forgive me. Or, maybe she might. There was so much mystery around the Mira family, and inquiries regarding the Mira family had only intensified in the most secure and classified channels. Frank knew where Ray and Julia Mira were, and had been monitoring their activities. He was careful about what information he shared with the agency, and what he did not share. However, he still couldn't find Marc and Liz. They had just vanished. He sat in his car in the garage and stared out through the windshield. Sudden knocking on his window startled him out of his thoughts.

"Hey sweetie!" said Sue, smiling. "I'm sorry, did I wake

you?" she asked sarcastically. "Dinner's almost ready."

Frank lowered the window. "What's for dinner?"

"Burgers. When you come inside and grill them, dinner will be ready," said Sue.

Frank noticed the stress lines on her face, messed up hair, and the bags under her eyes. "The girls really put you through the wringer today, didn't they?"

"You think?" said Sue. She walked back inside the house. "Each day is a new adventure. You should hang out one of these days and see for yourself."

"Here we go." said Frank.

The rain started again to pitter-patter against the kitchen window. Frank closed the door quietly and hung up his coat. "Another long day for both of us, I suppose."

"Frank, those girls are driving me crazy." said Sue.

"They're just four years old." said Frank.

"Yeah, but there are three of them, Frank." Sue paused to catch her breath. "Three of them and one of me. How on earth did we manage to get triplets?"

"I can start taking some more time off work to help out," said Frank. He scratched his head and looked around the room. "What happened to the microwave?"

Sue laughed and dropped into a chair at the table. "The kids figured out what happens if you put metal objects in it and turn it on." She looked curiously at Frank.

"What is it?" asked Frank. "Are you ok?"

"You seem unusually relaxed," said Sue. "Everything alright at work?"

"Yeah, things at work are letting up quite a bit, actually. No more traveling to Delaware for at least a couple of months," said Frank. "In fact, I'm going to take the rest of the week off."

"You can't do that," said Sue. "We need the hours. We need the money."

Frank pulled out his tablet and laid it in front of her on the table. "I got a bonus. We'll be ok."

Sue pulled the tablet closer and smiled. "That's wonderful. We can even pay down some bills with that," she placed her hand lovingly on his. "Can you really stay and help out for a bit?"

Frank cleared his throat and looked at Sue. "There's something we need to talk about."

"My parents, right?"

"Yes, your parents," said Frank.

"They contacted you again, didn't they?"

"They just wanted to know if you're ok."

"Tell them I'm ok then," said Sue, sounding less enthusiastic.

"I did." Frank's smile melted to a frown. "Something seems different with them." Of course, Frank had been monitoring Ray and Jules for years, and even knew a lot more about them than did their estranged daughter.

"Did they say anything about Marc?" asked Sue. "I miss Marc. I wonder if he and Liz were ever able to have kids."

"They won't say anything about Marc and Liz," said Frank. He knew that his real employer would love to know Marc and Liz's whereabouts. Therefore, Frank also wished he knew, so he could protect them, and guard another possible way this could all lead back to his own wife and family. As long as the agency knew precious little, the chances of them tracing the information back was slim.

"Maybe someday they'll reach out to us on their own."

said Sue.

"Yeah, hopefully," said Frank. "Anyway, you should reach out to them, maybe go spend some time with your folks. I can watch the kids."

"You'd do that?" asked Sue.

"Well, of course," said Frank. "That means, of course, that you would need to talk to them."

"I'll think about it." she said.

Frank turned around to see three little four-year-old girls staring up at him. "Eve, Anja, Kinley!"

"Daddy!" they yelled in unison.

"You guys need to be nicer to mommy," said Frank. "She told me about the microwave."

Sue sat as if contemplating a major life decision, not hearing anything the kids were saying. Suddenly, she blurted "I'll do it, Frank. Give me their weird arcane super-secret contact info, and I'll make some arrangements for a visit."

"Do what, mommy?" asked Eve.

"I think it's time you girls met some cousins," said Sue. She smiled at Frank. "But first, I think mommy's going on a little vacation to visit grandma and grandpa."

Finally, thought Frank. I'm really looking forward to some more time with the kids, and maybe Sue will come back with contact information for Marc and Liz. If Sue and the girls are going to be safe from the IC, it's only because I can ensure that safety.

Nothing's coming between me and my family, thought Frank, no matter what kind of agreements or contracts I made.

* * *

The sweeping coastal cliffs of Puerto Rico provided the privacy Ray and Jules had always desired for their work. Now, several years later, their villa had provided a fun and safe getaway for the rest of the family. Sue did visit now and then, and even brought the kids once. Of course, a lack of understanding here and there led to arguments. Finally, Sue decided she wouldn't return. However, Frank's plan to make contact with Marc and Liz succeeded, and Sue's disagreements with her parents didn't stop her from reconnecting with her brother, Marc. They had been apart for so long, and they had a lot of catching up to do.

What's more, her triplets became really good friends with their cousins Jacque and Arec. The boys even spent a few summers in Newport while Marc and Liz were away on business. All the while, Frank tried to learn more and more why the agency wanted to know more about the Miras — especially Marc and Liz. He had even offered to watch Jacque and Arec while they were away doing whatever it is that they did. However, each offer was always turned down. They had already made arrangements. In time, Frank was able to learn more about the officers they would leave behind to watch their boys. Frank was sure he would be able to learn more of Marc and Liz's dealings from the security teams they used, but they proved to be even more of a mystery than Marc and Liz.

Something was going on, and Frank, despite all of his training and resources, couldn't figure it out. On the other hand, he couldn't push too hard for fear of exposing his own wife, Sue, as being related to the rest of the Mira family.

Finally, whether Frank got the information he wanted or not, it didn't matter. He and Sue were glad to finally have connections with family. It was something Frank missed, being an only child himself. As time passed and the children got older, they drifted apart. Sue decided it would be best for them to just keep to themselves in Newport. Frank, having received more and more responsibility, was home less and less.

Sue became suspicious of his activities away from home. The agency was requiring more and more of his time on remote assignments – the kind that he could not talk about at all. All she knew is that he had been dealing with sensitive equipment for which he had signed nondisclosure agreements. Over time, Sue was able to put more pieces together. Frank's work seemed always to involve some mysterious person known as "The Director". To her, it felt more and more like the IC was the least of their worries.

Mr. T became acquainted with Frank through various projects at the school where Frank played out his fake role as an electronics technician. Frank was always grateful to take jobs at the school since it put him close to home. Mr. T was happy to offer those projects, so he had an opportunity to check up on Sue and her family. It also gave Mr. T opportunities to learn more about the new and growing threats Vinton and his team were facing.

The Director was already known to Mr. T. He and his son, a young Agent Thomas, had already been investigating him, and some possible connections between The Director and Seraphim.

Mr. T felt comfortable with the security of the Stephens family. He was more concerned about Marc and Liz. Agent Thomas had expressed concerns that they were too vulnerable.

We're spread too thin, thought Agent Thomas, and the strength and influence of the enemy is growing too fast.

Ray and Jules were getting old, and they were feeling it. Finally, Ray was no longer saying "six more months and it will be ready." The time had come to train Arec in earnest, and to help him understand what they and his parents had been preparing him for. The Rocket Handbook is ready, thought Ray. I just hope that Arec is ready for it.

"Oh, I can't wait to see Arec! Their visit last summer seems like a lifetime ago," said Jules. "I wish they could both come this time."

"Jacque's sixteen now," said Ray. "He probably feels like he has better things to do than to hang out with his grandparents."

"Soccer camp?" asked Jules. "You think soccer camp is better than his yearly visit with us?"

"It's not about what we think, Jules," said Ray. He sighed. "Just be happy that Arec still looks forward to coming. Enjoy it before he grows up."

"Let's see, Arec is nine years old now," said Jules. "That means he's got five more years before his brains start to fall out."

Ray smiled. "I like to think of him as being only one year away from his corpus callosum being fully formed in his noggin."

Jules sneered at Ray. "Of course, you'd like to think that," she said. "Just don't scare him this year. That knife stunt you pulled last year went a bit too far, Ray."

"Hey, that was both of us," said Ray. "Remember?"

"Yes, yes. Of course." Jules smirked and tapped her fingers rhythmically on the glass table. She always did that when she was nervous. "It was my idea though to convince him that it was all a dream. Marc and Liz never brought it up."

"Why would they?" asked Ray. "Besides, they know what we're doing. They know what we're trying to prepare him for."

It was at a secluded location that Marc and Liz dropped off Arec. One of the best parts of these visits to the island was the trip in his parent's aircraft. He didn't even know whether to call it a helicopter or a jet. It was neither, and when Arec asked his parents about it, they said that they would explain when he was older. They always said that.

"Mom, dad," said Arec on the way to the island, "You have a lot of explaining to do."

Marc and Liz smiled to each other. "All in good time," said Marc. "If I'm not mistaken, your grandparents have a surprise for you."

Ray and Jules were there to meet Arec. When Arec turned back around, his parents had left as quietly as they had arrived.

I feel so alone this time, thought Arec. I wish Jacque could have come. He wondered why Jacque would rather go to soccer camp, or be with girls.

At the end of day two, Arec again prepared for

bedtime. The sun was going down, and he couldn't stop yawning. Grandma and grandpa were so excited for me to come, thought Arec. But, today they seemed so distracted with their work. Grandpa even suggested sending me home early this year. Something was wrong. Arec overheard something about a warning from Mr. T, and that he had lost contact with his son, Thomas.

"Who's Mr. T?" asked Arec as he poked his head into his grandparents' study. "And what's wrong with his son, Thomas?"

"They are friends of the family," said Jules, looking nervously at Ray. "At least, one of them for sure still is," said Jules. "Let's get you to bed, dear. We'll talk more tomorrow."

The wind started to howl throughout the villa, causing papers to rustle.

Marc and Liz sat up in bed almost at the same time, and Liz flipped on the light. A distinct alarm echoed throughout the room.

"1:00 am," said Marc. "Seriously?"

Liz was already scrambling for her tablet that was making the alarm sound — not a normal alarm, but the kind that wakes you up no matter what time of night it is. It was an emergency, and only the direst circumstance would warrant it being triggered. After tapping madly on her tablet, she turned to her husband. "I can't get through to them, Marc!" She flew out of bed and put on some clothes.

"I'm right behind you," said Marc, his voice shaking.

He looked at his tablet. Arec's transmitter was located at the emergency extraction point off the coast of Puerto Rico, but Ray and Julia's transmitters were nowhere to be seen.

"I can't find them, Marc," said Liz frantically. "Let's go. We've gotta go now."

Arec had made so many trips to stay with his grandparents, that they had all grown more and more comfortable with the idea that nothing would go wrong. They had developed a nearly undetectable air transport, they had worked so hard to train Arec (as young as he was), and they had created an emergency protocol with Ray and Jules – named "plan C" by Ray. They hoped that they'd never need it, but they knew that there would really only be one reason to use it. They just hoped that if Seraphim came after their son, they would all be ready.

Liz fought back panic as memories of that fateful night they lost Callum flooded back into her mind.

"Liz, let's go!" said Marc.

It was only thirty minutes after the alarm sounded that their aircraft silently touched down in near pitch-darkness on a private and secluded clearing. The crashing of waves was heard nearby, and in the distance out across the channel they could barely make out the steep cliffs on an isolated island where Ray and Jules' villa sat under the moonlight.

"Right there, Marc," said Liz. "He's laying down at the edge of the clearing!"

Marc cradled Arec in his arms and felt for a pulse. "He's ok, just unconscious. He's been hit," said Marc as he pulled a small dart from his neck. "He seems to have weathered the tube transport just fine."

Liz, tears streaming down her face, looked all around and saw some lights in the distance on the island. "Marc, look!"

"Yes, we need to go." said Marc.

"Marc, plan C. We need to complete plan C now!" said Liz. "They initiated it, now we need to complete it. It's what we agreed to do. It's what they'd insist we do."

"Yes, I know... but they're my parents," said Marc. His face was pale and his jaw dropped. "I can't do it."

"We have no choice, Marc!" said Liz. "You know what's at stake. You know who we're dealing with. The villa is gone, and they are probably already gone as well."

"Yes, I know," said Marc, silently. With hands shaking, he pulled out his tablet and entered a command. There was a place for each of their thumbs on the display next to a warning, written by Marc himself.

"Ok, let's do this," said Liz. "Agreed?"

"Agreed." said Marc.

They both placed their thumbs on the display and the ten second countdown initiated. Within seconds, the silent aircraft disappeared into the black of night. In the distance, Marc and Liz heard a dull boom and felt a subtle shockwave followed by an eerie calm. Arec was safe, an unseen enemy had been driven from Ray and Julia's property, and their research was secured. Plan C was a success but only with a huge price.

"I'm going to miss them too, Marc," said Liz. "I'm really sorry." Marc hung his head and sobbed. Liz put her hand on his. "We did the right thing. It's what they would have wanted us to do."

"Yes, I know. It's what we promised them we'd do," said Marc. "Doesn't make it any easier. They both stroked

Arec's wet hair.

Liz looked up at Marc. She was sure Marc had the same question in his mind. How would they tell Arec and Jacque that they had lost their grandparents?

CHAPTER NINE

The Report

A straight line of soldiers stood in formation at the back of the dimly-lit room. In front of them stood their captain. An uneasiness hung in the crisp conditioned air of the small steel-walled office. Another mission had ended, and now it was time to report. The leader was revered among his men, and they had only ever known him as "the captain".

The captain's accomplishments had written a lot of recent world history, but his name was unknown to the world. In the most recent ten years alone, he had led missions that brought numerous dictators to their knees. Under his command, wars had been thwarted. He had fired the shots that took down the last known, and most feared terrorist leaders. For the captain, however, the most meaningful accomplishment had been to help establish the most influential organization on the planet, and he didn't even know its name. No one did. Those involved had also been invisible. The identities of the captain and his men had been cleared from all records. The organization they served didn't exist to anyone but him, his men and his commanding officer.

Despite the extraordinary accomplishments of the captain's team, it was the mysterious and specific orders from the captain's commanding officer that usually led them to their successes. The captain had learned to follow every order. He knew that his orders were always first-hand. They were always from the top. His orders always benefitted from the latest intelligence. Missions were very simple that way: follow orders and succeed, disobey and fail.

The captain's commanding officer was a neatly groomed man in a dark tailored suit sitting before them behind a large desk. That man was a mystery to even the few who had worked directly with him, and to them, he had only ever been known as "the director". He always wore the same dark suit. His hair was dark and long, most of the time covering part of his youthful face. His well-groomed beard concealed any hint of personality or weakness. He was also particular about the neatness of his clothing.

The captain had been completely confident in his own abilities and those of his men. Perhaps he'd been too confident. Reporting a failure was something he'd done seldom in his career, but it was part of the job. This time, it was different. Their mission was different and the stakes were so much higher than the director had let on. On top of that, the game had changed, and so had the rules. Their target was able to do things that they could not understand. The captain had followed every order perfectly, but somehow he and his team had still come up short. Somehow, they had failed.

The room was completely silent as the director casually reviewed the captain's report. For the captain, the silence was painful. He's drawing this out, he thought as he stood patiently at attention. He felt tired and stretched, as if a poisonous seed of doubt was eating away at his will. How could this happen? he thought. After all I've done, how could it come to this?

The captain and his men had served their cause so well. Their unit alone had been able to steer and manipulate the Investor Consortium. Given their record, one failure could certainly be excused. Once the circumstances were known, the director would certainly forgive. The captain showed no fear, in spite of his doubts, and now it was his responsibility to report on a painful and embarrassing failure. It's all part of the game, he thought. Somehow, that thought provided no comfort.

The director had earned an unparalleled reputation, but ironically very little was known about him. His men had learned that he was not to be trifled with, and if he wanted anything from any government or organization in any part of the world, he got it. He seemed unstoppable. No one knew where he had come from, only that he had been one of the subjects studied by the organization as a small child. Now he ran the operation. The director had personally chosen the captain and each of his fifteen men for his most sensitive assignments. It had been five years since the captain and his men had decided to leave their families, friends, identities, and citizenships behind. They had chosen to serve a more noble cause, one that would bring order from chaos.

Finally, thought the captain, there was an influential and well-funded operation that would make real change in the world. The ends justified the means. He had seen enough blood spilt in his career for political gain. He'd had enough of the corrupt Investor Consortium, and now it was time to devote his skills to a greater cause – and there could be no greater cause than absolute and irrevocable world peace. All mankind would soon have no choice but to accept their new and improved government. After all, the people, through selfishness and complacency, had chosen it. It was the inaction and laziness of the average citizen that had architected the very government they said that they had hated for so long.

In the new order, every point of view would be embraced, every idea valued, and every moral accepted. There would finally be absolute social justice and governmental protection through a new world alliance. Because of the commitments the captain and his men had made, they had no country of their own. With the director, they would establish a new country, built on a foundation of strength and dominance. All over the world they were setting the stage for the greatest achievement ever wrought by man. Peace. There would be peace through technological supremacy, and the director seemed always to be ahead of the technological wave. He was beyond powerful, doing things none of them could explain. Their hope for the world was in the palm of his hand, yet no one knew his name.

Despite their edge, the critical five-year long mission had failed. The captain and his men had come with bad news. They knew that the director had already read the report and that an accounting was just a formality. A dead serious formality. The director looked up at the captain. His silent stare somehow tore away at his formidable iron will, causing it to unravel and fray in front of his men. The fifteen soldiers remained in formation behind the captain. Like their leader, they were all seasoned experts, and they had also seen things they could not explain. They each knew that the captain would be held responsible for their failure.

"Explain, captain," commanded the director from behind his large mahogany desk. He broke his stare on the captain and turned to face the dark floor-to-ceiling window behind him. To the captain and his men, only the back of the director's head and shoulders were now visible in the dimly-lit office. He leaned back in his slender chair as he stared out into the dark of night. The director was irrationally annoyed that the window stood in his way. He didn't like anything standing between him and anything else. He despised offices and buildings. He was tired of limitations. He'd had the best soldiers on the planet at his command, and they had still failed.

The captain, tall and dressed in a white reflective body suit, stepped forward. Like a few of the others, his suit was still soaked with salt water from their mission. With crisp resolve, he started to explain. "Sir, the team requires more time. We—"

"—Failure is unacceptable," interrupted the director. "I know what you did and did not do. Did I not explain to you, captain, the importance of this particular mission?" He stood and folded his arms, still with his back to them and staring out the window. "Why is the old couple not secured?"

"They–" stammered the captain, "–they were not found." The other soldiers, also dressed in the same white body suits standing behind him remained silent and still. The captain straightened. "I will not waste your time with reasons for our failure." For the captain, it stung to even say the word "failure".

"Very wise, captain," sneered the man in the dark suit. "That decision may have just extended your lease on this miserable planet."

"Yes sir." said the captain.

The director smiled, then sneered. "What of the boy? How on earth did you fail to secure the boy?"

"Sir, we, I mean I, pursued the boy. He was on a rock out in the water. We shot him with tranquilizers, but then he just disappeared." said the captain. "He was evidently ready for our assault. Our divers found nothing. Our scans detected nothing in or around the rock."

The man in the suit pounded his fist on the arm of his chair, then took a deep breath and straightened his tie. "He's nine. Nine years old. You can't retrieve a nine-year-old boy?" he said calmly.

The captain continued. "The grandparents, they planned for his escape. I made the call for the assault, and the men performed admirably, and I have–"

The director turned around swiftly and faced the captain. "You have failed," he said as he reached into his pocket. The room hushed and only the sound of the ventilation was heard. The captain held his breath and took a step backward as the man in the dark suit smiled and pulled out a small bottle of eye drops, and quickly treated both of his eyes.

"Yes sir," said the captain. He gritted his teeth. "May I

complete my explanation, sir?" He tried to sound tough, but his tone fell short of confidence. He started sweating, and a coldness washed over him.

"You mean, there's really something to explain?" asked the director sarcastically. He stared into the eyes of the captain. "Continue, at your own risk."

The captain stared back into the director's face. He had stood in this office to report his progress many times. Every time he had good news to share, but this time it was different. The man in the suit had seemed so confident before. Now, he looked harder around the edges, disheveled, and tired. Their last mission was somehow personal. It must have been personal, thought the captain. Something was wrong – he'd never seen the director like this before. As the director stepped forward out of the shadows, they could now see clearly that his eyes were bloodshot.

The captain usually had a lot to say about their mission, but this time he struggled for words. He and his men had monitored the mysterious old couple in Puerto Rico for years. They could have easily taken them many times, but the captain had his orders. It was not the right time. The old couple had something the director needed, and apparently it was the grandson. A punk kid, and somehow he had escaped them. All targets had escaped.

The captain swallowed nervously and continued. "We engaged the coastal villa as directed. Somehow they knew we were coming. The place went dark well into our approach. Upon our arrival, a destructive event obliterated the entire house. Everything was disintegrated, leaving little trace of the villa and no trace of anything or anyone."

"You mean, it was cleaned. Correct?" asked the man in the dark suit.

"Yes sir, the place was cleaned," answered the captain. "But it wasn't us, we didn't do it. We had no choice but to stand back and watch until it was finished. We had no choice."

The director casually unfolded his arms and pulled a small flat metallic case from his pocket. He placed it on the desk between him and the captain. "So, it was a cleaner device like this, only much bigger. Correct?" asked the director.

The captain took a step back, as did the fifteen others behind him. "Yes sir."

A soft blue glow appeared around the director. The captain and his men had been briefed on the details of the cleaner device, but had never understood the blue glow that the director could create around himself. A rumor had spread in their tight circle that it was one of the assets the director's scientists had been developing. They understood that it could shield a person from just about anything, but not much more than that. The room was silent with fear, but also curiosity.

"Don't make excuses, captain. You always have a choice," said the director.

"But, sir, I wasn't excusing anything," said the captain, "I can do this. Give us another chance, sir! We have some possible leads on the boy." he said. A fresh bead of sweat streamed down the side of the captain's face. "There's more, and I didn't put it in the report."

"Oh?" said the director, obviously amused at the captain's attempt to hold back intel for insurance. "It had better be good."

The captain raised his hand, and a second later, he caught a small drive tossed to him from one of the men behind him. "We were able to obtain what seems to be one of the old couple's first research logs," said the captain. "Look for yourself, it's short but insightful. Your decryption algorithms proved most useful."

The blue glow around the director vanished. He smiled and took the small drive. "You already reviewed the log, then?" asked the director.

"Yes sir," said the captain, "I did not want to waste your time with irrelevant intel."

"I will determine what is relevant, and what is not." said the director.

"Yes sir," said the captain. "My sincere apologies, sir."

The man in the dark suit removed the cap from the end of the drive and pinched the metallic end between his fingers. A few seconds later, he saw the following flash before his eyes:

Personal Research Logs
Dr. Raymond Mira
Dr. Julia Mira

Ray's been developing a new kind of neutrino detector. Since he won't write about it, I will.

It's like none other ever designed, only a fraction of the size of a normal neutrino detector. Ray even mentioned something about the discovery of a new particle. It's unconfirmed, but so much of his work is already so theoretical. Anyway, I like physics, particularly particle physics, but it never quite excited me the same way as geology or oceanography.

Ray tried to explain the significance of their most recent discovery. He said that all living and non-living material, whether a tree, a rock, an animal or a glass of water, all break down to the same basic molecules. Those molecules are composed of atoms. Atoms are composed of a number of different types of subatomic particles. I can't remember the names, but he said there are two basic types of subatomic particles: the type that carry force, and the type that have mass. The type that have mass combine to form other types of matter. The other type, force carriers, provide currents and fields that facilitate interaction between the different mass particles. Ray then smiled and said, "Simple, right?" Yeah, right.

Anyway, Ray apparently discovered a new type of force carrier particle, a boson particle of some sort, that is responsible for determining when other force carriers assign a different mass to the mass particles. It's supposed to be the particle that determines when and on what particles mass adjustments occur. I think I got that right. Anyway, Ray explained it this way: there's a ball sitting on a table. Both the table and the ball have mass, because of the elemental force of gravity, they rest against each other. He said that there are force carrier particles that determine the mass of the particles in each object. Ray said that by manipulating the newly discovered particles, it was possible to adjust the mass of the ball so that it would fall through the table.

Sounded crazy to me and a little bit dangerous. He explained further that there really is no void. He said that if we had the ability to see all matter, we'd also see that there is no void. He said that it all matters, and then he laughed. I didn't get his nerdy joke at the time.

-Julia

"Interesting. Is that all?" asked the director. He stared coolly at the captain as he leaned back in a hard, black leather chair.

"Yes sir. The rest was evidently lost in the explosion

that took down the old couple's villa, sir," said the captain.

The man in the dark suit threw the drive into the trash. "So, how did you come across that little bit of intel?"

"We intercepted a transmission from the area around the villa," said the captain, "But we couldn't lock on the source. Also, the transmission was encrypted in morse code."

"What?" said the director. "That's ridiculous – that's not encryption. Why could you not retrieve the rest of the logs?"

"I was just going to say," said the captain uncomfortably, "That it took two of your teams in India to capture the stream. It was being projected from a neutrino factory somewhere to the north of Puerto Rico."

"Right. So, once you captured the data stream, you had to interpret the morse code." said the director. "But I don't care about that. What of the neutrino factory?"

"We were unable to locate the factory," said the captain. "We read in the brief that we might have to intercept particle emission streams and decrypt, but we weren't expecting–"

"–You weren't prepared," interrupted the director. "If you had followed my instructions, you would not have wasted time on trivial matters. You could have easily captured the entire stream, and found the neutrino factory."

The captain shifted and looked around the room. "Uh, yes sir. I suppose, sir. The situation was quite irregular."

"Indeed," the director smiled and hovered a pointed finger over the small steel cleaner device and pressed the top. It opened to show a small pulsing red circle. "Your little bit of intel is interesting, but not interesting enough," said the director. Again, a blue glow appeared around the director, but this time it was brighter. The captain's men stayed at attention.

"Yes sir," said the captain after an uneasy pause. He knew what was going to happen, he had seen the same thing happen to many others who had failed before him. He looked into the bloodshot eyes of the director and contemplated one last maneuver. He knew that his men would help him if he could take the director down, with or without his mysterious blue glowing shield.

As if the director could perceive his thoughts, he looked beyond the captain to the other soldiers. They remained at attention out of respect for their leader, but the director knew that they feared him the most. The captain had led them well. As far as he was concerned, this one blemish is all that tainted an otherwise incredible record. On the other hand, what should have been a simple extraction had become an embarrassing failure. It showed weakness on the part of the director to have chosen him. Their failure in Puerto Rico had been a catastrophe. He would now have to deal with the local authorities, U.S. government authorities, and orchestrate yet another massive cover up. Of course, the director wouldn't do any of that himself, but it did slow down his plans and force schedule adjustments. He had sent the captain and his élite troops into every other kind of conflict, and however difficult it seemed, they had always accomplished their missions. The captain had been one of the best. Perhaps it was not right to dispose of him for this one mistake, he thought. The blue glow lessened slightly around the director.

The captain remained frozen at attention. More sweat

poured down his face. I'm showing too much fear, thought the captain. Last chance to make a move. He shot his hand forward with deadly precision, but he wasn't fast enough.

The dark suit man gently touched the small pulsing red circle. A bright flash tore through the room. The window behind the desk blew out in a cloud of glass particles. The desk shattered into tiny wooden shards that flew out in a shockwave that knocked the captain to the floor. The shock of the blast tossed the others against the wall. They fell to the floor, stunned and writhing in pain.

The blue glow around the dark suit man faded away. He straightened his tie and crouched down to check the pulse of the captain. He was still alive but unconscious. The blast burned most of his clothing away and blood trickled from one of his ears. There were bloody gashes all over his body. He looked up to see the others slowly composing themselves to again stand at attention. "Men. Your captain lives because of his stellar record," said the director. "Let his failure be your strength."

"Yes, sir!" they all yelled in unison. They were bloodied, but all stood at attention. It was an honor to serve the director, and to serve in such a noble cause. They would bring honor and strength to their new country and to the world. The ends without question justified the means, and in their view, the means were relatively compassionate. Their technological prowess would force every nation to bow to peace and security. Terrorists and dictators would continue to fall before them, with or without the pitiful man now laying on the floor.

The director stepped over the unconscious captain and approached the others. They all had a single yellow band on their otherwise white reflective body suits. It was the sign of the most élite in their ranks. Two yellow bands, signifying the rank of captain, were still barely visible on the arm of the man on the floor. A new captain would now have to be commissioned, and he already knew who it would be. He no longer needed a soldier with a stellar record, but one with amazing strength and speed. He would need to be able to work alone and detached from his men. He would require a less conventional set of principles. For the first time, his choice of captain would be a soldier who was less precise, and more ruthless.

The director walked to the soldier in the middle. He was noticeably taller and larger than the others. "You are now the captain," said the director.

"Yes sir!" said the soldier. A proud grin slowly formed on his face.

The director touched the soldier's arm and a second yellow band appeared. The director straightened his dark suit coat, then turned and stepped back over the soldier. That man, whom the others had called their captain, remained motionless on the floor. The director turned around, knelt, and touched the man's limp arm. Both yellow bands disappeared. The director stood back up and walked casually through the pile of splintered wood that had been his desk. His perfectly clean dark suit contrasted greatly against the dusty mess of the office. Again, he stared out into the night. This time, no bullet-proof window panes obstructed his view, and a cool breeze whistled through the room. He liked it. "You already have your orders, captain! Take that man off my floor, clean him up, wipe his memory, and leave him where he'll be found. I'm sure his family will be glad to see him again after all these years. He no longer exists to us or to any other operation, anywhere."

An uneasy silence hung in the room as the men remained at attention. It was a gesture of respect for the banished man who had been their captain.

Enough, thought the director. "Move! Don't fail me again. I don't care if it takes years. You have everything you need. Find the boy. He's all that matters now." said the director. "Understood, captain?"

"Yes sir!" replied the new captain.

"I want regular updates. We're closing this site. You will receive notice of our new headquarters. Understood?"

"Yes sir!" said the captain. With perfect silence, they all vanished from the room.

The director smiled. He had trained them well. The night sky was cloudy. A storm was approaching. He marveled at the majesty of the earth. He felt an insatiable need to control it. He tried to imagine how much longer he would have to deal with all of these weak people and disorganized governments. There was nothing but weakness and selfishness all around him. Fear. Hopelessness. Lust for power. Nations were conspiring against other nations, and he was in the middle of all of it. The director would stand by and watch them all destroy each other, like a tank full of betta fish. Others had forced the director into this wretched, inspired, and ruthless organization. He had no memory of his youth. He knew he had a family, but could not remember their faces. He had been taken from them and it had never been explained to him why. As the child grew older, he discovered why he'd been taken. He learned more quickly than they did. He became stronger than any of them.

Soon enough, he turned his captives' tactics against them. Like numerous other test subjects, the organization had analyzed him, they had operated on him, and they had cut into his body to see what made him tick. He could take it no more, and his reciprocation was efficient and ruthless. When he was done with them, there was no trail to follow, and no one left to oppose him.

The young, lost man became the director. Others would call him the dark suit man. He was a person of many names. He improved the methods of his captors and broadened their goals. He would make the world a better place for everyone and nothing would stand in his way. No one would ever do to others what had been done to him. In just a few years, he became the intelligent center of a silent storm that would bring the world together, and no nation would ever know who he was until he willed it. His would be the last and final world order. His would be the last act of terror.

It had been a long time since the director had to move his headquarters. He hated that the old couple had been at the root of his only failures. Ironically, it was also their research that had contributed to his success. Where had those old people found such ground-breaking discoveries? he wondered. He could find no backing from any government or corporation anywhere. It was unlikely that they had just made their amazing discoveries from nothing. He had tried to find their source and their funding, but found nothing. Why hadn't they sought to capitalize on such wonderful technological achievement? No matter what the answers were to his questions, the director had already decided that he would be the one to bring their discoveries to the world for the sake of global order and peace.

But now he had failed to obtain the bulk of the old couple's research, and their boy had escaped. Now it was time to focus on the boy, and that boy's parents might have the answers he sought. If they were any bit as proficient as the old couple, it would surely prove a challenge to find them – but he must find them. The boy was already nine years old. Before too long, he would be stronger, wiser, and more prepared. It would be more difficult to take him. How had he escaped? thought the director. How could he have eluded his best men? He remembered his own proficiency at a young age – his ability to outwit and outmaneuver others older and more experienced than himself. Maybe... he thought. The director gritted his teeth and sneered into the darkness of night. There could be no more failures handed to him by the Mira family. Many of his men were waiting in line to become captain, and they all knew the consequences of failure. The director had the finest minds in the world compartmentalized into an intricate system of innocuous think-tanks embedded in governments and institutions all over the earth, and they were all at his command. Thus far, they had all proven adept at cracking whatever revolutionary data he was able to obtain. Perhaps the recovered research log from the old couple would yield some clues.

The director pondered the content of the log. His long black tie waved in the breeze, and he hastily tucked it back into his neatly buttoned suit coat. The old couple had obviously been researching subatomic particles, but why? he thought. She mentioned force carrier particles and mass particles. Much of what the old lady wrote in her log had already been discovered. However, the ability to control mass – that was truly compelling. The director had already developed expanded ways to disassemble and collide matter, but to control the mass of matter? The possibilities seemed unlimited.

The director spun around and pounded a panel on the wall. It slid open to show a pulsing red circle which he then tapped without hesitation. A brilliant white flash emanated from the room. It expanded and consumed the entire wing of the business park. Within seconds, the building was silently leveled to the ground. The man in the dark suit casually walked away from where the building once stood. His blue glowing outline was the last part of him to disappear into the darkness of the woods. Sirens could be heard in the distance.

Finally, the last chapter of his operation had begun, and the director had removed most opposition. There were still some who stood in his way, but they would soon be eliminated and their knowledge would be employed for the good of all humanity. Many in history have tried to create order and peace through dominance, thought the man in the dark suit, but I'm better than all of them. I hold in my hands a power they never had, but at the same time, I am thoughtful and generous...

...After all, I did let that poor captain live.

CHAPTER TEN

Change Of Plans

DAYTONA BEACH, FLORIDA

"Liz," called a voice from the other end of the room, "Where'd you put my tablet?"

"Seriously? You're always losing that thing," said Liz. "Last place I saw it was on the dresser."

"Ah, yes. It fell on the floor," said Marc. "Thanks."

She stopped and looked thoughtfully at her husband. "Do you think he's ready for this?" she asked.

"Arec?" said Marc, "He's been wanting this for over a year. Besides, we can't keep dodging his questions. He's fourteen, too smart, and may already know more than we think."

"There's only so much he could know," said Liz. "But, I was mostly concerned about his last trip to your parent's place. I'm not sure it would be wise to bring all that back up. He's made so much progress."

Marc stopped and stared at the wall. "Well, yeah, but he needs to know the truth. I was hoping that we could talk about that with him on the trip. Don't you think he's ready to know the rest? It's been five years, after all." he said. He turned to Liz. "Five years of us not explaining what happened. Five years of him asking, and us ignoring him or changing the subject. He's not brought it up for a few months now. It's gotta be tearing him up inside. He's giving up on us, and he's probably been blaming himself for what happened." he said. "Arec is old enough. He's ready."

"Why would he feel like that was all his fault?" asked Liz. "He doesn't even really know what happened."

"He was only nine years old. He got away," said Marc. He locked down and tossed his tablet into an open bag on the floor. "He probably feels that–"

"–He could have done something to help your folks," said Liz. "That's obviously irrational though."

"The point is that we need to talk to him about it," said Marc. "I think I need to talk about it too," he smiled and gave Liz a hug.

"Hang in there. It will all be better soon," said Liz.

"Yeah. I hope so, for our family's sake," said Marc. He walked toward the doorway leading to the hallway. "I'm going to check on Arec."

"Me too." said Liz.

They quietly opened his door. He was sound asleep.

"We were right to not let him go to his brother's party, right?" asked Liz. "I feel bad."

"Well, it's 1:00 am now. We're planning to leave at five. It's probably good for him to get some sleep." said Marc. "Besides, Jacque and his friends aren't exactly the best guys to hang out with. A fourteen year old hanging out with a bunch of twenty-somethings?"

"But it's his brother. Jacque would have looked out for him," said Liz. "I just want him to have a normal life. Part of me hates that we have to pull him into this whole family legacy thing."

"You know as well as I do that we're doing the right thing," said Marc. "He was made for this. Quite literally, in retrospect. Don't you see that?"

"Yeah. I guess," she said. "I just hope your folks completed the prelim training before, you know." Liz regretted the way the words were coming out of her mouth.

"We'll finish anything they left undone," said Marc. "We've both observed him. Seems like they did a pretty good job." He held her hand. "He'll do just fine."

"Well, he's a Mira. It's in his blood I guess," she said. "You know, we're going to have to tell him about his grandparent's work."

"All in good time," said Marc. "We're still trying to figure all of that out. How are we supposed to explain it to Arec? We've got to stay focused on Arec and his progress. He's different from his peers. Smarter, faster. We should just focus on him, and how he was born. He's going to want to know." He smiled at Liz nervously.

"Oh, that will be a fun discussion," said Liz. "Wish we still had that data we got from your parents, and especially the—."

"—It was better that it disappeared with my parents," interrupted Marc. "They did the right thing, cleaning away their place with everything in it. I hate to think of what would happen if any of their research had fallen into the wrong hands."

"Especially that creepy guy in the dark suit," said Liz.

"We're intercepting him on this mission. It's really our first offensive. You realize that, right?"

"Depends on how you define offensive," said Marc. He smiled, trying to hide his anxiety. "We're just monitoring his activity. That also gives us a better view of what he's planning next, what he's thinking and where he might strike," said Marc.

"Are you sure it's wise to start Arec out on this assignment?" asked Liz.

"There's no better assignment if we want him to understand what he'll be up against. Besides, we're not going to make contact. We just need to find out what they're up to and then get out." said Marc. "We'd better finish packing."

"Can you go downstairs and make us some hot chocolate?" asked Liz. "I can finish your bag."

"Sounds good," said Marc. He smiled and quietly leapt down the stairs.

Part of the routine of leaving on an assignment was to make a call to their office to send for a pair of armed agents. Arec had always thought of them as babysitters. She couldn't wait to bring him along this time. No babysitters. On the other hand, she loved that he had always been so safe and protected at home while they were away on an assignment. She had a hard time even imagining her children in danger. That was always part of the deal; she and Marc's expertise on critical issues, and in return, their children would always have a complete security detail.

As Liz folded clothes she thought about how lucky she was to be a mother. It was only because of the research of Marc's parents that they could even have their own children. Jacque was always Arec's closest friend growing up, but when Jacque moved out, the two of them started to grow apart. Jacque was nothing like Arec, but Liz and Marc loved them both just the same. One thing was certain, Arec and Jacque were still loyal to each other, despite their differences.

Liz having lost track of time, looked at the clock. "Marc, honey, are you almost done down there?"

No answer.

She stood up and walked to the top of the stairs. "Marc?" she said. The hairs on her arms stood up. There was a slight breeze drifting through the house. An irregular breeze, as if a window was left open somewhere. She turned and looked down the lit hallway. Arec's room was next to their's, and further down the hallway, there were two other rooms and a bathroom. All the doors were shut but one. She looked down and saw impressions in the carpet.

Someone was there.

"Liz?" said Marc from the bottom of the stairs. "You called? Hot chocolate's almost ready."

Marc could see Liz standing in the hallway near the top of the stairs. She was still and facing forward, just outside of their bedroom. "I'll be up in a few minutes," he said loudly. All of his senses told him that something was wrong. Marc's body tensed, and then relaxed as his well-trained instincts took over. Liz's body language told him all he needed to know. He leapt up the stairs without making any noise and stopped a few paces from the hallway. Marc looked into her eyes, but she kept staring forward. He looked at her left hand. The middle finger twitched and then she touched her middle finger to her palm. It meant that there was something straight ahead, but she couldn't make it out. Their own special form of sign language had come in handy many times before on dangerous assignments, but they never had to use it in their own home.

Liz was relieved that Marc was there, but continued to look straight ahead. Various scenarios flashed through her mind, and they all included having to protect Arec in the room right next to her. She knew that she would die before letting anyone past her. She looked down at the carpet and could see new foot impressions appearing in her direction about ten feet away. She clenched her fist; a sign to Marc that she was going to attack.

Marc's heart started to race. Even with all of his advanced tactical training, he did not feel ready for this. Not in their own home. How did they find us? he wondered. He gritted his teeth, pointed toward Arec's door, and clenched his fist. It was a sign to Liz that he was ready. Marc pressed a small button on his watch. The distress signal was instantly sent, but it would be a handful of minutes before anyone arrived. They would do what they could do until help arrived. Marc nodded to Liz signaling that he was ready.

Liz's movements were a blur as she dropped and slid forward with a strike, but something countered and knocked her to the floor. Marc leapt from around the corner and flew feet first through the air. He struck an invisible target, and a dull pop sound could be heard. The wall shook and a large indentation in the sheet rock appeared in the adjacent wall. They've improved their cloaking capabilities, thought Marc. He fought to suppress his fear as he forced the primary objective into his mind:

they must keep this intruder distracted from Arec.

As Liz tried to get up, something struck her side, causing her to fly sideways. She hit the wall with enough force to put another hole in the opposite wall. Some framed photos on the wall fell and crashed to the floor. Liz rolled backward and leapt up as blood trickled from the corner of her mouth. Marc and Liz stood together and waited. All was quiet. They scanned the carpet for activity. Marc saw it first. As the blade was thrust forward, Liz shifted slightly to avoid major internal damage as it entered her side. The knife ripped back out, spraying blood all over the wall beside her. She dropped to her knees but then rolled backward and kicked straight up, slamming the intruder against the wall. Marc then quickly thrust his palm forward with deadly speed. They heard the intruder hit the wall again, stumble, and fall backward through a doorway further down the hallway.

Marc looked at Liz's side. There was a wide gash through her shirt and blood was running down her leg.

She nodded to Marc. "I'm ok. No permanent damage," she said as she forced a smile.

They slowly and silently walked toward the doorway at the end of the hall. Without any warning, Marc was struck from the side. His head hit the wall and a sharp pain ripped through his skull as he fell to the floor. His vision was blurry. He laid there stunned while he watched Liz strike out, then get blocked. She spun around and it seemed like she started to lift off of the floor. Liz thrashed wildly as she was thrown back down the hallway. She hit the floor and rolled, leaving streaks of blood on the carpet. The intruder kicked her in the side repeatedly, but she held in her screams.

Marc pulled himself up and limped down the hallway. Who was this? he thought. He's so strong. Marc gritted his teeth and stumbled toward the other end of the hallway where Liz had been thrown. As he got close to her, something started to drag her toward their bedroom. He limped faster and lunged into the bedroom. He was able to get a hold of a part of the intruder. Perhaps an arm. He spun around and dropped his weight against the joint of his opponent. He felt a pop and the intruder grunted in pain, letting up just long enough to let Marc spin backward and thrust his elbow into his opponent. He heard the intruder drop to the floor and looked over to Liz who was now slumped over the bed. She was losing blood. He knew there wasn't much time. He started to feel like he had failed his family. He turned around and immediately felt something hit his face. All went dark.

Marc woke up at the end of the hallway. The intruder had tied his hands to Liz's. Her skin was cold and clammy, but he still felt a pulse. With blurry vision, he could see down the hallway. The intruder had opened Arec's door. Marc tried to yell, but duct tape blocked any sound he tried to make. He couldn't see Liz's face. As far as he could tell, she was unconscious. Their opponent was obviously skilled. In fact, he was extremely skilled. Marc realized that they had the same training that he and Liz had received. Rage grew within him, and he wondered if there were any more intruders. He turned to his right and looked through the opened door into a dark and vacant guest bedroom. A warm breeze and the smell of the night air filled his nostrils. The curtains drifted lightly to the side revealing a large clean circular hole in the window pane.

As Marc continued to stare into the room, someone

entered the hole in the window. This one was not cloaked, but dressed head to toe in dark clothing. He gave a familiar motion with his hand, signaling to Marc that he was one of the agents responding to his distress signal. The agent checked Liz's pulse and walked past them down the hall. As he approached the master bedroom, the intruder became visible. Marc's hope faded as he saw the intruder and the agent in black shake hands. What? thought Marc. They both turned to look at Marc and Liz. As the intruder and the agent each removed their masks, Mark could only groan in despair through the several layers of heavy black duct tape that was starting to tear at his skin. He knew them both − but the agent, that's what shocked him the most. Neither he nor Liz had seen him for years, and now it seemed he had joined the enemy. How could we be so betrayed? thought Marc. Where had he and Liz gone wrong? What about Arec? Marc started to panic. It had been so long since there had been an attack on their family. Why now? he thought. Marc felt Liz's wrist again and sensed a weak pulse.

"You shouldn't have let him see you," said the agent. "They were expecting me, not you."

"Doesn't matter," said the intruder, "They'll both be dead soon anyway. I was thinking that we'd just let her bleed to death."

The agent shook his head. "That'll make a big mess. Already enough to clean up," he said. "We should be more precise, efficient, and clean, don't you think?"

"Just shut up and do as you're told, and there won't be any problems," said the intruder. "You're the hired one here. I'm in charge."

"Yes, sir." said the agent.

The intruder sneered as he looked the agent up and down. "You used to be a to be an agent for the Mira's, didn't you? My employer must really trust you to hire you for this assignment, traitor. Throw the love birds in their bedroom closet." ordered the intruder. "It's insulated pretty well. We can keep them there until we know what to do with them. I wanna get every last bit of intel outta them, and then we'll finish them off."

"What about the boy?" asked the agent.

"I knocked him out with a trank. He'll be asleep for a while," said the intruder. "He's the prize, after all. Don't want him damaged."

"Prize for whom, may I ask?" whispered the agent.

"Not sure I trust you with that information. Not yet, anyway," said the intruder.

"Fine. You help me carry them to the closet then, unless of course you want me to slowly drag them down the hallway," said the agent.

The intruder sneered, grabbed the agent, and held him against the wall. "I make the orders here, not you," said the intruder. "Are we clear on that?"

The agent shook himself loose. "Fine. Can I cut their legs loose then?"

The intruder grumbled as he whipped out a long knife and swiped it passed Marc and Liz, cutting some of the nylon cords and duct tape. "Satisfied?"

"Yes, sir." said the agent as he lifted up Marc and Liz.

Marc hoped for an opportunity to take both of them out, but his rage was swiftly swept aside as Liz's hand briefly tightened on his. She was starting to feel warmer, but she also started to shake. She's going into shock, he thought. He had to save them, save his family. There was so much to do, and Arec was a big part of it. He wondered what the intruder meant when he called Arec a prize. What would they do to him? He wasn't ready for all this.

The agent dragged them down the hallway and through the double doors leading to the master suite.

As they approached the closet, the intruder kicked them into the closet. "Don't let them out," said the intruder. "Keep an eye on them. I'm gonna go look around downstairs."

After a few minutes, the agent turned to Marc. "I'm here to help," he whispered.

Marc growled from behind the duct tape.

The agent smiled, drew a knife, and swung it across Marc's face. It opened a small slit in the tape.

"What do you think you're doing?" hissed Marc. "I am going to make sure your life is a living h—"

"—No you're not. Your intruder there is my closest link to the enemy – someone who I have been tracking for years. I have worked too hard to jeopardize all that now." said the agent. "We've known each other a long time. Trust me. I'll protect your boy."

Marc heaved a sigh of relief. "I thought you had turned on us."

The agent smiled. "Not a chance."

"Arec's the one who will finish my parent's research," said Marc. "He must be protected at all cost."

"Yes, I know," said the agent. "I'll try to get to the source of all of this madness from our friend."

"Liz has lost a lot of blood. I think we're losing her," mumbled Marc through the tape. "Cut the ropes a little and I'll get the rest of the way out."

The agent looked behind nervously. "No, he'll notice," he said. "You know as well as I do who we're dealing with here."

"Where's the other agent?" asked Marc. "Where's your real partner?"

"I checked in and took one slot. I skipped the rendezvous with the other agent to get here first," said the agent. 'Not sure how the other guy would deal with all this."

"Protect Arec at all cost," said Marc. "He's not been briefed. He doesn't know anything."

"Nothing?" asked the agent. "What am I supposed to tell him?"

"Don't worry about all that, just get him to the checkpoint. The others will know what to do, and I'll take care of the rest," said Marc. "Meanwhile, I need to get his mother patched up."

They heard the front door open and footsteps downstairs. "Oh no, the other agent is here," whispered Marc. "He's not going to be ready for this - no time to warn him." They heard a scuffle and some banging. Something metal hit the floor and they heard a few loud screams and then a muffled yell. The back door opened and the noise disappeared outside.

"I'll check on the other guy when I get a chance," said the agent. "How are you getting out of here? What's your plan?"

"The tube," said Marc. He did his best to smile behind the duct tape. "It's here, in the closet."

"Here? Where?" asked the agent. "Listen, you can't go yet. Our friend must be the last one to see you or else he'll think that I let you go. I can't have my cover blown, for

Arec's sake."

"Agreed," said Marc. "After we're gone, the liquid in the tube will need to re-oxygenate. Takes about eighteen hours. Keep Arec safe for eighteen hours and then tell him to go to the closet. He'll figure out the rest."

"What if he needs to leave earlier than that?" asked the agent.

"He'll drown if he tries to use the tube before it's recharged," said Marc. He heard the sound of footsteps. Marc looked up at the agent. "You're going to have to do something to make sure he knows you're on his side." He nodded to the agent as the intruder entered to room. Without warning, the agent back-handed the side of Marc's face. Marc exaggerated the force of the blow by twisting sideways. At the same time, he dislocated his own shoulder, giving him the angle he needed to start to loosen the remainder of the nylon cords that bound him.

The intruder smiled, then glared at the agent. "You think that they're ready to talk?"

"I don't think so," said the agent. He stood up and dusted off his hands. "Just thought I'd beat him up a little. He still had too much attitude."

"Really?" The intruder turned and stooped down to glare at Marc. "Do you have any idea how painfully I'm going to tear your family apart if you don't play nice?" he said. "First, I want you to tell me—"

Marc was finally able to free his own hands. He swung his hand around and struck him in the groin. The intruder groaned and stumbled backward. Marc then kicked the intruder through the bedroom door and back into the hallway. He hit the floor and rolled in pain. Marc removed the tape from his face. "I don't care what you want," he said. Marc then kicked the intruder in the side. Liz stood up and followed Marc into the hallway. The intruder blocked Marc's next kick, leapt up, and slammed Marc into the wall. He then turned toward Liz as she tried to stagger back into the bedroom.

The intruder followed Liz, then turned to the agent. "Beat Mr. Mira down and tie him back up," he said to the agent. "I'll take care of his wifey," The agent nodded and dragged Marc back into the bedroom.

Liz, only partially conscious, stumbled and fell to her knees as she reached the middle of the hallway. There was a shotgun in the hallway closet, but she knew that she'd never make it. Despair entered her mind as the intruder dragged her back to the bedroom.

"Time to secure these two troublemakers so we can deal with the boy," sneered the intruder. He opened the large closet door, and as he did so, he examined the weight of the door. "Nice and solid," he said. He grabbed Liz and dragged her into the closet. The intruder turned on the closet light and examined the walls. He chuckled and threw Liz against one of the closet walls. Stacks of boxes and shoes toppled on top of her. "Stay!" he yelled. He turned and walked back out of the closet. "It's secure. Toss him in there as well, and we'll see how much they really appreciate food and water, provided the lady doesn't bleed out first."

The agent threw Marc into the closet as well, then turned and smiled at the intruder. It was a smile that he didn't have to fake. He knew this was Marc and Liz's best chance of escape. Once they were away and safe, the equation was drastically simplified. The agent would then be able to ensure the safety of the boy and gain the trust of the intruder; a monster who threatened the entire Mira family. The agent would also be one step closer to knowing the intentions of their real enemy.

The intruder smiled back at the agent with satisfaction and then turned to sneer at both Marc and Liz as they sat on the floor of the closet. Liz sneered at the intruder but then paled as the pool of red on the carpet underneath her grew.

"You're a coward," grunted Marc, "You're not getting anything out of us."

The intruder straightened his shirt. "Well, I already have what I came for," he said as he turned and nodded toward Arec's bedroom door.

As the agent stood behind the intruder, he nodded and winked at Marc and Liz, trying to hide his sadness. This was the moment they had all trained for, but for which none of them was ready. The enemy had made the first move and had struck with ferociousness.

The intruder slammed the closet door shut, and turned to glare at the agent. "Nicely done, traitor," said the intruder. "If you continue to perform this well, then I may just recommend you to my employer for a more permanent role on my team."

Moments later, the closet door made a loud clicking sound. The intruder spun back around and attempted to open the closet door, but it was unusually heavy for a closet door. They could feel a jolt through the floor and a some shaking, followed by various mechanical humming in the walls.

"What the? Where's that noise coming from?" asked the intruder. He drew his gun and aimed it at the door. As he was about the unload a few rounds, the door clicked again. He pulled the door open, but Marc and Liz were gone.

The agent fought successfully to conceal his relief. "What did you do?" he yelled, trying to sound angry. "Where did they go?"

"What? I didn't do anything. I checked it out!" The intruder growled and leapt into the closet. He poked around in every corner, shut the door, locked it, and then just stood there. Nothing. They were gone.

The intruder threw the door back open and glared at the agent who was now standing there with his gun drawn and aiming it at him.

"What are you gonna do, shoot me?" blurted the intruder.

"Wasn't sure who was gonna come leaping back out of that magical closet," answered the agent. His act of sounding ignorant appeared to be paying off.

"Well, put that thing away," said the intruder, "We've still got the kid." As he walked by the agent, he turned and punched him in the face.

The agent turned sharply and fought the urge to swing back, knowing very well that he could have dropped him in a second. "What was that for?" asked the agent, trying to sound hurt. "Wasn't my idea to put them in the closet."

"I just wanted to hit someone," said the intruder. "Deal with it. We need to clean up this mess and get ready to play the friendly agent game for young Mr. Mira."

"One question," said the agent. "Who's your employer? I wanna know what I'm getting myself into here."

"Well, what was the name of the person who hired you?" asked the intruder.

"The contract confirmation message I received was sent

by the Office of the Director," said the agent. "A bit too vague, in my opinion."

"That's all you need to know." The intruder laughed and headed for the stairs. "Make yourself useful, and clean up this mess before morning." He paused and turned back to the agent. "Keep your opinions to yourself."

CHAPTER ELEVEN
Baby Sitters

Arec opens his eyes, but the room is dark, only barely lit by the glowing display of a clock on the dresser and the moonlight coming through the window. The breeze is cool. The ocean air coming through the half-open window fills his nostrils. He can hear the relaxing rush of waves and the familiar tinkling sounds of a tin mobile scattered with sea shells. It twists slowly in the breeze. He's about to drift back to the warm comfort of sleep, but he's startled by some activity down the hall. Some rustling and commotion can be heard from his grandparents' study. They're just working, they're always working, he thinks as his eyes close. Usually, they work late into the night. Even with their busy schedules, they love to have Arec out to visit for a few weeks each summer at their cliff-top home on the beautiful coast of Puerto Rico. They always make time to teach him something – how to navigate steep terrain; how to skip rocks on the beach; how to lift heavy things despite his small size; how to leap onto moving objects; what to look for in a person's face to find out if

213

they're hiding something; how to accurately fire a handgun blindfolded.

He wonders if other kids also have grandparents that teach them all of those things. He's not sure if it's his mom and dad that he misses, or if he really just wants to play with kids his age during the last few days of his visit. Ideas of fun things to do the next day fill his mind, but the weight of fatigue on his eyelids cause them to peacefully close.

The breeze turns into a howling wind, making the mobile spin even faster. The commotion in the study down the hall intensifies, and the wind whistling through his room makes it more difficult to hear the details of a conversation in the study. There's silence, then footsteps. He drifts back to sleep. The window slams shut and he sits up. The room is pitch dark except for the faint glow of the clock which soon vanishes as well. Footsteps and shapes are moving all around him. Arec is gently but forcefully pulled out of his bed and led into the hallway. "Wait, I have to go to the bathroom!" he says.

"Be silent dear, no time for that," says his grandma. She strokes his hair as he's led down the darkened hallway toward the back door.

"Remember what we've taught you. Remember your exercises," whispers his grandpa as he opens the door. He motions for Arec to sit down on the back porch against the house just beside the door opening. He wraps a wool blanket around Arec and turns to walk back toward the door.

The moonlight provides enough visibility to make out the silhouette of his grandmother as she kisses her hand and places it on his forehead. Tears flow down her face.

Why is she crying? wonders Arec. Why are all the lights turned off in the house? Why is the porch light turned off?

"Is there a storm coming?" asks Arec.

No response.

He's still drowsy as he sits on the ground, wrapped in the dark blanket. His eyes burn with fatigue. His grandfather crouches down in front of Arec. "You'll be fine," he says. He turns to look back toward the door where his grandmother is standing. She nods at her husband.

The old man's face looks stern yet loving. He points over Arec's shoulder out into the darkness of the woods surrounding the yard of their beautiful villa which is located on the top of a bluff overlooking the beach far below. "Trail, rock, jump. Understood?" says his grandfather.

Arec's chest tightens and panic sets in. "No, I don't want to go alone," he says. "It's dark. I'm scared." The wind whistles through the trees and faint pulsing sounds could now be heard all around them. He wipes his nose on his pajama sleeve.

"I'm sorry Arec. It's too dangerous," says his grandmother. "You'll be ok."

Grandfather stands and ruffles Arec's hair as he turns to walk away. Arec jumps up and grabs the back of his shirt. He can feel the softly worn fabric of his flannel shirt between his small fingers. "Grandpa, where are you going?" asks Arec. "Why can't I come? Why are we outside?"

The old man smiles broadly, but his eyes fill with sadness. "We need to go, but you need to stay," he says. "Follow the evacuation instructions. Listen to your parents. We didn't want to leave like this, we're so sorry." There seems to be more that he wants to say, but he stops himself. "Never forget what we've taught you. We love you." He turns and rushes toward the house pausing briefly to look back. "Arec, run!" he says.

Arec's grandmother now holds a firearm in one hand and a rifle with a scope in the other, which she tosses to her husband. They both turn and run back through the doorway and into the darkness of the house before Arec can say goodbye.

I never got to say goodbye, thinks Arec. Goosebumps cover his arms and back as another cool breeze whips through the villa, briefly throwing aside part of his wool blanket covering.

The pulsing sound in the air increases. As a sudden gust blows by, Arec's eyes fill with dust, and the sound of gunshots crack through the night air. He steps back and the blanket drops to the ground. Arec fights the urge to run back into the house, and quickly runs the other direction to find cover in the familiar shrubs along the back edge of the yard. He can barely see the back door through the darkness and the dust from across the yard, and all of the lights on the house are dark. There's a blinding flash followed by a shock wave that sends Arec to the ground, then silence. He smells wood dust in the air and hears the sound of shattering wood. The familiar silhouette of the villa is now gone. How? thinks Arec. He is about to emerge from his hiding place when dozens of piercing spotlights emerge from the cliff below and scan the yard around the area where the house stood. They converge on the back porch area where Arec had been sitting, and then start to trace paths across the yard. The pulsing sound increases. To Arec, it seems as if a hundred unseen eyes are looking for him. He remembers that his grandfather told him to run. Why? he asks himself. He chokes back the urge to cry and starts to run. He leaves the gated part of the yard and runs down a trail. It's steep and dark, and he knows it well, but he's never walked it at night. As he turns a corner, he trips and falls into some thick brush next to the trail. Arec hits his head and the pain is intense. He reaches up and feels a wetness in his hair. His vision, the pain, and then everything else fades away. He curls up into a ball and drifts off into a place of silence and warmth.

As Arec started to wake, he felt his head for a wound. Nothing. He sighed with relief. It was just the nightmare again. He opened his eyes and squinted, but his vision was blurred Arec stared at the ceiling. I wonder how many times I have to endure that stupid nightmare, he thought. It was different this time. It was deeper, darker and so real. His head pounded. He had twisted and turned so many times while sleeping that he had wrapped himself up into a cocoon of blankets. He shifted slightly and then rolled right off the bed and onto the floor. His barely opened eyes shunned the morning light. It hurt. Everything hurt. He could not remember the night before. This was not a natural pain. He felt like he had been beaten in his sleep, but there were no bruises. As Arec moved his limbs, the pain all over his body started to fade. Only a sharp pounding headache remained.

The events in the nightmare had taken place five years

before. Now, at the age of fourteen, he was getting tired of those dreams. He felt doomed to re-live, over and over again, the last moments he could remember from the last night he spent at his grandparents' villa in Puerto Rico the night that they disappeared. In general, his memory of that trip had faded over time, but each time he had the nightmare, he remembered another detail. By now he had remembered most of that night, but there were still holes. He missed his grandparents, how they always had fun with him but always treated him with respect. They had a lot of fun together, and never treated him like a little kid.

He tried to remember the last moments of his time on the island, how he escaped, and the trip back home. He hated having those nightmares, but each time he hoped that he would remember just enough to start answering the really big questions. That pulsing sound in the air he heard as he ran from the villa down toward the beach – that part was new. He had forgotten about the pulsing. It was strong enough to shake him. Just the memory of it now made his head throb even more with pain, making feel sick.

He lay on the floor, still wrapped in a blanket like a burrito, and again stared up at the ceiling. He finally noticed the alarm clock that had been beeping at him. He managed to free an arm from the blanket and yank the power cord out of the wall. Silence. Of course, now he wanted to know the time. He turned to look at the dark, blank, and lifeless clock. Arec cursed at the clock, as if it was mocking him.

Standing was a chore, but not just because of the bedding wrapped tightly around him. He started to feel as if he had just gotten off a nauseating carnival ride. He was startled by the sounds that came from his stomach, and started to smell bacon. Breakfast, he thought. Just what I need! Mom and dad are the best. This is going to be the best Saturday ever. Somehow he would have to put Puerto Rico and the disappearance of his grandparents behind him. It had only been five years, but it also seemed like a distant memory. Arec's loving and attentive parents had seldom spoken of it and he had never really understood why. I've always been afraid to bring it up, thought Arec. Could I have done anything to help them? I was just a kid. Maybe. I feel like I could have, I'm just not sure how.

Arec stumbled toward the door, trying to recall again how he had spent the last few hours, or even the last few days, before going to bed. His hand started to shake as he raised it to the door knob. Fatigue? he guessed. He didn't feel right at all. I'll feel better after getting something to eat, he thought. Birds were chirping outside, and although his vision was still blurry, he could tell that it was a beautiful sunny day. Arec sighed loudly. I can't wait to put all that behind me, once and for all. It's time to finally join my parents on an assignment.

Arec turned the doorknob with resolve, and at the same time some more of his memory of the day before started to trickle back into his mind. For a few days, his parents had mentioned that he was finally old enough to take on a business trip. Here it was, almost nine in the morning. Why didn't they wake me up? he thought. I never sleep in.

There was only one explanation.

Arec's body tensed. No, not again, he thought. They never leave without telling me, or did they? His headache pain was replaced by anxiety. He remembered now that his parents were planning to leave early in the morning. He reached back toward the dresser and grabbed his phone. They were supposed to leave at five in the morning. "Oh no," he said. He looked across the room to the bag he had packed. He looked at his phone, but there were no new messages from his parents.

Arec opened his door. Everything looked so clean. He ran down the stairs and the smell of freshly cooked bacon was strong enough to almost make him forget why he was upset. A lump grew in his throat, and he wiped his eyes quickly. Arec was too old to cry like a baby. Every time Arec's parents left town, two agents were assigned to watch over him from their office. The last thing Arec wanted do was cry in front of the baby sitters. I'm too old for this crap, thought Arec. As he walked into the kitchen, two uniformed agents were cooking up an impressive pile of bacon. Ah, crud, he thought. It's been almost two years since I've had baby sitters. I used to really look forward to the time I got to spend with these guys. But now? How would they deal with a fourteen-year-old kid? I'm too old for their games. Arec decided not to try and hide his frustration. "What's going on? Why didn't I get to say goodbye to them? That's so not cool." he said.

They didn't answer or even look at him or pause. One of the agents was sitting at the island in the kitchen snickering at the funny pages in the morning paper while eating pancakes. The other one was wearing his mother's frilly apron and frying more bacon as if a plate-full wasn't enough for one breakfast.

Arec felt that maybe this was a peace offering. At least these guys were trying to start things off well. "Don't you think that's enough bacon?" asked Arec.

The taller agent at the stove turned, spatula in hand. He held it like a weapon. "Hey, young Mr. Mira, I trust you slept well last night?"

"You can call me Arec, and yes, I slept really really well. Too well, and what a mother of a headache. What did you guys slip me last night?" He meant it as a joke, but started to wonder if they had actually drugged him.

"Oh, that was your folks' idea – we had nothing to do with that." said the agent cooking the bacon.

"So, I was drugged? Seriously?" asked Arec. He suppressed his anger, seeing the situation as an opportunity to get some information. "When did they leave? What time did you guys show up? Didn't hear a thing."

The agent didn't answer. He smiled, picked up the plate of bacon, and faced Arec. "Hungry? You can freeze the extra pieces," he said as he held the plate in front of Arec. "I'm Agent Neese and my partner there is Agent Locke."

They didn't exactly fit the mold Arec was familiar with, but it had been a few years, and he was older now. He grabbed a piece of bacon. "So, are you the senior guy, Agent Neese?" asked Arec.

"Yes, sir," answered Neese. He stood at attention.

Arec mockingly stood at attention as well. "At ease, soldier!"

Neese relaxed a bit and wryly smiled. "We're probably the last people you wanted to see," he said.

"Correct-o-mundo," said Arec as he grabbed some bacon from the plate. "Where'd my parents go this time? I was supposed to leave with them early this morning."

"Sorry kid. Apparently a change of plans," said Neese, "And you know the rules. Assignment data is classified.

Even for you."

"Yeah, okay." Arec wasn't really mentally up to all of this yet. "What's the schedule then? How long will my folks be away?" asked Arec, who was now trying to keep track of all the unanswered questions he'd asked so far. He still couldn't believe that they'd just take off without telling him, especially when he thought he was going with them. Before Arec could ask another question, both agents froze and looked in the direction of the front door. Something got their attention, but Arec didn't really care. He just wanted them to start answering questions.

Agent Locke rose from the kitchen island, put the paper down, drew his gun, and stood behind the entrance to the kitchen just out of view of the entry way. Somehow in the same action he'd managed to also grab a large knife out of the block on the counter and hold it aside his raised firearm.

Some sort of act to impress me? thought Arec, or is there really something going on here? Either way, they've got my attention. Arec remembered when he was younger how the agents would include him in fake security drills. He would follow along as best he could, and they would coach him on what to do if there was a real emergency. "I'm really not in the mood for this right now, guys," said Arec.

Agent Neese waved to Arec to get over to the far side of the dining room next to the kitchen. He then drew his gun and walked toward the front door. Locke stayed in the kitchen between Arec and Neese. Arec rolled his eyes in disgust. "I'm really too old for those commando games, guys," said Arec.

Locke froze, maintaining his focus on the kitchen

entrance. Neese was slowly walking toward the front door while Locke stayed with Arec in the kitchen. Locke ignored Arec's protest and kept his aim poised on the walkway leading to the kitchen. "Expecting company at o-nine-hundred on a Saturday morning?" whispered agent Locke.

Arec started to wonder if this really was a drill. I'm not sure what the show is all about, maybe I'll just play along, thought Arec. "Nope. Wasn't expecting anyone, agent man," mocked Arec. "Hear something, I presume?" Arec casually walked past Locke, not really expecting an answer to his question.

Arec approached Neese, who stood with his gun aimed a few paces from the front door. The only thing that could keep them from hearing a pin drop was the sound of Arec's bacon-munching, which, unfortunately, didn't seem to annoy the agents at all. Arec followed closely behind Neese as he approached the door. He turned briefly to see that Locke was now behind him, now aiming his gun and the large knife at the door. A tall silhouette could be seen through the privacy glass in the front door. The doorbell rang and Arec jumped slightly, but he knew right away who it was. He stepped around Neese and parted the narrow curtain to look through the side window. It was Arec's tall twenty-one year old burger flipping, disheveled and obviously hung-over brother. He was leaning against the door frame with one hand and rubbing his forehead with the other.

"Hey, it's just Jacque," said Arec. He turned around and Neese was no longer there, but back in the kitchen at the stove and Locke was again seated at the island reading the comics.

Whoa, thought Arec, I always loved the way these guys got around like ninjas. Arec opened the front door and Jacque strolled right in. He always reminded Arec of the Shaggy character from the old Scooby-Doo cartoons.

"Hey bro," said Jacque, "The guys dropped me off – thought I could catch some morning grub." His gaze shifted from Arec to the kitchen. "Is that bacon I smell?" he asked.

"Umm, yeah" was all Arec could say before he lunged around him and made a beeline toward the smell. "Good to see you too, Jacque," mumbled Arec. It had been a few years since he'd moved out on his own, but he still managed to spend a lot of time around the house. His burger-flipping job was walking distance from his apartment closer to downtown. Every once in awhile after a late night party over at his friend's place after work, he would come on over and mooch a free breakfast before crashing on the sofa. Despite his weird, annoying, and sponge-like nature, Arec was always thankful to have a brother like Jacque.

A little annoyed, Arec closed the front door and walked back into the kitchen. Jacque was sitting next to Agent Locke, and they were both munching on bacon and laughing at comics. "Jacque, allow me to introduce my latest baby-sitters. Agents Locke and Neese."

"It's a pleasure to meet you," said Jacque, "Baby-sitter agent dudes."

Neese just stood there, spatula in hand. He stared coolly at Arec from the stove. "Long enough to warrant extended supervision and protection," he said bluntly. He continued to stand there, twirling the bacon spatula like a baton.

"Excuse me?" said Arec. "What are you talking about?"

"Before you answered the door, you asked us how long your parents would be gone," answered Neese. He turned back to the stove. "Long enough to warrant extended supervision and protection," he said again.

"Ah, right. Thanks." Arec had a hard time hiding his dissatisfaction with the answer he got. It was canned and meaningless. He looked back over to Jacque who had paused from comic reading to stare at Arec.

Jacque smiled broadly. "Nice boxers, Arec," he said as bits of bacon fell out of his full mouth as he spoke. He laughed and nudged Locke who seemed uninterested. "Arec, you missed out on a killer party last night."

"Mom and dad wouldn't let me go, not this time." said Arec.

"Why not?" asked Jacque. He frowned and continued to shove bacon and pancakes into his mouth. "We don't spend much time together anymore."

"Yeah, I wanted to go," said Arec glancing at agent Neese, "But mom said that I should get some sleep. I was going to go on their trip with them this time."

"Yeah, right, Arec," said Jacque. He stopped eating and looked at Arec. "Wait. Seriously?"

"Yeah, had a bag packed and everything," said Arec. "We were supposed to leave early this morning."

"Weird," said Jacque as he continued to eat, "They usually text me when they're leaving town. Never heard anything. Maybe this is another one of those tests for you."

"Hmm, yeah, maybe," said Arec. "Either way, sounds like they had a last minute change of plans."

Jacque stopped eating again and looked at Arec. "Got

any pain meds handy? My head is pounding."

Locke, without breaking his concentration on the newspaper, put a medicine bottle on the counter in front of Jacque.

"Thanks!" said Jacque. "So, what do you mean by change of plans? What did they say before they left?"

"Nothing," said Arec, "I just woke up with a splitting headache and these guys were here," Neese smirked and twirled the spatula in his hand.

"So, they didn't wake you or anything?" asked Jacque. "That's weird. It's been at least a year since they've gone out of town."

"The agents drugged me," said Arec. He glared at Locke, who didn't seem to notice. "That's why I slept in."

"Yeah, you never sleep in, freak." said Jacque.

Arec braced himself with one hand on the counter while he rubbed his forehead.

"Like I said, the sedative was your folks' idea," said Neese. "They didn't want you waking before they left." He put some fresh bacon on the pan.

Arec thought it was strange that he was making so much food. Why so much bacon? he thought. Arec glared accusingly at Neese. "I seriously doubt my folks would ever do anything like that," said Arec. "Did you guys also drug our breakfast?"

Jacque the comedian placed his hands around his own neck and screamed as bits of food fell out of his mouth. He then went limp and flopped onto the counter, scattering bacon all around him. He looked up and started laughing with a piece of bacon stuck to the side of his face. "Arec, the food's fine. You gotta loosen up, dude," said Jacque. "Remember the time we slipped the laxative in Jimmy's hot chocolate during that concert at school? His pants were all dripping before he even left the room."

Locke, only slightly amused this time, chuckled and turned back to the paper. Arec was the only one who noticed Neese holstering his gun. He's on-edge, thought Arec.

"Arec, these guys are ok, not like the goons you had last time mom and dad left town," said Jacque. "And they sure can cook." Neese walked over and put a new load of hotcakes on his plate and winked at Arec. "Thanks, agent Neese," said Jacque as he looked at Arec. "Eat something, might make that headache go bye-bye. It's sure doing something for my hangover."

"I don't have a hangover," blurted Arec. He was getting annoyed.

Neese turned to Arec. "Listen boys, it might be a bit until you see your folks again, but you will." Arec couldn't help but to be skeptical, and Neese could tell he was uncomfortable with him. Neese continued. "We don't have much intel about their mission. It's a need-to-know type of thing. Not a whole lot to share with you. Dig?"

Neese didn't speak like an agent. Maybe he's trying to talk hip to impress us, thought Arec. "So, what intel can you share?" Arec flashed a quick grin at Jacque. They both knew the drill: keep it juvenile, hold your cards close, and never stop trying to get more information.

Jacque clumsily pushed his plate aside which ruffled Locke's neatly laid out newspaper. "You guys can be straight with us," said Jacque with a smirk. "How long are they gone this time? You can tell us that, right?"

Locke flashed a concerned expression at Neese who just nodded in the negative.

Something is up with these guys, thought Arec. Mom and dad are always there to introduce us to the agents who are assigned to us and this time they just split. Gone. Without a word, no goodbye. I didn't get to say goodbye to my grandparents either.

A seed of anger grew within Arec. Being drugged was not any standard procedure he'd ever been aware of, or even warned of. He also knew that his parents would never do that to him. He could tell that Jacque was also tipped-off. They both knew that something wasn't right.

CHAPTER TWELVE
Bad Day At the Office

Neese turned off the stove, untied the frilly apron he was wearing and hung it on the pantry door. Locke folded the newspaper, stood up, and stretched.

"Well?" asked Arec.

Neese's eyes kindled with a fire Arec had not noticed until now. "Well, what?" he said.

"What about our parents?" asked Arec. "Anything you can share with us about their trip?" Arec tried to sound as earnest and juvenile as possible. Arec had a sinking feeling that they had just started down a road with no way to turn around and go back. Agents were always well groomed, respectful and cordial. Their sense of duty was always unmistakable, their ability to protect was never in question. Arec had taken those attributes for granted too long. Neese was starting to tax the level of confidence he had in agents.

"Yeah," said Jacque, "Just seems weird that you can't tell us anything. That's really lame."

Neese still didn't answer, but instead stared down at

Arec. His hair was tousled and matted at the bottom as if sweat had saturated it then dried. His uniform collar was stretched and there seemed to be sweat stains. His face was poised and disciplined, but lines of stress seemed more apparent now that the friendly bacon-flipping act had faded. I think it's all an act, thought Arec. But why? Not sure about Locke, but Neese is definitely hiding a lot. I don't think he's supposed to be here. Arec looked over to Locke who was now leaning against the wall, folding his arms. Arec's anger grew, and so did his fear.

Jacque stared at Arec as if to try to blast him telepathically with his concerns. Jacque had often said that such a thing as telepathy was possible. He was funny like that, very superstitious. Either way, Jacque always had a good sense of things being awry. He just never knew what, exactly. "Seriously? Why so lame, you guys?" said Jacque.

Neese forced a smile. He walked up to Arec and put a hand on his shoulder. "We are not your average agents," he said. "We've been assigned to you because of unusual circumstances surrounding your parents."

"What circumstances are you talking about?" asked Arec. "Are they in trouble?"

Neese smile broadened to a wide grin. "They're in Puerto Rico. I believe you know the place."

Arec's face paled. "Puerto Rico? Why?" He felt Neese's hand tighten on his shoulder. What disturbed Arec more than the fact that Neese was lying, was that he was now trying to get information about a topic Arec didn't want to discuss. He's got a lot of nerve, thought Arec. He also noticed for the first time some faint discoloration on his sleeve and the front of his uniform shirt. The observation of small facts helped keep Arec from losing control of his emotions. He straightened and glared up at Neese. Arec's mind started to race. I think I know what's going on, I've got to be patient. I've got to let this play out. Neese is afraid of something. I can see it in his eyes. Arec took a step back.

Neese smiled. "You were there when your grandparents disappeared. What happened? What did you see? You share intel with us, we'll share with you."

"Hey, what's the point in not sharing information about our parents with us?" asked Jacque. "Why the lame games? And you, agent Locke, don't seem to want to say anything. You dudes are weird." He ate some more bacon and smiled proudly at Arec.

"We don't have to tell you anything," said Arec. "And I'll ask the questions, Agent Neese." Arec's heart was pounding so hard he feared it would show through his shirt. "Now, what can you guys tell us about our grandparents?"

"We don't know anything," said Neese, but Arec could tell that it was another lie. Neese sneered slightly, "I thought that maybe you could tell us."

"Seriously?" blurted Jacque, "Do you guys know how to answer any questions, or are you gonna just keep being lame?"

"You like the word lame," said Locke, "Don't you?"

"He speaks!" said Jacque. "And yes, I like that word 'cause it describes you guys perfectly." He looked at Arec and smiled. "We're just gonna go now. I've got my own place. Arec and I will hang out there, and you can just hang here and cook. We'll be back for grub at dinner time."

"I don't think so," said agent Neese. "You boys aren't

going anywhere." Neese could feel the tension in the room increase exponentially. "We are sworn to do our job, and our job is to protect you."

"From what?" asked Arec. "You gonna explain anything to us?"

"I already stated our terms," said Neese, "You tell us what you know about your grandparents first, and we'll go from there."

"Lame, lame, lame!" said Jacque. He knew that was the very last thing on the planet Arec wanted to discuss with anyone. "That's two lames for Neese, and one lame for Locke."

"But, you're from the office," said Arec. His doubts were growing about that, but he played along anyway. "Don't you guys already know everything there is to know about my grandparents and what happened there? Don't you have to know all of that in order to adequately protect us?"

Neese's deceptions were becoming more and more obvious. He looked uncomfortable. He realized that Arec wasn't just going to fold and tell everything he knew.

"What are you afraid of, Agent Neese?" asked Arec.

Neese's face was calm, but Arec could sense his anger level was climbing. He clenched his fists. He hated that this punk kid could read him so easily. They had clearly underestimated him.

Arec glared up at Neese. "What really happened to my parents?"

Locke abruptly stepped forward between Arec and Neese and held out a box of popsicles. "Why don't we all have a treat? It's a warm day and it sure would be refreshing, right?" asked Locke. He slapped the box of popsicles against Neese's chest and glared at him sternly. "Right?" He turned and also looked at Jacque.

"Very well," grunted Neese. He glared at Arec and turned to walk away.

"Oh, popsicles," said Jacque, "Not so lame. Thanks, Locke. You're still lame though."

As Neese walked away, Arec noticed that there was a torn belt loop on the back of his uniform trousers, and there were what seemed like scuff marks on the sides of his pant leg. Maybe from a fight? thought Arec. If so, with whom? I wonder what mom and dad would want us to do?

"We'll take ours outside." said Jacque.

Locke smiled as he licked a popsicle. "Suit yourself. Just don't go anywhere." He followed Neese out of the kitchen.

"Yeah, lame," said Jacque. Locke left the room and Jacque turned to Arec. "Well, that was weird, and a little freaky."

Arec walked quickly toward the back door. "Good call Jacque," he said, "I kinda feel sick. That bacon's sitting in me like a lead brick."

By now it was getting close to lunchtime and the sun beamed over the tops of the trees. Shadows retreated and morning dew by now had evaporated. Jacque was happy to get out of the house. They walked a bit of a distance out into the deep backyard and then stopped. Arec surveyed the grass around them, moving it around with the tip of his shoe.

Jacque watched him curiously. "What are you looking for?" he asked.

Arec turned and squinted as he looked back toward the house. "Well, there are two possibilities. Either these agents really are different like Neese said–"

"Or?" asked Jacque.

Arec walked over to an area where it looked like some grass had been disturbed and flattened, revealing some of the soil underneath. "–Or, these guys are not from the office at all. They're not here to help," said Arec. "I think they tried something with mom and dad. They didn't get what they wanted, and now they wanna try with us."

Jacque was annoyed. "Seriously? How could you know that? What could they possibly want from us?"

"Information. I don't know. Either way, it's just a theory." said Arec.

"Yeah, a lame theory," said Jacque. "How about this theory: they're just a couple of creepy agents from mom and dad's office." Jacque walked over and looked more closely at the same area of disturbed grass. "So, what's up with the grass?"

"There was a struggle here," said Arec, "The grass has been raked here to try and cover it up. They're trying to cover up something."

"Yeah, who knows what happened while you were drugged," said Jacque. "So, you think mom and dad are ok?"

"I don't know," said Arec. "Always felt so safe around the agents, but these guys creep me out."

"Yeah, these guys are lame," said Jacque. "Thankfully I don't work until Monday. But even if I did have to work this weekend, I wouldn't go anywhere and leave you with those lame-os."

"If they were working with mom and dad," said Arec, "They would know more about their assignment. They wouldn't have just left the way they did, unless it was an emergency."

"So, you don't think this is one of their training drills?" asked Jacque.

"No, not this time," said Arec. "They would have said goodbye. Somehow they would have said goodbye."

"Arec, listen, we really don't know how much these guys know." said Jacque, "Maybe they're just messing with us."

"But why? That doesn't make sense. Agents joke sometimes, but they don't mess around. You know that." said Arec. "Jacque, they're lying. I can tell."

"Yeah, I know you can," said Jacque. "You're the best poker player around. So, let's say you're right, and not lame. What are they lying about?"

"As far as I can tell, mom and dad are alive," said Arec. "Locke is hard to read, but Neese is—"

"—Lame?" said Jacque, smiling.

"Geez, c'mon Jacque. I'm serious. You're always such a screwball." said Arec.

"Yeah, sorry," said Jacque. "Guess I'm still feeling messed up from last night."

"Well, that's gonna have to stop now." said Arec.

"Yeah, don't be lame. Hate it when you get all preachy at me," said Jacque. "So, what about Neese?"

"He's lying about everything," said Arec. "He really doesn't know where mom and dad are, and he's really mad about them. Not sure why. Also, he wants something. Not sure what. It has to do with what grandma and grandpa were working on though."

"You got all that just from reading Neese's body language and stuff?" asked Jacque. "You're gonna have to teach me how to do that mind-reading stuff. Grandma tried to teach me once, but I couldn't do it."

"It's not mind reading or telepathy, or any of that crap," said Arec. "It's just observation and body language. Analysis of aberrations in speech patterns."

"Aber-what?" asked Jacque. "Dude, you're lame when you throw big words at me like that."

"Just trust me," said Arec, "We need to find out what they want."

"Hey, you got it bro." Jacque looked cautiously toward the house and then stepped closer to Arec. "So, if these guys are not from the office, where are the real agents, the ones that are supposed to be here?"

"Let's verify who they are," said Arec. "We'll ask to see their identification. If they try to deny us verification of identity, then we know for sure that we're in trouble."

"Sounds like a not-so-lame plan," said Jacque, "Maybe I could–"

"–Jacque, stop talking," interrupted Arec. He noticed that both agents were standing at the dining room window with binoculars watching them. Arec turned his back to the house and looked at Jacque. "Oh man," he said.

"Oh man, what?" whispered Jacque as he turned and looked toward the house. "Are they coming?"

"No, but they can tell what we've been saying," said Arec, "They've been watching us."

"So what?" said Jacque. "It's not like we're bugged."

"Jacque, agents can lip-read," said Arec. "Thankfully, we haven't been facing them very long, so they couldn't have read that much of our conversation."

"Seriously?" said Jacque. "Don't you think that maybe you're being a little paranoid?"

Arec rolled his eyes. "Trust me," said Arec.

As they approached the house. Neese and Locke walked outside and just stood there on the patio. "Having fun in the sun, boys?" asked Neese. "Remember not to wander off now without telling us first. We are supposed to protect you and we can't if you disappear," said Neese.

"Like our parents?" said Arec.

Neese smiled and whisked out his identification card. "You wanted to see this?" he asked. His grin changed to a sneer.

Jacque looked at Arec in shock. He realized that Arec had been right. The question was just how much of their conversation they had heard.

Locke also walked up and held out his identification card. They each had their thumb over one end of their card, activating a small blue light in the middle. A person needing to check their identity would put their thumb over the other end of the card. The light in the middle would indicate whether or not the cardholder was valid.

Keep cool, thought Arec. "Yeah. We just wanted to make sure you guys were legit since our folks never introduced us," said Arec. He knew that he had to conceal as best he could how nervous he was. This whole game would change if the agents didn't check-out. Arec thought through a myriad of escape scenarios, but none of them seemed to work in their favor.

"That's cool with you dudes, right?" asked Jacque.

"That's reasonable," said Locke. "Go ahead."

Arec placed his thumb over the spot on the other end of Locke's card. The blue light started to spin in a circle and then turned green. Arec then placed his thumb over the other end of Neese's card and it turned green also. When Neese started to pull the card away, Arec tightened his grip to take a closer look at the card. He noted the serial number, and also that the hole where a cord passes through had been torn out.

Arec looked up innocently at Neese. He was tall, and the way the shadows cast on his face only added to his ominous appearance. "Agent Neese," said Arec, "Where's your ID card lanyard?"

"Right here," said Neese as he pulled it out of his shirt, "The cord tore out of the card while playing ball. Happens all the time - cheap cards." Neese jerked the card away, and as he did so Arec could see a cut on his wrist just beneath the cuff of his uniform shirt.

"And what about the cut?" asked Arec. "How'd you get hurt? You guys never get hurt."

"Really rough ball game, kid. You ever play ball?" answered Neese.

"You called me kid. No agent has ever called me that," said Arec. He stepped back and so did Jacque. "Also, both of your cards are loaners, no names on them. Also, I can tell by the serial numbers that they're both senior agent cards. Only one of you should be a senior. Can you explain that?" asked Arec.

"Both cards checked out. That's all you boys need to know," said Locke. "Let's stop the game of twenty questions."

"Oh, I have a lot more questions than that." said Arec.

Neese chuckled and looked out to where Arec and Jacque had been talking. "Not sure you really wanna go there."

"Listen, Mr. Mira. The lights turned green," said Locke. "They check out. Just drop it."

"Yeah, I saw that," said Arec. Something is very wrong,

thought Arec. They're hiding so much from us. "Where are our parents?"

Agent Neese and agent Locke silently stood there as Arec and Jacque turned to walk back into the house.

"Remember what we said, don't go anywhere." said Neese.

"We're just going to walk around out front. No worries, lame-os," said Jacque. He closed the door behind him.

"The kid knows, or at least suspects, too much." said Neese.

Locke looked at his watch. "Let's give him a little more time to cough up some info voluntarily," he said.

Neese turned and glared at Locke. "I have no problems disposing of you along with them," said Neese. They walked further out into the yard. Neese kicked around some of the loose clumps of grass and smiled at Locke.

"Is that where you took care of the other agent?" asked Locke. "Where did you put the body?"

"He's buried over there in the garden," said Neese. "Didn't put up much of a fight. Definitely a new guy," he said. He walked back toward the door to the house. "They don't train them like they used to," said Neese. "Keep an eye on the boys."

"And you?" asked Locke.

"Me? I'll be watching you, of course." Neese winked and walked back into the house.

Locke smiled and looked at the irregularly spaced piles of compost and soil in the garden on the other side of the yard. Locke turned around and looked over the top of the Mira's two-story house. The sun was starting to get lower in the sky, and the breeze was warm. He turned around and looked at the tall trees flanking the back fence of the yard. Some were narrow, others had thicker trunks, but they all swayed gently in the breeze. Agent Locke exhaled deeply as he walked back toward the house.

CHAPTER THIRTEEN
Maple Syrup

Arec and Jacque walked around the side of the house and out into the front yard. They squinted in the warm afternoon sunlight. "Jacque, we've got a really big problem. Those guys are not from the office," whispered Arec. He turned to see if the agents were watching them from any of the windows in the house.

Jacque also looked nervously toward the house. "Yeah, you were right about the lip-reading, I'll give you that, but the lights turned green on their id badges," said Jacque. "They checked out, right?"

"That only proves that they have agent status. They may have gone bad," said Arec. "And no. I'm not paranoid."

Jacque couldn't dispute that. Arec was almost always rational. "Ok, fine. How do the id badges know that they are agents?" asked Jacque. "Checks their fingerprints somehow?"

"Nope," said Arec. "There's some sort of chemical in their blood that the card detects."

Arec looked back toward the door. A chill ran down his back. He could now barely see the silhouette of the two agents walking around behind one of the front windows. "Something else I noticed," said Arec, "Agent Neese has gone to some trouble to remove what could be blood stains on his shirt and sleeve."

"Who's blood?" asked Jacque.

"Think about it, Jacque."

"Mom and dad's?"

"Don't know. I need some maple syrup," said Arec.

"What?" whispered Jacque. "Are you hungry?"

"No," said Arec. "Maple is the reagent for the chemical in the agents' blood."

"Oh yeah, of course," said Jacque sarcastically. "What the heck is a reagent?"

"It's something you use to cause a reaction to occur with something else," said Arec. "You use it to validate the presence of a particular substance. In this case, maple will reveal the presence of the blood of an agent."

Jacque laughed, and then frowned. "Wait, you're serious? How do you know that?" he said.

"Grandma and grandpa," said Arec. "Didn't you ever pay attention to what they taught us?"

"So, you don't think it's mom and dad's blood?" asked Jacque.

"Jacque, you were right to wonder where the other agents are," said Arec, "The agents that are supposed to be here protecting us."

"Well, yeah," said Jacque proudly, "I was right 'cause I'm not lame. Also, I'm starting to think that mom and dad were into a bit more than publishing educational books."

"It's pretty clear they never had anything to do with book publishing at all," said Arec. "All I've been able to dig up is something about a rocket handbook."

"So, you think that maybe Neese is looking for that?" asked Jacque. "He wants to build a rocket? That doesn't make any sense."

"I agree," said Arec. "Maybe it's a code name for one of mom and dad's projects that they never wanted to talk about. I thought that they'd start letting me in on more details on their trip, but that obviously isn't happening."

"Ok, this whole thing just seems so far-fetched. It all smacks of lame-ness," said Jacque, shaking his head. He put his hand on Arec's shoulder. "Dude, mom and dad are pretty smart and resourceful. They do that Crab Magoo, and Katmandu, or whatever. They can kick butt. I'm sure they're ok." said Jacque, but his expression started to show concern.

"It's Krav Maga and Tae Kwon Do," said Arec, "And no, they're not ok," said Arec. "These so-called agents did something to mom and dad, and I think we're next."

"Ok, we need to settle down and think, Arec," said Jacque. "What would mom and dad have done to warn us? They must have tried something, right?"

Arec felt a cold sweat. He nervously ran his fingers through his hair. "I don't know," said Arec.

"So, why would our grandparents possibly have wanted to develop a reagent for agent blood?" asked Jacque.

"It's meant as a way of identifying them if their blood is found, I guess." said Arec.

"I don't get it. Who would need to identify the blood of an agent?" asked Jacque. "Just to verify that they aren't lame-os posing as real agents? Doesn't seem to be working too well for us."

"They've gone to a lot of trouble to try and fool us into thinking that they're legit." said Arec.

"But, why do we even need agents?" asked Jacque. "Why did grandma and grandpa? Why do mom and dad?"

"Jacque, what if Neese and Locke killed the agents that are supposed to be here, and then they took their place," said Arec. "I think that the stains on Neese's shirt are blood stains from the real agents." He frowned and looked at Jacque. "Could also be from mom or dad."

"Yeah, I get what you're saying, but I still think that's a pretty paranoid theory you've got there," said Jacque, seeming now to be a bit more nervous. "If you're right, what do we do now?"

"I don't know. Let's rule out the agent theory first," said Arec.

"And just how do we do that?" asked Jacque. "Arec, we've gotta call the police or something."

"No way. They're agents. They're monitoring any transmission to and from this area." said Arec. "You know that. We'd be dead or gone before they'd even get here."

"If your suspicions are right, that is," said Jacque. "I think you're being paranoid."

"If I'm wrong, why do we need to call the police?" asked Arec.

"Oh yeah," said Jacque. "Ok, this whole thing is just lame. Our family sucks. I hate agents. What's your plan with the maple syrup?"

"When we go inside, let's go to the kitchen," said Arec. "When I distract them, you grab the maple syrup container on the counter. Go to the sink, and fill it mostly up with water. Close it and shake it up quietly. When I give you the signal, throw it to me and I'll take care of the rest. If I'm right, we'll know pretty quick if Neese has traces of agent blood on him." Arec smiled.

Jacque grimaced. "If you're right? How will we know? He's gonna beat the crap out of us! I don't like that guy at all. There's something about Neese that scares the crap outta me. Your plan sounds lame."

"I don't know what the reagent does, but the reaction is supposed to be instant and obvious." said Arec.

"Ok, but if we get killed, I blame you," said Jacque. He was starting to freak out, but still kept his sense of humor. Arec knew that he would have to lean on Jacque quite a bit. He was glad that he wasn't alone.

As they turned and walked back toward the house, the agents could no longer be seen through the window. I wonder if we'll ever make it out of this alive, thought Arec. Agents are highly trained and can do things normal people can't even imagine doing.

As they walked back toward the house, Arec remembered an incident when he was only six. He'd lost control of his bike and rode straight into a busy road. It happened while their parents were away and the agents were in charge. Arec couldn't stop his bike. He saw a large truck speeding down the road. When he tried to stop, he fell off his bike in the middle of the road. Just as the truck was about to hit him, an agent flew in out of nowhere and snatched him right up off the road and then set him down on the other side of the road. They found out later that the truck's brakes had failed. It slammed into a huge oak tree in front of the neighbor's place and burst into flames. The agent didn't have a scratch. Arec remembered looking up and seeing the agent's smile as he dusted him off and checked for injuries.

Neither Neese nor Locke has that smile, thought Arec.

"I don't know if I'm up to this," said Jacque. "Those agent guys are lame, but they're also scary."

"We'll be ok." he said. "Just keep an eye on me."

"Yeah? Who's gonna keep an eye on us?" asked Jacque. "We're on our own, dude."

As they approached the house, the sunlight beamed through the tops of several tall trees in the back yard. Arec noticed a quick flash of light from the top of one of the taller trees. "Did you see that up there?" asked Arec.

"See what?" asked Jacque.

"A flash in the trees." said Arec.

"Didn't see it. Maybe just a bird or a plane." said Jacque.

Arec and Jacque casually strolled through the front door. The house seemed lifeless and dim. Arec paused and looked around. I've really enjoyed this place, he thought. It's been nice. A lot of good memories. I'm going to miss it. Something definitely seemed wrong, out of place. Also, all of the blinds were shut, but a breeze could be felt throughout the house.

"Come on, let's go eat some breakfast for lunch. I'm starving," said Jacque. He winked. Arec smiled, but he wasn't hungry. "Yeah, sounds good."

Agent Neese had prepared a pot of coffee while they were outside. The smell of roasted beans filled the kitchen. "Welcome back. Ready for a late lunch?" asked Neese as he leaned back and casually brought a white mug to his lips. He seemed confident and relaxed, as if he knew something that Arec and Jacque did not.

Arec knew in an instant that Neese had again been lip reading their conversation. Arec didn't look to Jacque but could sense that Jacque was thinking the same thing. How much of our conversation did they read? thought Arec. He scrolled back through his memory, analyzing which way they had faced in front of the house. Another cold chill swept over him as he realized that with some effort, Neese and Locke could have read their entire conversation. We have to get out of here, thought Arec. Running isn't an option, not yet anyway.

Jacque looked nervous. His stomach rumbled in the quiet room. Jacque looked sheepishly at Neese. "Yeah, I'm down with some of that leftover breakfast food," said Jacque. He always got hungry when he was nervous. It was quite the opposite with Arec.

Arec sat down at the kitchen island and filled his plate with a stack of now cold rubbery pancakes. The smell of breakfast lingered in the room. The bacon was gone, just pancakes.

Neese was facing Arec, leaning against the stove flipping a coin between his knuckles. One corner of his mouth was turned up in a wry smile. Locke was sitting next to Arec, and still reading the comics page of the morning paper and chuckling. The afternoon sun shined through the window behind them, flooding the room with natural light. New details now seemed more obvious than before with Neese. Lines and creases on his face became more noticeable, as well as bags under his eyes. He also had a general sense of animosity that seemed to grow with each minute. Neese just stood there and glared at Arec.

Locke seemed blithely unaware of Neese's growing aggressiveness. Probably the classic good-cop, bad-cop thing, thought Arec. He tried to focus on his food and ignore Neese's stares. He could hear Jacque behind him at the sink rinsing some dishes. The water seemed to run for an eternity. Something was definitely wrong with Neese. Locke seemed strangely peaceful. As the sound of running water ceased, Arec knew that Jacque was ready with the syrup container. I hope this works, thought Arec. He tried not to think about what might happen to them if they failed.

Neese's coin flipping paused. "You gonna stare at those hot cakes for the rest of the afternoon, kid?". He chuckled and continued to flip around his coin.

"Jacque, can you pass me the syrup?" asked Arec.

"Sure thing," he answered. He tossed it to Arec.

Neese rolled his eyes but then without a second's warning was showered with watered down maple syrup. It sprayed all over his face and the front of his shirt and sleeves.

Arec was still holding the now mostly empty container of syrup like a cannon when Neese spun around and knocked it out of his hand, simultaneously forcing Arec's face against the countertop with a paralyzing arm hold. Arec gasped in pain while Neese started to choke him with his other hand.

Locke leisurely folded the newspaper and stood next to Neese, folding his arms. He yawned and smiled.

"Let him go!" yelled Jacque.

Neese sneered and stood back. Arec gasped and coughed violently. He glared up at Neese from across the kitchen island.

Neese was surprisingly calm as he slowly and deliberately ran his long fingers through his hair. "Well, now that was very unwise," said Neese, not aware of the bright yellow splatter and smear marks that were starting to appear all over the front of his shirt and up one sleeve.

Bingo, thought Arec. Jacque just stood there in amazement.

The room was completely silent except for the hum of the refrigerator and the faint sound of a jet flying overhead. Locke was still folding his arms as he looked carefully at Neese.

Neese ran his hand across the front of his shirt and looked at the sticky watered-down syrup on his palm. He raised his arm and inspected the yellow marks all over his sleeve. He smiled and wiped his hands off on a wet dish rag. "So, young Mr. Mira. Did you get the intel you were looking for?" asked Neese. "Just what exactly did you think that little stunt would accomplish?"

"Well," said Jacque, "Now we know for sure that you're truly, radically, lame."

Neese didn't even seem to hear Jacque. His expression almost seemed mechanical. He keeps his emotions in check very well, thought Arec, but I can still see the hatred in his eyes. He took out the other agents, and he will continue to kill until he gets what he wants. His aggression reveals weakness. Mom and dad always said that an aggressive person always loses ground. I just hope he loses a ton of ground before he kills Jacque and me.

"I know that you killed the real agents." said Arec.

"You assume too much. You have no idea what you're getting yourself into, kid," said Neese. He grabbed a wet washcloth off the counter, leaned back against the stove, and casually started to wipe the sticky mess from his shirt.

"What did you do to our parents?" asked Jacque.

"I have no interest in speaking to you," said Neese. "As far as I'm concerned, you should already be dead. You shouldn't even be here." He looked to Locke who swiftly pulled out his gun, but kept it aimed at the floor.

"Wait," said Arec. It was now clear to Arec that they viewed Jacque as expendable. Arec knew they'd try and use him for leverage. He couldn't let anything happen to Jacque. Mom and dad, where are you? thought Arec. He looked up and glared at Neese. "What do you want?"

Neese just kept looking down at his shirt as he wiped up watered-down maple syrup. "I will assume control of your parents' work. I will take everything," answered Neese. "After I've extracted all codes and any other intel from you that I need, I'll eliminate you, just like I did your grandparents. Then I'll finish off your parents."

"Ah, so they're alive." said Arec.

"Alive, for now." said Neese.

Arec could tell he was bluffing about his parents. "And what if I refuse?" said Arec.

"Oh, I'm not concerned about that," said Neese. He glanced over at Jacque as he continued to wipe off his shirt. "Your lame-o brother there will be a quivering mess on the floor, begging for you to tell me whatever I want to know."

Arec knew Neese wasn't bluffing about Jacque.

CHAPTER FOURTEEN

Odd Man Out

"Arec," said Jacque, "Don't worry about me. Just don't give the lame-o what he wants." Jacque tried to act tough, but Arec knew that he was terrified.

Neese smirked, then threw the wet washcloth he had been using up into the air. In a blur, he then struck Arec in the face and in a second blinding strike, thrust his palm forward. Arec flew backward through the air, knocked over a chair, and hit the edge of the dining room table.

Neese held out his hand and caught the washcloth as it fell back down through the air. He continued to wipe down his shirt. The cold grin on his face hinted that Neese had waited a long time to do that.

"Leave him alone!" said Jacque. He reached down to help Arec up. Arec propped himself up as he struggled to breathe. Blood ran from the corner of his mouth.

"So, young Mr. Mira, I'll make it very simple for you," said Neese. "Hand over everything you know and cooperate, and I'll spare your parents' lives. I may even let your brother live as well."

"No, you won't," he said. Arec stood up straight and stared back at Neese. The pain in his chest and the side of his face was excruciating. "You did something to my parents, but I don't think you know where they are," said Arec. "You want me to cooperate? Try telling the truth for once."

"Fine," said Neese. "How about this. You cooperate, and I won't kill Jacque."

Arec wiped the side of his mouth where he'd been hit and looked at the smear of blood left behind on his arm. He felt different than he ever had before. With a strange feeling of confidence, the situation now seemed clearer. Adrenalin coursed through Arec's veins, and at the same time memories of his grandparents' training flooded his mind. Everything depends on me now, thought Arec. He fought to suppress his panic. The side of his face where he'd been hit throbbed with pain. Neese did something to my parents, and they might need help, he thought.

Arec knew that it would be a mistake to let Neese see any fear or weakness. He casually walked back to the kitchen island and sat down on the same stool he had been sitting on directly across the counter from Neese, who continued to wipe off his uniform shirt.

Locke still stood a few feet from Neese near the stove. He had been quietly watching as he fiddled with a toothpick in his mouth. Arec noticed that his expression was a bit more serious now and that he was watching Arec and Jacque very closely.

"You're no agent. You're too sloppy, Neese." said Arec. "And Jacque's right. You're extremely lame."

Neese glared at Arec and laughed. "So I've heard," said Neese. He seemed surprised at Arec's confidence. Neese dropped the washcloth to the floor and smiled. "I heard that you're a child prodigy, some sort of genius," said Neese. "If you really were that smart, you'd know by now that there's no possibility of a happy ending for you." He paused slightly, revealing a hint of uncertainty. Neese was worried about something but tried to conceal his concern. He could tell that Arec could see right through him and that angered him even more. Neese's hint of doubt gave way to resolve as he leaned forward across the counter and stared at Arec. "I don't think you're very smart at all. Just a punk kid," said Neese. "Apparently I need to be clearer with my intentions." He arched back and twisted sideways, bringing one arm back to swing while he lowered the other to simultaneously unholster his sidearm. As Neese raised his weapon in a swift fluid motion, his expression betrayed the anger he had been trying to hide.

Arec analyzed every one of Neese's movements. Everything around him seemed to slow down, but he seemed to be able to move much more quickly. His mind started to race. There were so many things he hadn't noticed until now, and it all started to come together. No introduction from his parents, the look on Neese's face when they first met, the way Neese spoke and moved, Neese's surprise at Jacque's arrival, Neese's messed up and sweaty hair, torn clothing, evidence of a major struggle in the yard, the suspicious ID cards, the signal from the tree tops, the opened blinds over the kitchen sink, and proof that there was the blood of another agent all over Neese's shirt.

All of the facts strung themselves together into a scenario that Neese apparently had not considered. Arec thought of that signal he had seen in the top of the tree as they were walking back into the house. Maybe one of those agents, sent to help him, was still alive. Maybe he had just been waiting for the right moment to make his move. That agent could turn the tables on Neese and remove him from the equation, that is if he wasn't too beat up to do something. Either way, if that possibility was real, it would play out at any moment. Somehow he knew that there was no better time than now. Arec calculated all of the bits of evidence and data. He started to see the bigger picture. What might seem crazy was actually the only rational explanation.

Still, something wasn't quite right. Arec watched in slow motion as Neese continued to move his firearm, not toward him, but toward Jacque. Arec had to move faster. From his memory, he measured the distance from the house to where he and Jacque had been standing earlier out in the front yard. He then estimated the height of the tall tree behind the house where he'd seen the flash. He calculated a vector from the top of the tree to the window over the sink, which lined up pretty well with where Neese now stood in front of him. Neese would never know what hit him, or who hit him, thought Arec. Neese was about to fix his aim on Jacque; only a few tenths of a second left. That's it, thought Arec. I'm blocking the target. When I move out of the way, the other agent will have a clear shot. The only question is Locke. What will he do? Arec hated that he had to respond this way to Neese, but his hand had been forced. Jacque would die if he didn't act, and Arec couldn't afford to pass up a chance to have Neese removed. Knowing that Neese was about to die, Arec decided to focus his attention instead on Locke. The rest would just have to play out on its own. It was out of his hands.

Time was up and Neese was starting to pull on the trigger. Arec swiveled on his stool and laid down sideways so that his torso was at the same level as the counter top. The target was now clear. Just as Arec dropped down, a cracking sound rang through the room followed by another shot from Neese, then silence. Neese just stood there, his stare now empty but fixed forward as if Arec was still sitting across the counter from him. Neese's arm went limp and his gun fell to the floor. He staggered backward, hit the stove and dropped lifeless to the floor.

Jacque knocked over a glass of orange juice on the table as he stumbled backward from the table. "What the crap?" he said. For Jacque, Neese's strike at Arec, their brief exchange, and then Neese hitting the ground had just taken a few seconds. Jacque backed up against the wall, then looked down and noticed the fresh bullet hole in the table top just a few feet from where he'd been sitting. His face was pale. Jacque's surprised reaction had drawn Locke's attention long enough to buy Arec a few precious seconds. Arec suddenly found himself at the base of the kitchen island, holding Neese's gun. He was aiming it at Locke.

Locke immediately aimed his gun at Arec. His expression was a mixture of shock and amazement.

Arec scanned the scene before him long enough to assess what had happened. Neese was laying face up on the floor in an unnatural pose. His lifeless eyes stared blankly at the ceiling. A neat hole had been made in his forehead, and from that hole, a thin red stream started to drip down the side of his face. Another wound was visible near the center of his chest. Two expertly-placed instant-kill shots, but somehow Neese had still been able to fire a single shot at Jacque. It was a close call.

Jacque was still trying to figure out what had happened. "What did you do, Arec?" asked Jacque. "Or was it Locke? What happened to Neese? How did you get over there so fast?"

To Arec, Locke now seemed oddly relaxed as he kept his gun aimed at him. He could easily eliminate me, thought Arec, but then he wouldn't be able to get any of the information out of me that Neese had wanted. If Locke goes for Jacque, I could eliminate him. It was clear that Locke was now backed into the proverbial corner. Then again, Locke gave no indication that it was an unfavorable situation.

"Arec!" said Jacque. "What do you think you're doing? Do you know how to use that thing? Shoot him!"

Locke's expression was still and calculated. He kept his aim on Arec. "Jacque, Arec is quite capable with a gun," said Locke. He kept his stare on Arec. "Isn't that right, Mr. Mira?" asked Locke.

"I–I'm not sure," said Arec, shaking his head slightly. More memories of the time with his grandparents flooded back into his mind. "What do you mean?" A horrible ache started to rip through the top of his head.

"Arec," said Locke, "How did you do that?"

"What, Neese? No, I didn't shoot him," said Arec. He kept Neese's gun aimed at Locke, and tried to shake off the headache.

"No, not that. You passed right through the kitchen island," said Locke.

"How did Arec do... what?" asked Jacque. He turned to Arec. "What's going on? What the heck is Locke talking about?"

Locke paused and then glared at Arec. "There was no time for you to dive to the floor, crawl around that island, and then grab Neese's gun," said Locke. He turned to Jacque. "Arec somehow went right through the four-foot wide kitchen island." He was going to continue, but stopped and stared past Jacque at the wall, suddenly realizing how ridiculous all of that sounded. Locke turned again and glared at Arec. "How did you get Neese's gun so quickly?"

"I don't know, Locke," said Arec. "But I didn't kill Neese. I know you didn't do it either." Arec's stare now pierced Locke. "Was it the other agent?"

"Very good," said Locke, smiling. "The other agent needed a clear shot." Locke looked briefly to the window over the kitchen sink.

Arec looked at the window as well. Even though the blinds had been closed all around the house, someone had opened the blinds over the sink. Rays of sun beamed through the window, warming the room. The signal in the trees was for Locke, thought Arec. It was Locke who opened the blinds before we came back into the house. It had to be Locke. He had opened the blinds to provide the other agent with a clear shot at Neese.

"Who needed a clear shot?" Jacque asked. He was still composing himself. "What other agent are you talking about?"

Arec relaxed his aim on Locke, stood up, and walked over to the window. He fingered the hole in the now broken glass pane in the kitchen window and stared out into the backyard and up into the tall trees. "Agent Locke, I'm not sure what's going on. Maybe you can explain," said Arec.

Locke kept his gun aimed at Arec.

Jacque was about to ask a question when Arec interrupted. He knew what Jacque was going to ask. "Jacque," said Arec. "Locke's junior partner is out there - the one Neese thought he had eliminated." Arec turned and casually walked over to Locke who was now aiming at Arec's head.

Jacque was confused. "Then, what about–"

"–Agent Locke?" said Arec. "We also know that Agent Locke is not from the office." Arec smirked at Locke. "We already knew that."

"We did? How did we know that? Dude, you were just as clueless as me." said Jacque.

"Jacque, I tried to explain that to you earlier." said Arec.

Jacque sat down. "Whatever, just forget it. So, are you just going to let him shoot us? You could have taken him out."

"I think that Locke is here to help us," said Arec. "Otherwise, we'd already be dead."

Jacque sneered at Locke. "Yeah right," he said, "He's probably just playing us, like Neese."

"Jacque, he could have taken you out, but he didn't." Arec placed his hand on Locke's gun. "Agent Locke, somehow you are the agent that has been assigned to me, I'm just not sure how." Arec smiled and rattled off a long string of numbers and letters.

"That's enough," said Locke, "Only needed the first twenty-four characters in that authorization code." Locke lowered his sidearm. "You got that code from your grandparents, didn't you?" he asked.

"They taught it to me using a weird phrase." said Arec, "It just popped into my head."

"I recommend that you get out of the habit of saying things out loud that pop into your head," said Locke. He holstered his gun and straightened his shirt. "Neese was a real agent, but also a real enemy to your family. He was working for someone. I have been trying to find out who for a long time, ever since Neese started to work for your parents. He was highly trusted and very dangerous. You and Jacque are both very fortunate that you're still alive." said Locke. "I had hoped to learn more before his elimination."

"So, Neese knew our parents well?" asked Arec. "What about you?"

Locke paused and smiled. He looked down at Neese's body and sighed loudly. "I knew your grandparents, and I know your parents," he said. "As did my father."

"They never mentioned the name Locke." said Arec.

"Locke, how can we trust you?" asked Jacque. "How do we know you're not just pulling a Neese on us?"

As Locke walked up to Jacque, he again stumbled backward and hit the wall. Locke smiled and stopped. "Jacque, your parents died when you were two years old. The Puerto Rican government agreed to put you in the Mira's protective care shortly thereafter. You are now twenty-one years old, you have a scar on the back of your left leg, your favorite color is purple, and you love tuna on your pizza."

"Ok, so what?" said Jacque. "Where did the scar on my leg come from then?" He looked nervously at Arec and back at Locke.

"We don't have time for this, boys," said Locke.

"There's a lot to do."

"Don't be lame," said Jacque, "I wanna be sure. You can't blame us for being nervous."

"Fine. When you were nine you cut your leg while climbing under a chain link fence during school," said Locke. "I was the really young junior agent sent to pick you up and I also treated your leg."

"That was you?" asked Jacque. "So, answer this then, what was I given when I was picked up from the school?"

Locke smiled. "A red white and blue popsicle. You liked it because it was patriotic. You held it up and started to sing the national anthem." said Locke. "Are we done?"

Arec remembered earlier how Locke had offered the same kind of popsicle as a treat. A signal for us from Locke? thought Arec. Brilliant. Perhaps Locke was trying to tip-off Jacque.

"Holy crap. Yeah. I haven't thought about that for a long time." said Jacque. His brief smile turned again to a sneer and he pointed at Locke. "So, why didn't you help us?"

"I did help you. You're still alive, aren't you?" said Locke. "Also, it was your parents who told me to keep an eye out for trouble. My investigation led me right to the guy who had gained your parent's trust. They had suspected that there was a mole, leaking information. Sure enough, it turned out to be Neese."

"And it was my parents who called for you, right?" asked Arec.

"Yes, that's correct," said Locke. He paused and frowned. "Listen, your mom was in rough shape by the time I arrived. I just couldn't get the word to your parents about Neese fast enough."

Locke again looked at the lifeless body of Neese on the floor. He pulled out a knife and swiftly cut through the fabric of Neese's right sleeve and tore it down. Underneath was a pearly-white skin-tight fabric. Two yellow stripes around his arm were clearly visible, and they were pulsing. "Captain," said Locke grimly.

"What? Captain who?" asked Jacque.

"Neese was the captain." said Locke.

"Captain of what?" asked Arec.

"Captain of the starship lame-o." said Jacque.

"You boys are in a lot of danger," said Locke. "Arec, Neese is nothing compared the guy who wants to get his hands on you. Neese was his right-hand guy. We need to get ready to leave. They're already on their way."

"Wait," said Arec. "Who? Who's on their way? And what about my parents. Where are they?"

"Arec, I can't explain right now. You have to trust me," said Locke.

"We're not going anywhere until you tell us what happened to our parents," said Arec. "How's my dad? Is my mom alive? Tell me. That's an order."

Locke looked nervously at his watch and back at Arec. "Your father is fine. Your mother is, well, she's still pretty injured," said Locke. "Like I said, by the time I got here, Neese had beat her up pretty badly."

"Where did they go?" asked Jacque. "Why didn't they take Arec with them?"

"They were lucky to get away," said Locke. "Your mom was losing a lot of blood. Neese had us against a wall." Locke looked at them and frowned. "Your dad made the call, and I think he made the right call. He knew I would be here to take care of Arec. Jacque, we didn't plan on you showing up."

"Yeah, I never plan on Jacque either," said Arec. "He always seems to show up at unexpected times."

Jacque punched Arec in the arm. "Dude, you're lame. You should just always plan on my random, unpredictable appearances," said Jacque. "You know how much I love my single, spontaneous life."

"Well, time for a lifestyle change," said Locke. "That is, if you want to live."

"What is it with everyone preaching at me today?" whispered Jacque.

"Agent Locke, who is coming?" asked Arec. "Why do they want me so badly?"

"Why don't you tell me how you flew right through that kitchen island?" asked Locke. "You need to be straight with me if I'm to effectively protect you boys."

"I already told you that I have no idea what you're talking about." said Arec.

Locke peered at Arec skeptically, and back at Jacque who shrugged innocently. "We have a little time, since Neese's men didn't plan their next move to happen until later tonight," said Locke. "See those pulsing yellow bands on Neese's arm?"

"That's a signal for others to come?" asked Jacque.

"That's right," said Locke. "So, we've got to get out of here."

"Go where? What's the plan?" asked Arec.

"I need to get you boys to the checkpoint," said Locke. "Welcome to your first assignment, Mr. Mira. Not quite how anyone planned to get you rolling, but we'll just make the best of it. No more training exercises. This one's for real."

"What about that other agent?" asked Jacque.

Locke smiled. "My partner? Yeah, he's about to come through that door."

Just as Locke turned around, a badly beaten man in a torn and dirty agent uniform pushed open the door. One of his eyes was swollen shut. He also limped badly and one arm was twisted in an unnatural direction. Blood covered his uniform and he was very pale. He had a large sniper rifle slung over his shoulder and aimed a handgun at Arec.

"He's already been cleared," said Locke, "Stand down."

The badly injured agent looked around. When he saw Locke, he collapsed on the hardwood floor.

Locke picked up the agent and placed him carefully on the dining room table. "I'll tend to him," said Locke. "You two better get ready to leave. Arec, better start remembering those exercises. Things may get dicey until your ride out of here is ready."

"Ride?" asked Arec. "Like, a car?"

"Nope, not like that. It's upstairs in your parents' closet," said Locke.

"What's in their closet? Bicycles? Jet packs?" asked Arec.

"I'll show you in a minute. Some method of escape that your folks came up with," said Locke. "My hands are full here." He started to apply some first aid to the other agent. "Neese's guys are probably still expecting a communication or status from him. At the very least, Neese's death triggered an alert. We've gotta hurry."

"Yeah, I think we understand that." Arec drew Neese's gun.

Jacque stepped away from Arec. "What are you doing with that? Guess it will come in handy, right?" asked

Jacque nervously. "Maybe we could fire off a few rounds in the back yard, you know, for practice?"

"Nope." Arec spun it 45 degrees, and inspected the handle and then the underside of the barrel. With one hand, he ejected the clip and all of the rounds. He then spun it back around, cracked it on the counter, and removed the barrel and spring. A small pill-shaped device fell out from behind the spring. He dropped all of the pieces onto the floor next to Neese's body and stepped on the pill, crushing it to pieces. It made a snapping sound and started to smoke. "Don't want to have anything left behind from that guy," said Arec. "You never know what he may have rigged."

Jacque stared at the pile of parts and rounds scattered on the floor. "Arec, how did you do that? What was that thing?" he asked.

"A transmitter," said Locke. "Arec, you're starting to remember some things?" he asked.

"I don't know, maybe," said Arec. "Grandpa used to time me to see how fast I could take one of those guns apart and put it back together. Pretty much the same kind of gun, actually."

"Yeah, but how did you know what that pill thing was?" asked Jacque.

"It just seemed logical that there would be a tracking device in his gun; that whoever Neese worked for would want to track him," said Arec, "I would." Arec looked at Locke. "So, I guess I'm making the call then."

"That's right," said Locke, smiling proudly. "It's your call now. I'm here to help. We've got a few things to do in a short amount of time. I recommend that you eat something while you can."

"Sounds like a plan," said Arec. "So, how long do we have?"

Locke paused, and the other agent groaned with pain. "Well, the ride won't be recharged for two hours."

"Recharged? What kind of rides could there possibly be in a closet? Are they rechargeable bikes? Scooters?" asked Arec.

"Their closet isn't very big," said Jacque. "You could maybe fit a few bicycles, but certainly not a motorcycle."

"No, it's nothing close to what you're thinking," said Locke. "Listen, I gotta fix up my partner here. We'll likely have company within the hour," said Locke. "We need options until the ride is ready. Any ideas?"

"Well, I have no idea what kind of ride you're talking about, but we can use our parent's car." said Arec.

"Shouldn't we call for help?" asked Jacque.

Locke started sewing some stitches on the other agent. He placed a rolled up rag in his mouth for him to bite down on. "Jacque," said Locke, "Can you please hand me the small spray bottle in the top of that first aid kit?"

Arec was getting impatient. "Well, other than running, I can't think of anything else," he said.

"We can't outrun them, and calling the authorities would be an extraordinarily bad idea," said Locke. "They'd never stand a chance and we've got to keep all of this contained." Locke stopped, snapped off a piece of cabinet moulding, and held it up to the other agent's leg. He looked at the agent then took the rolled up rag out of his mouth. "Had better days, Agent Cooley?"

"This is only my eighth field assignment," said Cooley in a hoarse voice. "You'll need to reset the bones before applying a splint."

"Yes, of course," said Locke. He placed the rag back into Cooley's mouth. "On three."

Cooley grasped onto the sides of the table and screamed as Locke pulled swiftly on his ankle and then twisted. A loud popping sound could be heard. With his good arm, Cooley gripped the table so hard that he broke off part of the edging around the table. "Sorry, Agent Cooley," said Locke. He placed the splint and turned to Arec and Jacque, who were both staring at Locke in shock. Cooley spat out the rag and lowered himself from the table. He seemed to suddenly be doing much better, but was still in rough shape.

"Whoa. Never seen that before," said Jacque.

"Yeah, and never wanna see that again," said Arec. "So, mom and dad's car, then?"

"Sounds like that's our best option," said Locke. "We'll lead them away, provide a distraction, and you guys can circle back. By then the tube will be recharged."

"Tube? Recharged?" asked Jacque. "What tube?"

Locke smiled. "I don't know much about it. It's some sort of a fluid-filled tube that enables high-speed transport."

"What the heck are you talking about?" asked Jacque.

"In mom and dad's closet?" blurted Arec. "I've been in that closet enough to know that there's nothing in there but a bunch of old stuff."

"I'll let your folks explain," said Locke impatiently. "It's their closet, their tube. I never liked the idea, but it is an emergency."

"Their tube? Why can't you explain?" asked Jacque.

Locke sighed. "Because I don't know!" he growled. "Listen, I'm not supposed to know. Got it?"

After Locke finished setting Cooley's broken arm, he sat up on the table. "Listen, guys. Agent Locke is right. The first objective is to get you to the checkpoint. We'll make sure you get there in one piece, or die trying."

"Ok, that's it," said Arec. "What is worth dying for here? You guys gotta give us something to work on."

Cooley looked at Locke.

"Ok, but you have to understand that the more you know, the more danger you'll be in," said Locke. "And your folks would not like that."

"I dcn't care, Agent Locke." said Arec.

"Ok," said Locke, "All I know is that your grandparents chose you to carry on their work after your parents. They chose you to succeed your parents in guarding some pretty extremely sensitive research. That research must be kept frcm people like Neese at all cost." said Locke. He leaned closer to Arec. "You have been trained for this job your whole life, and it's my job to protect you."

"Any idea why my parents never thought to mention any of that?" asked Arec.

"Yeak," said Jacque, "That doesn't make any sense. We never really knew anything about what our parents or grandpaents did."

"Sorry. What I've said is all I know about that," said Locke. "Those who hunt you believe that they have noble and good intentions. They will never stop. They will die trying to find you, and I will die if needed to protect you."

"But why?" asked Arec. "I just don't understand what this is all about," said Arec. He started to walk away.

"Mr. Mira," said Locke. Arec stopped but didn't turn around. "When you get up in the morning, what gives you hope?" he asked.

"Hope? My parents, my grandparents. My family gives me hope, but now they're all disappearing." said Arec.

"Yes, of course," said Locke. "What else?"

Arec turned around and glared at Locke. "I hope that someday my nightmares will go away." Arec's shoulders drooped and his head hung down. "I hope that our parents are ok and that we'll see our grandparents again."

"Well, let's see if we can make all of that happen, shall we?" said Locke.

"What kind of research are we really talking about here?" asked Arec. "What were they researching?"

"No one knows. Not yet anyway," said Cooley. "We've been hoping that you would be the one who'd know all of that."

"But how?" asked Jacque.

Locke smiled. "All in good time, Mr. Mira. First step, the checkpoint. At the checkpoint, you'll receive a book." said Locke. "A very different book. Your father said that he would make arrangements for you to get it."

"Let me guess, a rocket handbook?" asked Arec.

Locke smiled and looked at Cooley. "That's what your folks called it," said Locke, "I guess they've already mentioned it then?"

Arec smiled. "Well, not sure I was supposed to hear it when they said it," he said. "I asked for more information, but they refused. They just always passed it off as unimportant and changed the subject."

"Agent Locke," said Jacque, "Were they building a rocket?"

"Not sure," said Locke. He looked down at Neese's body. "One thing I do know. Neese was looking for that book. I thought that I could keep the situation here under control as long as he didn't find it, but I was wrong."

"I really complicated stuff, didn't I?" said Jacque.

"Well, yes. But thanks to you Jacque, Arec's not in this alone," said Locke. "And thanks to your buddies at work, you're still alive. Neese wouldn't tell me, but I'm pretty sure he was waiting for you to return home last night so he could get rid of you."

"Well, it seems like a lot of his plans didn't turn out his way," said Jacque. "I'm glad he wasn't able to do more damage than he did."

Agent Locke frowned. "The night is young, boys."

CHAPTER FIFTEEN

Company

The sun was going down and the shadows lengthened. A slightly cooler breeze blew through the house. Arec held up his hand and wiggled his fingers in the breeze. "Agent Locke, why did Neese open all the windows?"

"Neese wanted to be able to hear outside," said Locke. "Not sure why. He was spooked by something."

"He was bluffing about our parents," said Arec. "Maybe he thought they'd come back with reinforcements."

"Perhaps," said Locke. "We could certainly use their help."

"So, agent Locke, what can you tell us about the soldiers that are coming?" asked Arec.

"You already know better than anyone," said Locke. "I understand that you've seen them before." Arec put his hands in his pockets and started to walk out of the room. "Arec, stop. I know this is uncomfortable, but we need to talk about what happened when your grandparents disappeared," said Locke.

"My parents never wanted to talk about any of that."

said Arec.

Cooley didn't break his stare through the rifle scope. "Now would be a good time for some intel, Mr. Mira," he said. "Something's not right out there. Too quiet, so dark, and there's something wrong in the breeze."

"It was a long time ago," said Arec. "It was dark. I was running away. I never even got to say goodbye to them."

"Arec," said Locke, "Please try to remember. Anything will help."

"All of the lights were off," said Arec. "There were small beams of light everywhere, dropping out of the sky and coming up from the cliffs below."

"Your grandparents villa. What happened to it?" asked Locke. "Did your grandparents warn you of anything?"

"It all happened so fast." Arec looked uncomfortable. "I don't know. Maybe they said something. I don't remember." he said. Arec stared at the floor and closed his eyes. "There was a pulsing sound," said Arec. "I heard it several times after the lights showed up."

Locke frowned and looked at Cooley, whose attention was now focussed on their conversation.

Cooley slowly lowered his rifle and turned to Locke. "Sounds like the guys we ran into a few years ago," he said.

"So, what did you guys do?" asked Jacque.

"We ran," said Locke. "We couldn't see them. They were cloaked somehow." He pulled out his gun and checked the clip. "We should get ready to go."

"So, our plan B is the car?" asked Jacque. "You said we have about thirty minutes, right?"

"That was ten minutes ago," said Locke. "Mr. Mira, we need to turn off all of the lights. Can you and Jacque do that? We're going to keep a lookout for guests."

Arec and Jacque ran around the house turning off lights and opening blinds. When they got to the top of the stairs, they stopped. "Do you smell that?" asked Arec.

"Smell what?" asked Jacque as he stuck out his nose, looked around and sniffed.

"Carpet cleaner, kinda bleachy too," said Arec. He knelt down and smelled the carpet. "It's been pretty thoroughly cleaned."

"Big deal," said Jacque. "Maybe mom and dad cleaned the carpets before...," he looked at Arec and frowned. "Ok, why would they do that?"

"They wouldn't," said Arec. "Not in the middle of the night."

"What are you thinking then?" asked Jacque.

Arec knelt down and tugged at the edge of the carpet. He pulled it out slightly from under the floor moulding. Dark red stains were visible all along the edge of the moulding. He looked up at Jacque. "Looks like blood stains. A lot of them."

They looked up and down the hallway and then through the entrance to the master suite. Arec walked toward the room slowly. "Jacque. Someone cleaned all of this carpet recently, and they did a pretty thorough job of it. All up and down the hall." said Arec.

"It was Neese," said Locke. He stood at the top of the stairs.

"Geez, dude," said Jacque. "Don't sneak up on us like that."

Locke frowned as he looked at the carpet. "He didn't want to raise any suspicion," he said.

Arec glared at Locke. "The bacon, the smell of it all

flowing upstairs," said Arec. "That's why he made so much of it."

"Yes, that's right, he hoped it would cover the smell of the carpet cleaner." said Locke.

"Wow," said Jacque, "Another reason to dislike Neese. Ruined my appetite for bacon."

"Let's go take a look in mom and dad's closet," said Arec. They walked into the room.

"A few of the struggles with Neese happened in here," said Locke. "I'm really sorry I couldn't help them more."

Arec seemed to ignore Locke as he walked toward the closet on the far end of the bedroom.

"Well, see anything?" asked Jacque as he looked over Arec's shoulder.

"No, just a messy closet," said Arec. "Locke, I have no idea what kinda ride you're talking about."

Locke was about to say something when he was interrupted by the sound of a whistle. "It's zero-hour, people,' said Cooley from downstairs.

"Listen, I'm really sorry boys, but you have to come downstairs." He turned off the last remaining light in the hallway and started back down the stairs, pausing slightly. "You need to come now."

When they got to the front room, Cooley was aiming his sniper rifle toward the window facing the front yard. He was like a statue. It was hard to believe that he was so badly injured. "Something's not right. The breeze, I smell something, and it's too quiet," said Cooley as he peered through his scope.

"Keys,' said Locke. "Do you know where the keys are to the Suburban out front?"

Arec looked out the front window as well, trying to see

something, anything, through the darkness down the street in front of their house. The way Cooley was acting made them think that they'd be attacked any second. "The keys are always hung up over there by the desk in the kitchen," said Arec. He turned around and faced Locke. "You looked there already, didn't you?"

"That was the first place I looked, with the other keys," said Locke. "Neese probably hid them somewhere."

"Well, that's just great," said Jacque. "What now?"

"We can make due without them." grumbled Locke.

Cooley was still peering through the scope on his rifle. "It looks like the power for the entire block was just cut," he said as he grimaced and loaded a new clip into his assault rifle. With his one good arm, he adjusted the scope as he continued to look out the window.

"Why don't they just come and get us?" asked Jacque. "Why all the theatrics?"

"No theatrics, Jacque," said Locke. "It's part of a routine to keep a major offensive contained." He flipped a light switch on and off repeatedly. The room stayed dark.

Jacque pulled out his cell phone. "This will still work, right?"

"Nope," said Cooley. He was right. Cell service was dead.

"You guys have a radio, right?" asked Arec. "Maybe we can monitor that, or call for help."

"It's risky," said Locke. "They're likely monitoring all bands."

Arec walked over to the window and looked outside. Raindrops started to dot the driveway in the dim moonlight. The light rain and fog obscured their view. "Oh no," said Arec.

"Oh no, what?" asked Jacque. Then he felt it too, a faint pulsing sound in the air.

Cooley's rifle made a soft click sound. They all stared out the window. Down the road in the distance, and through the stormy haze and rain, they could start to make out a number of small spotlights. They seemed to dart in different directions as they approached.

Locke looked up, and then turned to look down the hall into the kitchen. Lights could also be seen through the trees beyond the back yard. They were surrounded, but with quite a large perimeter. Locke stood back from the window. "Time to go."

"The cleaner is ready," said Cooley. "Shall we make for the SUV and delay-detonate on the house? We could take out a lot of them that way." He held out a small flat steel case.

"Agent Locke, what's that?" asked Arec. "And why do you guys call it a cleaner?"

Locke smiled. "Again, you're one of the very few to have already seen it in action," said Locke. "It's the same kind of thing that leveled your grandparents' place. They probably set it off as a diversion, to buy your escape."

"So, they might be alive." whispered Arec.

"Sorry, not likely," said Locke. "You'll be briefed later, no time now."

"Well?" asked Cooley. "We're done here, right?"

"Yes, but no cleaner, not yet," said Locke. "The boys will need the house standing when they circle back." Locke looked to Arec, who seemed frozen with fear. "Are you ready, Arec?" he asked. "Are you sure your parents gave no instructions about an emergency escape?"

The pulsing sound started again, but this time it was

louder. "We should hop into the car and get outta here," said Arec. "You can hot-wire it or something, right?"

Locke continued to stare out the window. "Yes sir. Not a problem, it just takes more time, and we're out of that," said Locke. "You think this is what your folks would have wanted us to do?"

"Yes, I think so." Arec tried to sound confident, but he really didn't know. I'm not ready for this responsibility, he thought. If anything bad were to happen, if it was the wrong decision, I would be responsible, thought Arec. He tightened his jaw and swung open the front door. "Follow me to the car," he said.

Jacque ran to the vehicle and pulled open the driver's door. "It's unlocked!" he said. "That's weird, mom and dad never leave their car unlocked." Rain started to pour down even harder.

Locke pushed Jacque out of the way and sat in the driver's seat. "Get in, now!" he yelled to the others.

Arec and Jacque helped Cooley to the middle seat where he could stretch out his splinted leg, and then they hopped into the third-row seats. "Agent Locke, time to get this thing started!" said Arec. They closed the doors.

"Yes sir." Locke reached under the dash with a knife and pulled out some wires. After what seemed like an eternity, but actually only a few seconds, the ignition sounded and the large SUV roared to life. "Whoa, what has this thing got under the hood?" Locke was about to put it in gear, but then paused. The pulsing got louder and the light from the spotlights was close enough to shine on parts of the front yard. The rain pelted the roof of the vehicle. "Are you sure, Arec?" asked Locke. "Something's not right."

Jacque was getting impatient. He looked out the side window and pounded the wall. "Let's roll, man!" The tiny spotlights could be seen down the road and all over the neighborhood, they bounced up and down, and darted back and forth, as if they were each fixed to a person, but they just floated in the air. "Now now now!" yelled Jacque. Some of the neighbors were going outdoors to see what was going on.

"Yes, that's an order, Agent Locke!" said Arec. "We have little choice now anyway." The lights should have been all over them by now, but they held their perimeter. They were waiting for something.

Locke slammed it in drive and the vehicle accelerated with a leap down the road.

"We'll have to exit through a small field between two houses at the end of the cul-de-sac," said Arec, "And then drive through a construction area to get to the adjacent street."

The ride was so smooth that it hardly felt like they were off road. Agent Locke turned and made a beeline toward the interstate, going over curbs and through a park in the process. Despite the uneven terrain, the vehicle didn't seem to rock that much. "Well, that's just not right at all," said Locke. Without any warning, the vehicle jerked violently and swerved away from the interstate and down a dark side road. Locke frantically gripped the wheel to try and turn it.

"Problem?" asked Arec. "Where are we going?"

"The vehicle, it's no longer under my control," yelled Locke. Both of his hands were off the wheel and the brake and accelerator were disabled. "It's driving itself." Locke pulled out a knife and tore away the fuse box cover. He feverishly flipped around some wires and fuses, but nothing seemed to work. Locke pulled away a part of the dash and cover around the steering column and unholstered his sidearm. "Everyone plug your ears!" yelled Locke. He carefully fired a round into a section of the steering column. The vehicle bucked and swerved, but then jerked back. "Well, that didn't work," grumbled Locke.

Then something happened that alerted all of them. They felt the large SUV start to rise as it sped down a side road toward a wooded area in the distance away from the freeway. Strange hums and mechanical sounds could be heard in the walls and doors.

Locke turned around and looked at Arec who looked pale. "You know anything about this, boys?" yelled Locke. "This is quite the family car. Are you aware of any modifications your folks may have made to this thing?"

"Not that I know of," said Arec. "But that doesn't mean much. There's a lot I don't know."

"This is your parent's car, right?" asked Locke.

"Cooley, can you reach into the pocket behind the front passenger seat? It should have a bunch of candy wrappers. Butterfingers." said Arec.

"Nope. Nothing. Perfectly clean." said Cooley. He grunted and started to cough violently. Arec's heart sank, and a pit grew in his stomach.

The vehicle continued to glide forward uncontrollably. Locke tried to turn on the wipers to see where they were going, but they didn't work.

Locke glared at Arec. "This isn't good," he said.

"I don't understand," said Arec. "The plates, everything. It's identical."

"Except for the candy wrappers, dude," muttered Jacque. The inside of the windows were fogging up, and he was frantically wiping them with his sleeve.

Panic welled up within Arec. He had made such a hasty decision. He hadn't thought things through. "No, it's not our car," blurted Arec, shaking his head. "It's exactly the same kind of vehicle, but ours isn't brand new like this one. It can't be our car. I'm sorry! It just doesn't make sense! I thought I needed to make a decision, and this seemed like the best one at the time!"

"No time for apologies right now," said Cooley. "You all need to bail." He tried to open the doors on either side, they were all locked.

"Can't we just blow out the windows and climb out?" asked Jacque.

Locke raised his firearm and aimed at the windshield, but stopped, turned the gun around and bashed the glass with the butt. Nothing but a dull thud. "Bullet-proof glass," he said. "That would have been bad."

The vehicle accelerated and turned left, then right. They had no idea where it was taking them. It seemed to be hovering at least a few feet off the ground as it barreled through the air. Arec reached behind, removed the headrest, and slid over the seat into the cargo area. The only way out is through the tailgate, thought Arec. He stared out the rear window and saw that they were being followed in the distance by a large number of spotlights. They were closing in on them and the pulsing could again be heard. Arec thought he saw some of the lights dropping from the sky. He reached down and lifted up the floor panel to reveal a tool kit and tire iron.

Jacque leaned over the back of the seat. "What in the

heck are you doing back there?" he asked.

Locke was now in the middle row next to Cooley who was again coughing up blood and a lot more of it. Locke checked his vitals. "Cooley, you're really cold and going into shock."

"Not much time left for me, agent Locke." He held the small steel cleaner case close to his chest. His thumb was on the top of the case, and a bright red circle appeared. "You guys get out. Now! I'll take care of the hostiles." Locke knew the plan and also knew that Cooley wouldn't make it. He gritted his teeth in frustration as he turned around to lean over the back of the second-row seat. Arec was trying to open the tailgate. "You need to peel away the inside panel of the tailgate door!" yelled Locke. "Try the other side!"

Arec took the tire iron and jammed it into one side and pried back the panel. It snapped off. He reached through the cavity of the door with his arm in a weird angle. Arec's face wrinkled with pain.

"Arec, move to the side, I'll fire a round into the latching mechanism." said Locke.

"Not a good idea," said Arec. "What if it's all bullet-proof? The bullet could ricochet. I think I've got the latch on one side." He looked up at Jacque, who was staring intently out the back window. "Jacque, a little help, man!"

"You got it!" Jacque crawled over the seat and into the cargo area. Arec showed him where to insert his arm into the other side of the opening in the tailgate door.

"Now, grab the small thin steel bar and push it toward me. I am going to do the same thing from the other direction with the other bar. We need to do it together." yelled Arec. The tailgate cracked open, but they held it closed against the force of the door's lift support struts. Suddenly the sound of rushing air could be heard. They also heard the pulsing sound again.

Locke's face was stern and serious, more serious than they had seen before. "Okay guys, we exit to the sides, not straight out the back and slightly to the right. Duck, tuck, roll, and cover your head. Aim for the drainage ditches, they are filling with rain water. Got it?"

Jacque interrupted. "What about Cooley?"

Locke glared at Jacque. "Agent Cooley is doing his job," he said, "Now you need to do yours."

Arec already knew the plan. Cooley had saved them once already, and it looked like he would not cheat death a second time. Arec reached over the seat and grabbed Cooley's good hand. It was clammy and shaking, but his grip was firm. "Thanks, Agent Cooley," said Arec.

"Get back to your house, get to that checkpoint," whispered Cooley. "Find your parents. Listen to Agent Locke. Do what you need to do. Don't let your work fall into the wrong hands. Have faith in your family and you'll do just fine." He started coughing again.

Locke sat between Arec and Jacque and put a hand on each of their shoulders. "Remember what I told you. Those guys will continue to follow this thing long enough for us to get away. Cooley will provide the diversion." Locke turned and grasped Cooley's hand and nodded. "It was an honor to serve with you, Agent Cooley."

"Likewise. It was an honor to serve with the best," said Cooley. "Thanks."

"The best? Not sure about that," said Locke. "If I were the best, I could save you, and I can't save you."

"It's most important to save them," whispered Cooley.

His face was pale. He coughed again and this time blood came streaming out of the side of his mouth.

"Locke, do we meet somewhere after we jump?" asked Jacque.

"No, just head back to the house," said Locke. "You need to be fast. The escape route will be ready by the time you get back."

"Will they be able to follow us?" asked Arec.

"I don't know how it works. Just do your best. No other options." said Locke. He smiled. "Welcome to your first mission, Mr. Mira." Locke broke the support struts so the tailgate wouldn't fly open, and then pointed to the brush covered sides of the road that blurred by. "I'll exit left, you two exit right like I said. I'll buy you some extra time. Do what you need to do." he said. "The spotlights are part of some sort of special cloaking uniform. I've analyzed their movement patterns, they are man, not machine or drone. Highly trained, so be careful."

"Wait," said Arec, "How do we know what to do once we get to the closet?"

Locke swore under his breath. "Like I said, do your best. Your parents believed that you would be able to figure it out," said Locke patiently and with a smile. "You'll figure it out. I'll catch up later. Just get to that checkpoint."

"Wait, who are we supposed to trust once we get there?" asked Arec.

"Your aunt and uncle," said Locke. He looked down nervously as the vehicle started to lift off the ground. "Also, look for someone named Mr. T."

Arec paused, debating whether to ask another question. "What's your name?"

"Agent Locke."

"I mean your first name," said Arec.

Locke paused and sneered as he looked out the window. "It's Tommy. Now, we're starting to climb," yelled Locke. "Go!"

Locke held the tailgate door open long enough for them to each jump out. Arec and Jacque hit the muddy ground along the side of the road and rolled into a drainage ditch with a small muddy rushing stream. They crawled out of the water and up to the top of the embankment. Jacque groaned in pain a few feet away behind Arec. The rain started to fall even harder.

"Do you see that?" blurted Jacque, still panting and wincing as he held his arm. He pointed into the distance where they could still barely see the Suburban hovering above the ground and flying down the road. "Definitely not our Suburban."

The spotlights following the vehicle could be seen more clearly now because of the falling rain. The rain also revealed the faint outlines of human forms. It seemed as though the spotlights were fixed to their heads.

"Yeah, they are people with some sort of invisible covering. I wonder how that works," said Arec. "Pretty cool."

"Cool?" said Jacque. "We gotta get outta here, dude."

"Wait," said Arec, "Did you see where Locke landed?"

"No, you heard what he said," said Jacque. "Let's go."

As they were about to turn and run, the dark figures with the spotlights stopped and faced away from the vehicle, forming a perimeter as if to protect the escape of the Suburban as it leapt upward. At that moment, they could see Locke dive out of the back and disappear into the shadows on the other side of the road. The spotlights didn't seem to notice him and held their position, each facing outward in a big half-circle from the spot where the vehicle swooped up into the air. Just as it started to jump straight up into the sky, a huge flash could be seen from within the vehicle, and then a blue flame exploded outward on all sides. The vehicle jerked and arched back down toward the ground, hitting the road like an empty tin can with a hollow metallic thud. About half of the spotlights turned and approached the wreckage. A second blast spread outward, this time with an eerie crack which sent a shock blast through the nearest group of dark figures, causing several of the spotlights to go out.

"Wait," Jacque gasped, "There's no way agent Cooley could have–"

"–That's right." said Arec. "He's gone." Arec sat down on the side of a nearby ditch. "Thanks, agent Cooley," he whispered to himself.

CHAPTER SIXTEEN
The Ride

The remaining spotlights all turned toward the lifeless and hollow wreckage of the vehicle, and then fanned their attention back out to the surrounding area. Arec and Jacque froze. They couldn't breathe or move. Slowly, all of the spotlights converged on the area around them and started to close in. One by one their spotlights turned off, but the light rain bouncing off of them revealed their silhouettes.

Arec wiped his face on his sleeve. "C'mon Jacque. We've gotta go," whispered Arec. "We'll make it. We can outpace these guys. Have a little faith, will ya?"

"Faith?" blurted Jacque. "What does religion have to do with this?"

"Jacque, I'm talking about believing that we'll make it out of this, even if we don't know how," answered Arec. "That's called faith."

"Don't patronize me with your Sunday school crap," said Jacque. He crouched back down into the ditch. "Blind faith isn't gonna get us outta this mess."

"Not blind faith. Faith with a plan," said Arec. He started to climb out of the ditch away from the road.

Jacque didn't move. He was pale and shaking. "So, what's your plan then?" he asked.

"We need to run and hide until we get to the house," said Arec. "Let's go."

Jacque peered up over the top of the ditch. It was hard to tell how many there were, but they were definitely moving in their direction.

"Jacque, c'mon!" whispered Arec.

"They're invisible," said Jacque. "They can probably see better than us. There are more of them. They're trained killers. Explain to me how we'll outrun them?"

"I need you to believe that we can escape," said Arec. "I can't do this without you. I need your help. Don't chicken out on me."

Jacque remembered the promise he had made to himself to be there for Arec, for family. His fear started to fade and nothing else seemed to matter. "Okay, let's do it," whispered Jacque. "Nothing to go back to, I guess."

At first they had no idea where they were or how far away they were from home. As they ran, their legs numbed with adrenaline. Jacque fell a few times but got right back up. He was still holding his arm close to his side.

"Did you break it?" asked Arec.

"I think so, when we jumped out of the car. Hurts really bad," answered Jacque. "I'll be ok. Let's just keep going before I change my mind."

"I think that's the neighborhood there in the distance." said Arec.

As they started to run, they could hear and feel pulsing

sounds in the air above them. Spotlights dropped out of the sky through the trees in one direction and across some fields. Others appeared from the other side of a road in the opposite direction. There were no street lights, no house lights, nothing. The power in the whole area seemed to be out.

"Well, at least we can see where they are because of their spotlights," said Jacque. The spotlights in the distance all around them went dark. Arec and Jacque were almost surrounded and hopelessly outnumbered. "Sorry," said Jacque, "Maybe I'll just shut up now."

"We have to assume that they can still see us, that they figured out that night vision limitation," said Arec. "They're closing in on us, probably only a hundred yards away. Can't hear them, but they're coming fast."

"How do you know how close they are if we can't hear them?" asked Jacque. He looked behind as he ran, and could barely make out the silhouettes of their pursuers. "Wow, guess you're right. Do you think anyone will be there waiting for us at the house?"

"Yeah, pretty sure," said Arec. He tried to plan ahead, but every idea he thought of required getting into the house unnoticed. He also knew that their cloaked pursuers must already be there waiting for them. It didn't matter. They had no other option but to get into the house and make their way to their parent's closet. "Quick, turn this way," whispered Arec. They darted into a small wooded area between their neighborhood and the few houses behind them. Lifeless vehicles were strewn along the side of the road, and people were wandering around, dazed, in the darkness and the rain. Gunshots were heard in the distance. Arec and Jacque kept running.

"Maybe the neighbors will distract them and buy us some time." said Jacque.

"Just try and not stand out, or be seen by anyone – even if we know them." said Arec.

Finally, they hopped the fence and were back in the yard behind their house. They laid down in the dense shrubs at the edge of the yard. A few of the windows seemed to be broken and the back door was swung wide open. Yelling and gun shots could be heard from the street in front of the house.

"Seems like we're no longer being followed." whispered Jacque.

Jacque was just about to step out of their hiding place when, several dark figures quietly leapt over the fence behind them. They could only barely see the dark figures and couldn't tell how many there were. The figures paused and looked around, but not in their direction. More gunshots cracked through the night air. The dark figures turned and darted toward the house. Neighbors were yelling and there were now sounds of breaking glass and police sirens in the distance.

Before Arec could stop him, Jacque leapt out of the bushes and turned to face Arec. "Whew! That was a close call..." he said. Suddenly his voice cut short. Jacque froze and his eyes widened with fear. His arms flailed wildly in the air and it seemed like something was over his mouth and holding his head from behind. His legs thrashed around as his feet left the ground.

One of them was left behind to guard, thought Arec. Very clever. He could barely see the outline of the person holding Jacque, but he could see enough. Arec's body tightened and a fire welled up within him, but at the same time he was calm. He knew that Jacque didn't have much time. He also knew that they weren't there for Jacque. He's trying to bait me, thought Arec. He knew there was only one thing he could do. Arec leapt out of the bushes, slid sideways across the wet grass, flipped up feet first, and knocked down his near-invisible opponent. Jacque dropped to the ground and put his hands to his neck, gasping violently.

Arec knew he'd have to make this quick and silent. He had no time to think. He felt a rush of adrenaline as everything around him seemed to go into slow motion – like just before Neese was killed. Arec saw the outline of a dark figure strike at him through the rain. When his opponent's hand was within reach, Arec moved to the side. He caught and twisted his wrist with a sickening snap, bringing his opponent to what must have been his knees. Everything around him moved so slowly. Raindrops seemed to just hang in the air. Arec spun around behind his opponent and drove his elbow into the back of his neck. The dark figure dropped to the ground. The wind picked back up, and the raindrops fell quickly all around him. He turned around to see Jacque still laying on the ground a few feet away with one hand still over his own throat.

"Are you alright?" asked Arec. "Can you stand?"

"My neck. It hurts really bad," said Jacque with a raspy voice. "I'm ok."

The pain in Arec's head returned. He groaned and held his head as he dropped to his knees, shaking.

Jacque stood up cautiously. "Where did he go? I know he was here. He tried to kill me. You have to believe me. You ducked away and he ran off I think." Jacque said, panting. "Are you alright Arec?"

Arec didn't answer. He just reached out and tapped what seemed to be something in the air. Suddenly the person that attacked Jacque appeared. He laid still on the ground, dressed from head to toe in a jumpsuit. It was a pearly white color similar to Neese's.

"Whoa!" Jacque jumped back. "Is that him? What did you do? How?"

"He was going to kill you. I had to do something," said Arec.

"But, how'd you know? Did you kill him?" asked Jacque.

"He's unconscious. Not dead." said Arec.

Jacque stared at Arec in disbelief. "Arec, what is going on? How did you do all of that?"

"What do you mean?" asked Arec. "Sometimes it just seems like everything just moves so slowly. I don't know." He rubbed the sides of his head.

Jacque silently looked Arec up and down. His face was pale and there were scrapes on his face and neck. "You're scaring me bro. You've always been fast, but that was off the charts dude."

"I could have dislodged his axis from his atlas vertebra, killing him instantly," said Arec, "but I'm not a monster like Neese." said Arec.

"Right," said Jacque. "Vertebra, what? Is that biology or something?"

"Never mind," said Arec, "We need to go."

Jacque cautiously nudged the unconscious guy on the ground. "Shouldn't we grab his suit? Maybe we can use it."

Arec frowned and stared back at the house. "No time."

Jacque looked over the guy on the ground. He glistened like pearl, and there were small dark lenses over the eyes. There was a small device attached to the side of the head – a spotlight. "Spookies," whispered Jacque.

"What?"

"That's what I'm gonna name these guys. Spookies," said Jacque.

Arec rolled his eyes.

"You got a better name?" asked Jacque.

"No, I guess not." said Arec.

The yellow stripe on the intruder's arm started to pulse with a bright yellow glow.

"Look at that Jacque." said Arec.

"Yeah, like the stripes on Neese's arm," said Jacque, "But there's only one stripe on this one."

"Yeah, Neese was their leader. Let's get the crap out of here," said Arec. "We were lucky. I surprised him. I don't think I'll be able to do that again."

Jacque and Arec climbed up onto the roof and stood just outside the bedroom window.

"On three, I'll bash through the window." whispered Arec.

Jacque was about to say something, but then smiled, anticipating how Arec would respond. "No, I don't have a better plan," mumbled Jacque.

As soon as they broke through, there seemed to be a sudden silence all around them. Pulsing could be heard outside. Spotlights filled the back yard and running could be heard all around the house, then up the stairs.

"More of them are coming." whispered Arec.

"Yeah, they must have really been planning for a big fight." said Jacque.

"They're really expecting some serious resistance," said Arec. "I still don't know what they want."

"Doesn't matter now. How are we gonna use a closet to escape?" asked Jacque. "This is a lame plan, dude. What were mom and dad thinking?"

The bedroom door slammed open just as Arec and Jacque ran into the large closet and quietly shut the door. Arec tried to turn on the light, but it didn't work. They could hear running and banging all around them. They started to feel around in the darkness. It was really quiet, like the room was sound-proofed. Suddenly someone tried to force the closet door open, but Jacque quickly jerked back on the door handle. He quickly pressed the lock button on the handle. As soon as the lock engaged, a blue ring of light about four feet wide appeared in the middle of the floor. They heard the muffled sounds of gun shots being fired on the closet door. Jacque jumped back and fell to the floor, but no bullets came through.

"An armored door on the closet," said Arec. "Mom and dad put an armored door on their closet." He felt around frantically, straining his eyes to see anything.

"Armored or not, we have got to do something," said Jacque, "They'll break through that door somehow."

"The lights don't work, but I feel a cord to something," said Arec. He followed the cord to the wall of the closet. "It's plugged in." He felt around the mess of clothing on the floor. After moving some of the clothing around, Arec felt a few spots of dampness. "The floor is wet over here," he said.

"Yeah, smells metallic and kinda fishy." said Jacque.

Arec followed the cord to what felt like a small rectangular plastic box. It was open on one side and he could feel something smooth and round along the underside. "I think it's the black light to my old lizard cage," said Arec. He flipped the switch and the room lit with an array of eerie fluorescent colors. The damp area of the carpeted floor appeared dark, and dark streaks and a few spatters appeared around it and up the wall. "It's blood," said Arec.

"Ugh!" said Jacque, as he wiped his hand across his pant leg. It left behind a dark smear.

"Look at that, Jacque," said Arec. He shined the light on the back of the closet door. They could barely make out a faint and hastily-drawn message in blood:

d ok, m hurt

And below it:

neese bad trust tom

The "m" in "tom" trailed off to nothing.

"Agent Locke told me his name before we got separated." said Arec.

Jacque smiled as he looked at the message. "Let me guess. His name is Tom, right?"

"Tommy, actually." Arec looked down at his hand which looked dark under the black light. "Jacque," said Arec, "The dampness on the floor is probably mom's blood."

"Oh man, Arec. I think I feel sick," said Jacque, starting to hyperventilate.

Arec grabbed a sweater from a hook. "Here, breathe through this. You'll be fine," said Arec. "Don't be lame."

Jacque glared at Arec, then punched him in the arm. "Thanks."

The banging on the closet door paused for a few seconds, and then intensified.

"That message would have been really nice earlier." said Jacque.

"This was their last position." said Arec.

They both turned and looked at the glowing blue circle on the floor. "None of this makes any sense. Maybe mom and dad stashed some anti-spookie guns in here somewhere," said Jacque. He was terrified and a bit hysterical. "I don't want to die. No job. No apartment. No girlfriend. No nothing. I'm not ready to die. What the crap are we supposed to do now?"

Arec remembered what he was told to do the night his grandparents disappeared. Trail, rock, jump, thought Arec. Jump. That was the key. "Hey Jacque, watch this." Arec stood in the blue circle and jumped. The solid blue circle of light pulsed and started to spin. They felt a rumble and then the room shake. The area of the floor within the spinning blue circle slid down into the floor.

"Oh ok, what the heck is that?" asked Jacque.

Arec jumped into the hole that appeared in the floor of the closet. "Come on down, it's not that far. Seems pretty solid," said Arec.

Jacque carefully lowered himself down next to his brother. It was only a few feet deep. There were four pairs of foot restraints. As soon as they both strapped in, the floor lowered further another six feet or so, and the opening above them closed. Arec and Jacque faced each other in the tube. Straps came out and held them tight against the tube wall. "I'm not sure I like this," mumbled

Jacque. "What's happening? Why are we being strapped down? What are you not telling me, man?"

"Jacque," said Arec, "Some more of my memory is starting to come back to me from that night in Puerto Rico."

"Of course, it is," said Jacque. He frowned. "You mean that horrible experience that has given you nightmares for the past five years?"

"Yeah. I think I remember more of what happened, but I can't remember exactly." Then, it came to him. "Oh no," mumbled Arec. He started to pull at his straps. "No! Not again, I don't want to do this."

A loud drilling sound could be heard from the other side of the closet door.

"Settle down, Arec. They're gonna break through. What do we do?" asked Jacque. Arec was terrified. "Dude, what's going on? What's—" Jacque was interrupted by a weird sensation at his feet. He looked down to see blue liquid starting to pour into the tube. Within seconds, it had filled up to their knees.

Arec closed his eyes and held his breath, but then let it out. "I'm not sure you're gonna like this, Jacque." He held his breath again.

"Ah crap," yelled Jacque. "Yeah, already figured that out. I'm gonna get you for this, punk."

Arec started to panic. He pulled at his straps again but nothing would come loose. "Jacque, listen, you have to breathe it in. It sucks, but you have to drown in it. You can breathe the liquid."

"What? Why?" yelled Jacque.

The fluid was up to Arec's chin. He looked up to desperately gulp some more air, then the fluid covered his face. His arms and torso were still, but then he jerked around and convulsed. Jacque did the same within several seconds after Arec. They stared at each other through the blue liquid. Jacque was panicking. Arec waved to him to get his attention. He couldn't. Arec relaxed and big bubbles of air came out of his mouth. He winced as he breathed in the fluid, and then breathed it out. The last time he had done this, he was nine. The night he lost his grandparents.

Arec saw that Jacque had not yet exhaled. His cheeks were bulging with air and his face was red. Arec tried to talk to him, but, of course, no sound came out. He motioned to Jacque to exhale, which he finally did. The blue circle of light at their feet turned red and a panel opened in the tube wall between them which had two buttons. The top button read "Transport", and the bottom button read "Transport and Clean". There was a warning cover over the bottom button.

Arec and Jacque looked up and then smiled at each other. Arec gave a thumbs up and pointed at the cover. Jacque flipped it up, and Arec slammed the button.

All at once, there was a stinging shock, a thud, and a jolt which they could feel as it rippled through the fluid. Without warning, they dropped downward into darkness. Arec's last memory was looking up and seeing the blue disintegrating explosion of the cleaner tearing everything apart. As they descended, the path ahead faded like a brilliant blue dot into the darkness.

Everything went dark.

SEALAB XII, MILWAUKEE TRENCH, ATLANTIC OCEAN

Ray and Jules had left so quickly, that they forgot to power down the lab. Now, many years later, cups were still left out and doors left open. Seemingly random displays continued to faithfully spew out data updates and trending graphs, and the ventilation system dutifully hummed as conditioned air rustled papers here and there.

Many of the rooms in the Mira's small makeshift station were dark, but in one particular room, the lights were still bright. The holographic projection of the neutrino harvester's activity changed, and monitoring displays around the room leapt to life. It was a change Ray and Jules had hoped to be around to see.

However, plans had changed, and an unforeseen opposition had forced them to leave… but not before preparations could be made for the person who would complete their work. The lab waited patiently for its new researcher.

It was just a matter of time.

End of book one.

Next Book: Rocket Handbook, Book Two – Emergence